GREA WARNER

every day you & me

The characters and events in this book are fictitious. Any similarity to real persons, living or dead, places, or events is coincidental and not intended by the author.

If you purchase this book without a cover, you should be aware that this book may have been stolen property and reported as "unsold and destroyed" to the publisher. In such case the author has not received any payment for this "stripped book."

Every Day You & Me

ISBN (ebook) 978-1-964636-66-5
(print) 978-1-964636-67-2

Inkspell Publishing
207 Moonglow Circle #101
Murrells Inlet, SC 29576

Edited by Yezanira Venecia
Cover art by Emily's World of Design

OTHER BOOKS BY GREA WARNER

COUNTRY ROADS SERIES:
Country Roads
Almost Heaven
Take Me Home
Teardrop in My Eye
The Place I Belong
All My Memories

HEADS AND TAILS DUET:
Heads Carolina
Tails California

Whiskey Girl

The Broken Road

EVERY DUET:
Every Mile a Memory
Every Day You & Me

The Dance

DEDICATION

This one is for the readers who have loyally supported my books. Your desire to continue Maya's journey into motherhood is what prompted me to write *Every Day You & Me.* By doing so, I have a greater appreciation for the strength and courage of NICU families, babies, and the medical personnel who provide such critical care.

And, as always, for my family. Hawk may say it best: "Every mile traveled, every memory made, every day lived … I want them to be you and me." I am so very grateful for every moment.

GREA WARNER

CHAPTER ONE

"I like that it's a secret," I whispered while looping my arm through Hawk's and leaning in closer to him.

Placing his finger to his mouth in the universal quiet sign, he nodded. "But first, we need to get through this."

An abundance of greenery, pillar candles, and the white-cloth chairs we were sitting in created an elegant and romantic setting for Carter and Vanessa's nuptials. Carrying white hydrangeas, Vanessa wore a similarly colored, fluffy dress with a long train, and Carter was in a black suit with white shirt sans any kind of tie—he was too hip for such traditional attire. As best man, Finn stood beside his good friend/drummer, while Lara did the same as matron-of-honor for Vanessa. Rounding out those standing up for the couple on their special day were Carter's younger brother and sister.

Since both the ceremony and reception were taking place in the same Nashville venue, the staff needed to quickly transform the main area. The soaring room with exposed beams would go from rows of chairs and an aisle to one of food and linen-covered tables. To expedite the transition, the wedding party took pictures out front while the guests were asked to go to the temperature-controlled patio for cocktails.

Hawk and I, however, did not. *We* retreated to a secluded spot in the intimate, upper-level mezzanine. We had only made the decision to do so a couple days before and, luckily, the rules and laws of Tennessee said we could. So, we were. It was our turn for the exchanging of words, minus all the hoopla.

Both of us had that type of wedding before—his ending in divorce and mine leaving me a widow. This time around, we didn't want everyone making a fuss with parties, hugs, food, and … everything. We simply needed us … and the minister, of course. It was our secret.

Because of that, I didn't walk down steps or an aisle like Vanessa had. I didn't wear white. Although, my beaded dress was a soft cream hue. I also didn't have my father give me away, but I swear I could feel him with me. There was *no* family with me for that matter. And that would have been the truth even if we weren't saying our vows covertly.

Hawk was my family. He and the precious baby growing inside me were my life and my future. Since it was the last weekend of November, our "little bun's" actual arrival was still many months away. However, I counted him or her as our wedding witness, even though the state did not require one.

Adorning the darkest of blue suits, which coordinated with his tie and my eyes, Hawk gazed lovingly at me as the minister performed the wedding ceremony. While it was basic and quick, we did make sure to include some personal touches, too. I wore my late grandmother's necklace and had a trillium in my hair to honor the other side of my family's Canadian roots. In turn, Hawk wore his father's gold watch—one he rarely took out of the box—in memory of him. And we exchanged a few of our own words.

Accompanied by instrumental music playing below us in the historic building, I was the one who spoke first. "I was up most of last night trying to think of the perfect thing to say to you today."

"That's what all the shifting around and kicking me in bed has been about?" Hawk mock grumbled.

I shook my head. There was definitely something else on my mind disturbing my sleep, but I wasn't going to let it spoil our day. "You'd think it would be easy," I forged on. "I blog for a living. I use words constantly. But what do you write—say—to the most important person in your life on a day which means everything? I can't find the perfect words. I can't. I keep internally editing. I think it's because I will always want to add more. I don't want to just say them today. I want to say them for a lifetime." I was going completely rogue and off the cuff, which wasn't like me. "We both know that lifetimes, though …" I swallowed and cut myself off. I didn't need to say it. We both knew. "So, what I want to make sure to say today is, I am so thankful for"—I squeezed his hands—"you working for Finn, for me taking a girls' trip … for a bucket of ice." I paused as we both smiled at our first unforgettable meeting in the Keys. "It could have ended there. Thankfully, though, we both took chances—you with a kiss and me with a job—and we've had friends to help us along the way. It is that wonderfully complex. But it is also as beautifully simple as I love you." I tilted my head up and he dipped his so our lips could meet.

In contrast to my lengthy monologue, Hawk's vows were suited for those social media sites that have character count limitations. Yet, his words were beyond meaningful. "Every mile traveled, every memory made, every day lived … I want them to be you and me." He winked and added, "Me, too, Maya."

I recognized, of course, those final two words before my name as our *I love you*. "How'd you do that?" I whispered my exasperation and appreciation. "It was perfect."

"I've been thinking of and replaying them in my mind from the moment you accepted this ring." He encircled the engagement rock on my finger—the only symbol we would have of our union for a while since we decided to get married so spontaneously and had only gotten engaged a few weeks prior.

I shook my head. I'd met a number of macho men in my life, and Hawk was definitely a top contender. He didn't let a lot of people see the internal, soft, emotional side of him. But when he showed it to me, I could not be in more awe or love.

It was weird how different I felt after those couple minutes of words and the minister's proclamation of my new status as Mrs. Brannigan. I knew paper didn't make the commitment. The two people involved did. Somehow, though, formalizing our bond provided me a sense of calm and rejuvenation. It was like mystical doors had opened and I was breathing more completely than I, perhaps, ever had.

When we rejoined the formal wedding festivities out on the patio, my internal happiness must have shown right through. Smiling brightly, I was taking a selfie with my new secret husband when Finn and Lara approached us. Drinks in their hands, they were obviously done with *their* photo obligations.

"You're acting like *you* are the bride and groom," Lara noted my demeanor. "I mean, pretty soon, though, right? Did you pick a date?"

Finn must have noticed my look at Hawk because he hardly let his wife finish her question before proposing one himself. "Shit, you already did, didn't you?"

"What? Did what?" Lara looked at her husband.

"That's why you wanted to make sure you two could take off for a bit." Finn Murphy wasn't just Hawk's long-time employer. He was mine, too, although I had only joined the country music star's team six or so months prior.

While I looked at Hawk again—curious about Finn's time-off comment—Lara started putting the pieces together. "They did what … got married?"

I poked Hawk on his side. "Are we going somewhere?"

He rolled his eyes at Finn. "Thanks, man."

"What? Maya doesn't know? Rule number one: no

omissions from your wife."

"True," Lara seemed to give a particularly knowing look at her husband. "But is it also true that you are already married?"

When Lara opened her eyes wide at me, I looked at my husband. My husband! His shrug encouraged me to give up the guise, which was pretty much already over. "Yeah," I admitted. "Actually, a few minutes ago." I felt Hawk's hand affectionately playing around with mine. "We went upstairs and had the minister perform—"

"Oh my God! Congratulations!"

Lara's interruption and hug attack caused my hand to separate from Hawk's. I was laughing lightly and looking at him from behind Lara's embrace as he accepted Finn's congratulatory handshake. The men were much more than workmates. They were truly good friends.

"Oh." Lara suddenly pulled me away from her. "But I wanted to throw you a—"

"No. No. No. No." I declined any party or shower or whatever Lara had in mind. "We don't want all that." I reclaimed Hawk's hand. "Please. Okay? And wait to tell anyone. We don't want to take away from Vanessa and Carter's day."

"It was kind of last minute," Hawk added.

"But perfect." Then I got back to the question unanswered. "We're going somewhere?"

"Yeah, with those two." Hawk nodded toward the corner of the room where Carter and Vanessa stood.

"Oh." I hoped my one word came out without the sound of the disappointment I felt.

Finn had gifted his drummer a trip to Monte Carlo so the newlyweds could gamble and go on wine tours. It was perfect for the flashy couple, who loved that life and didn't want kids. Although I got along with both of them, it was far from my style and not where a pregnant me wanted to spend her honeymoon.

"Maya ..." Hawk shook his head and, boy, was I relieved

when he said, "Do you think I'm crazy? No. How about the Keys?" Although it was asked as a question, I was fairly confident he had already booked it. And then he confirmed. "Tomorrow."

That destination couldn't have made me happier. "Really?"

"I think we might have to be holed up in that room again." Even though he was referring to an extremely frightening experience, it was also what had propelled him and me to first meet and start our story.

As I curled myself onto Hawk's side, I replied the way he did when feeling free and easy. "Mayyybe."

Glancing at the spot on the patio that hosted a mic, stool, and guitar, Finn announced, "Looks like they're ready for me."

"You're not singing the next single, are you?"

As the "real" bride and groom entered the patio area, Finn answered his right-hand man. "It couldn't be a more perfect time … especially now." He swung his finger at Hawk and me.

"God, Finn," I exclaimed. "What is the song about? I want to promote."

My job for team Murphy was to assist his publicist, Reese. I was mostly in charge of a day-in-the-life blog, updating social media, and looking for anything with Finn's name on it. Yes, Reese would handle the releases and contacts, but I was always informed … except for that song, which seemed to be coated in complete secrecy.

"Hope you like it, Maya," Finn spoke to me and then to his wife, "You too, Beauty." He gave Lara a kiss, handed her his glass, and then started walking toward the mic.

"You haven't heard it?" I was shocked the singer's own wife wasn't privy to the new song.

"No. I'm in the dark as much as you. Though, in the past, if I don't know about a particular song, it's something extra special."

"Maybe you and I should be jealous," I jested to Lara.

"Hawk seems to know all about it. What exactly happens at these boys' weekends?" The only thing I knew about the song was that the lyrics were composed during their last getaway.

"Supposed to just be hunting and fishing," Hawk grumbled. "Give me his bourbon." He reached his hand out to Lara. "He owes me that much."

As Hawk took a swig, I commented, "You're making it seem like the song is awful."

"It's …" He shook his head, alongside a second sip. "No. You'll see."

Not needing an introduction, especially with the crowd of friends and friends-of-friends, Finn spoke into the mic, setting up the song. "For the newlyweds and for all them girls. This is called 'Boys' Weekend.' I hope you like it." And so started the vocals …

"It's the weekend we look forward to every year
An escape to the woods for good times and some beer

It's bro code, man cave, tunes, and some fishing
It's gambling and hunting and not doing dishes
There's no worries, no honeys, no fast-paced worlds
But why, oh, why, do we keep talking 'bout them girls?"

From the opening lines and chorus alone, I knew the latest Finn Murphy song was definitely not a sad, depressing tune like his "Dark and Dusty." As big of a hit and as beautifully done as that one was, I turned it off every time. It made me go back to a dark place of my own—losing my husband, Jeff. "Boys' Weekend" seemed to have the beat and tone of a classic country song but with a lighthearted, fun twist. It was a little unusual for Finn, but I could already see how it would be a hit.

The multi-award-winning country music artist looked directly at his wife as he started singing the next lines.

"I admit it, I started with pics of the kids
And vids of what both of them did
But after a few brewskis or two,
The stories came out about me and you
I explained to the guys—my bros in the band
What makes you the most beautiful"—he nodded at Lara—"*one in the land*"

It was obvious then that it was really a song about them—his wife and their kids, who were with Finn's mom during the adults-only wedding festivities. The lyrics were, indeed, going to be special like Lara had predicted. She wasn't one for the spotlight, and the family kept their private life pretty much that. It didn't mean, though, that it wasn't one robust with love. Finn and Lara Murphy were the ultimate relationship goals in my eyes. While being on Finn's concert tour all summer, I had personally been witness to their devotion to each other and their two children—Chance, age four, and Arinn, freshly minted age two. And since then, the family had truly become very good friends of mine.

Finn was right. I did like "Boys' Weekend." Not only was it sweet, but it would also be easy to promote. Fans loved songs that connected directly to the artist themselves. I was already beginning to think of hashtags for social media. First, though, I needed to refocus on the next round of lyrics.

"*A long time ago we were nothing but friends*
Our life now, though, has a happily ever after end
Strawberry blonde with eyes like the sea,
God, girl, what you do to a man like me

"*It's bro code, man cave, tunes, and some fishing*
It's gambling and hunting and not doing dishes
There's no worries, no honeys, no fast-paced worlds
But why, oh, why do we keep talking 'bout them girls"

When Hawk took another gulp of Finn's bourbon, I looked at him with curiosity. He truly was acting a little bizarre, and I knew it had to be about the song. But why?

"The drummer was next after a few hands of cards"

On the lyrical proclamation of Carter's profession, the groom raised both his hands in the air, as if the party gathered didn't already know he was the drummer. In contrast to Lara, Carter wasn't shy. He was a happy-go-lucky, talk-straight kind of guy. And his new bride had a similar personality.

Smiling and shaking his head, Finn continued singing.

"He easily concurred that he had fell hard
So in love with her dark eyes and matching hair
Long, loose waves of curls everywhere"

Oh, that was why Finn said it was the perfect time to premiere the song. I got it. It was a song about marriage. And Vanessa could not have been more thrilled, as her dark waves bounced with delight upon hearing the lyrics.

"Awww, this is perfect for their wedding." I nudged Hawk, who put his finger up to his mouth, urging me to listen.

"A casual fling was all they were s'posed to be"

Finn's lyrics made Vanessa shrug at her parents.

"But that all changed when he got down on one knee
Now forgoing his playboy ways
The two have made it to their wedding day"

"Woo-hoo!" Carter exclaimed midst lyric.

Finn chuckled a bit as he began his next line.

"*God, he said, what that girl can do to a man like me*

It's bro code, man cave, tunes, and some fishing
It's gambling and hunting and not doing dishes"

"I think I have the chorus down already," I proclaimed, starting the next couple words.

"Maya …" Hawk shook his head.

"*There's no worries, no honeys, no fast-paced worlds*
But why, oh, why do we keep talking 'bout them girls

I didn't expect it. He's a man of little words,
But whiskey made him spill about his girl
Sun-kissed hair brushing her shoulders and eyes,
They met by chance on a search for some ice"

Oh … my … God. I know my mouth dropped open, but I couldn't actually feel it. I was in such complete astonishment. Finn was singing about Hawk and me. The country music star's focus became solely on us, and I could tell Lara's was, too. But I was turning to my other side and looking at Hawk. Even though his mouth was perfectly straight, his hazel eyes were blinking and looking at me. I couldn't determine what his exact thoughts were, and I couldn't spend the time thinking about it. I had to listen.

"*Each letting go of things from their pasts*
To find a new love that'll forever last
Now there's a baby due sometime in May
And he loves it and its momma in every which way"

And then after the last round of the chorus, Finn ended the song with words that were more spoken than sung, "*I'm coming home, baby.*"

In the midst of the sound of applause, the singer

replaced the mic to the stand. Some of the wedding guests gathered around Vanessa and Carter. Others were talking with Finn.

My focus, though, was solely on one person and one person only. "Hawk …"

His response to my awe was to lift the corners of his mouth ever so slightly and take a final gulp of the bourbon. "What?"

It was true what the lyrics had said—Hawk was a man of few words. In that way, we were opposite, for sure. But, as he had proved in our vows, a lot of times it was quality, not quantity that mattered.

Right then, though, I needed more. "What? What? Hawk … God, that was … You … That was beautiful." Even if it was Finn who was singing it, I knew Hawk had some part in the song. "If we weren't already married, I would be down on my knee asking you."

"Well, I'm glad you said *yes* before hearing some silly song."

I ignored his attempt at being nonchalant. "It wasn't silly. It's how you feel."

That time his response was more truthfully heartfelt. "Yeah, but you already know that."

"I do." I stroked his cheeks and close-cut, dark-auburn beard. "And the people in our lives know, too. But still, it … it was special." I started putting the pieces together. "No wonder the song was such a secret."

Finn, who had made his way to our trio, interrupted. "Whatcha think?"

When I responded by throwing my arms around my boss, Hawk jokingly called out, "Hey, hey, not even an hour into our marriage and you have your hands—"

"On you." I switched partners quickly, giving my husband a much more secure and loving embrace than I had with Finn.

"And you," Hawk's finger pointed toward his friend. "So much for what happens at camp stays at camp."

Finn let out of small chuckle before addressing his wife. "Baby, you okay with me releasing it?"

"Sure," she agreed, adhering to her own man's side. "I loved it. Definitely one of my favorites."

"Maya? You're a yes?"

Finn was asking my opinion, which was kind but absolutely not necessary. First of all, his art was his choice. But second, uh, what an honor.

"Yes, of course," I agreed.

"You asking me?" My man's voice vibrated in my ear as I had my head on his chest.

"No, you don't get a say." Finn denied him and added a bro punch. "As cowriter, you'll get to come on stage if we win Song of the Year, though."

"Oh, brother." Hawk was like me in that sense—we both were behind-the-scenes people. He definitely preferred to stay off the stage but did a phenomenal job managing everything behind it.

And then there was the opposite personality. "All right, gals." Vanessa suddenly bounded into our group and put her arms around Lara and me, pulling us from our men. "Girl band. We're coming up with a sequel recording called 'Girls' Weekend.' Maya, you're a writer. We got this."

Lara was shaking her head at her fun friend as Hawk immediately denied such an event from happening. "No. Not even. She's preoccupied." And with that, he took my hand and led me back inside to the main room.

There was still some movement by the venue's personnel, but not the crowd and noise of the festivities on the patio. Hawk leaned against the exterior wall and brought me snug against him. We both seemed to look up to where we had only moments before became husband and wife.

After leaving the lovely memory of that moment sit for a second or two, Hawk asked, "You sure you're okay with the song?"

"Yeah." I smiled with complete ease. "It's not like anyone besides our friends know it's about us. I like that.

It's kind of cool … our insider secret."

"Sort of like our little ceremony earlier?"

"Yeah, hubby." I met my lips with his, and he readily reciprocated.

"How long do we have to keep up a presence here before we can start our honeymoon?"

"That's the beauty of this not actually being our reception—we don't have to do all the formalities."

Hawk's stomach rolled a little with silent laughter, and his eyes seemed to gleam. "Then I'm thinking we ditch now and head home."

"Hawk …" I *tsked.*

"Crap." His demeanor changed slightly. "I didn't think this through."

"What?"

I couldn't imagine an instance where "Mr. Meticulous" didn't have all the pieces in place. It was his job to keep everything in line and running seamlessly for Finn. Hawk observed and thought things out with precision. In fact, it was how Finn crowned him with the name we all knew him by. He has "Hawk" eyes. The first name he was given at birth was only used around close family and formalities like our marriage ceremony.

"Maybe I should have gotten us a hotel room or something?" he proposed.

"You said you did. We're *not* going to the Keys?" I thought that was confirmed. I was confused and a little disappointed.

"No, no, no. We are. Plane leaves tomorrow … late afternoon. I meant for tonight, here in Nashville."

"Tonight? Why?"

"It's our wedding night. It should be special." Ah, my strong yet sentimental man.

"A hotel in town would make it any more special?" I turned on the sentiment, too. "Home. Our home." I thought of Hawk's nearby townhome … the one I had moved into a few months before. "It couldn't be any more special than there."

"God, woman, you're the best." He placed his big hands on either side of my head.

"You're pretty damn great yourself." I kissed him again to punctuate my feelings. "And, you know, I really would like to get out of these shoes. If you're serious about leaving …"

"For the sake of your feet, of course," he agreed with a smirk.

"Of course."

"And we probably need to get you out of some other clothes, too."

"I mean, things might be getting a little tight." Three months into a first pregnancy did not warrant true tightness in a new dress, but, nevertheless, I played along.

"I love you, Maya."

God, I loved him, too. It still amazed me how much my life had changed since meeting him. I knew it came after a tremendous loss, and moving on at times had seemed impossible. But I was. I just had to believe that every day forward was going to be as beautiful as our wedding day.

My life had never been that way, though. Never. So, a part of me—the inner most, realistic part—clung to the fear that it all could be taken away again … just like that.

CHAPTER TWO

The white sheet was coming down on top of me. It was moving fast. I laid flat on my back beneath it, thinking all I had to do was move. I could sit up and swat it away. It should be that easy. But I felt stuck … paralyzed even. And then I started to panic. The sheet wasn't only coming down, but both of the sides were also squeezing in. I couldn't breathe. Damn my claustrophobia. I tried my arms again, but it was to no avail. All I could do was scream. When the horrified cry left my mouth, though, it came out silent. It was trapped, too.

Thankfully, the accumulating terror did accomplish one thing. It woke me. When I opened my eyes, the first thing I saw was a white sheet. It was above me, but it wasn't trying to suffocate me in any sense. It was safe and secure as part of the romantic tent Hawk had the hotel recreate before our arrival. With a mattress instead of pillows anchoring us, the blanket fort was supposed to be reminiscence of our first time in that same exact hotel room … the first time we met. And months later, I had treasured making love and falling asleep inside it the night before—day one of our honeymoon. That was until it subliminally transferred into the reoccurring nightmare I had been having for a few days.

I pursed my lips and began to try to regulate the tempo of my rapid breaths, which felt like a fan blowing at a decent speed. I knew it had been a dream. I didn't need to panic. I was safe. No sheet or person was breaking free. They couldn't take—

"Hey …" Hearing his voice, I slowly turned my head to see Hawk propping himself on his side via his elbow. "What's going on?" It was amazing how he could wake from a dead sleep and be so alert.

"Sorry." Just two more slow draws of breath out and I would be okay. One. "I, uh, didn't mean to wake you."

"Mai, what's wrong?"

"Just a bad dream." And two. Better. But maybe one more would help.

"About?" His hand rhythmically and gently stroked the side of my face that was closest to him.

"I don't know."

There was some truth in what I said. A lot of the dream evaporated instantly, but the ending part—right before the new addition of the suffocating sheet—always seemed to stick. I had no desire to relay it to Hawk, though. I wanted to solely be on our honeymoon with me in his arms.

"Really?" Obvious doubt dotted his question. "It's been going on pretty much all week. I know it's not you trying to think of some vows."

"No. Sorry." I felt bad about having been waking him for days. "I need you to hold me, okay?"

"Maya …" His sigh told me he knew I was deflecting, even if my request was legit and something we both treasured.

"Tight," I added. "You know how you do."

It was amazing how his secure arms wrapped around me helped my claustrophobia. You would have thought the constriction would be even more troublesome, but I had come to realize it wasn't the space I needed. It was the comfort. And Hawk was my personal breathing apparatus.

"Please." I assisted in my request by turning and curling

my body against his. "I can go back to sleep if you do."

He gave in by using a common Hawk phrase. "You got it."

***

I'm not sure which scent was stronger, the robust coffee or the salty sea air. Regardless, the two together seemed to be the perfect combination. I let my nose guide my bare feet to find the exact source. Even though it was only a little after sunrise, the hotel room's balcony floor was already warm to the touch … a significant difference from Nashville's cooler temps.

Sitting on one of the two striped beach chairs was a sight that was even better than the sweet smell. Hawk had his legs outstretched and his back toward me. Of course he was awake. He almost always was before me, despite going to sleep after. His gaze was on the turquoise water, which seemed to be lapping onto the still empty beach as if it was part of a perfectly timed orchestra.

I closed my eyes and breathed in again. This—I thought—is how life should be. This is the peace and joy that should be with us every day.

"I never experienced this balcony our first time here." Walking around the side of his chair, I leaned over and gave him a good-morning kiss.

"Nope. Curtains needed to stay closed. We definitely had to stay out of sight." He picked up a coffee mug from the small table next to him and handed it to me. "Decaf and should be hot. Unless you want to get the bucket and go look for some ice." He wrinkled his nose with his tease.

I tasted the beverage and sat on the chair next to his. "No. Don't need to necessarily relive that part."

"The part when you first met me in the hallway? I'm hurt." He mockingly put his hand up to his heart.

"If it didn't involve us hearing nearby gunshots and running into your room without me even knowing who you were …" I let out a light chuckle. "What do you suppose we will tell this kid about how we met?" Holding onto my belly, I felt a little swish of gas—a not-so-lovely joy of pregnancy. "I'm sure being barricaded and fearing for our lives isn't exactly what a child expert would recommend for story time."

Mid sip, he put down his own coffee and looked a little more directly at me. "That wasn't what the nightmare was about last night, was it?"

"No." Amazingly, all my thoughts of the hotel were positive, despite it being host to one of the most frightening experiences of my life. Because I associated it with our beginning, it did not cause an ounce of distress—awake or asleep. "Not at all."

"Well, that's good." His eyes swayed back and forth across mine before he spoke again. "Are you going to make me ask seventeen katrillion times before you tell me what's bothering you?"

"Seventeen katrillion …" I teased. "Is that more than a billion or less?"

"Maya …" My name came out partly as an exasperated sigh. "I think it's been at least five times now."

Because in the daylight everything seemed so much less threatening and I knew he would continue to ask, I told Hawk the truth. "I got a call a few days ago that he died."

"He—" His one word started as a question but was quickly aborted. "Oh. Why didn't you say something?" His tone may have sounded a bit angry to a passerby, but knowing him as I did, I understood it was more about concern and his need to protect.

I placed my coffee on the floor and rested my hand on top of his. "I know … If it has to do with me, it has to do with you." I recited something he had told me about the bond we shared—we were truly one.

"Damn straight."

I believed it—knew it—but still hated burdening him with things from my past, particularly when it concerned

Jeff. And also … "I didn't want it to have to do with me, though. I didn't want it to matter at all. I wanted to concentrate on us … on this." I caressed his hand.

"Well, it doesn't seem to be working."

"It is, though. I truly don't think about it at all during the day. But for some reason, my dreams won't let it go."

"What was the dream about specifically?" His voice was softer. "You do remember, don't you?"

My eyes shifted downward before meeting his again. "I don't really have a clear image, but I know it's Percy, and he's pulling at something I'm carrying. I'm not sure what it is. He wants to take it with him, but I won't let him. And I feel bad."

"You feel bad?" His hand moved from mine as he shifted in his seat to turn more directly toward me. "Why?"

I couldn't help but think the same question. Why would I ever feel bad about the man who killed my first husband? The only thing I had was a theory. "Maybe it's because I'm glad he … Percy"—I spit out the killer's name—"is dead. I mean, what kind of person is glad someone else died?"

"Oh, geez, Maya. A person who had their whole world upended by evil. That's who. And you feel that with good reason."

I love how even though it was my past with another man and I had only gotten to know Hawk over a year after the tragedy, he supported and understood all of what I felt regarding it. For that reason, I opened up a little more. "When they called and told me Percy died, it brought back seeing him in prison."

"I know you haven't wanted to talk about exactly what happened during your visit, but you have to know it tortures me only being able to imagine the worst."

I leaned over and pecked him a couple times with kisses of my appreciation. Then, after a breath, I decided to vocalize what went down in the prison a few weeks before. "He was nice." On Hawk's immediate disgruntled, deep throat sound, I clarified, "I mean … no. I mean … he wasn't like all brooding and angry and … I don't know." Hawk didn't try to disguise his headshake as I continued, "Percy did all of the talking. I was simply concentrating on breathing—catching my breath and not panicking."

That time Hawk's head movement was accompanied by an eye roll. He hadn't wanted me to face Percy Kellerman at all. It had been a bone of contention between the two of us. He knew it would—with due right—cause me an immense amount of emotional distress. And with me telling the specifics as we sat on that balcony, he learned it had been *physically* painful, too. But I stood by my decision, believing it was something I had owed both Jeff and myself.

"He wanted to say his piece," I continued. "He said that night he shot Jeff, he had been high because he'd just found out his illness was incurable. None of that ever came up at the trial. He hadn't told anyone."

"So that was his excuse for shooting someone? He found out he was sick?" Hawk's voice was a mixture of irritation and disbelief. "Tons of people are diagnosed with awful stuff and don't—"

"I know. He said he was only blowing off steam, shooting his gun off … minding his own business. That was all in the original testimony. The neighbors called the cops. Even though Jeff was clocked out and on his way home, he heard the call and went by himself because he was close. He should have waited. He should have waited for backup." Thinking of and relaying my deceased husband's final moments choked me up every time, and I took a second or two to wipe my watery eyes and continue. "The defense said Percy shooting Jeff was accidental and drug induced. But he said to me in that prison, Hawk … he said he did it because Jeff was a cop and he was raised to believe cops were like a disease, too. They were not good."

"For God's sake!" Hawk actually rose a little from his seat. "I would have ripped his head off."

"He wanted me to forgive him, but I couldn't."

"Of course you couldn't."

"I actually said I wouldn't. He wanted forgiveness, and he wanted to die." Once again sitting solidly back down, Hawk took my hand, which encouraged me to finish. "That's all. You know I wasn't in there long. I couldn't …"

"It felt like centuries." He related his side of the tale, having sat outside the prison gates waiting for me to reemerge that day. "If it's guilt you are feeling for not forgiving him, don't."

"Yeah, but I also think it's knowing he's gone is like letting one more piece of Jeff go. There's no living person to be angry with anymore. It's weird to be free of that. I know it's important for my wellbeing. I should concentrate on remembering the good times, not how it ended. It's a guilt for not holding on to that anger, or anything else, and being … happy. Because that's what I am. And there is no doubt in my mind that Jeff would have wanted that for me. I am so happy with you, Hawk."

"Aw, Mai, come here." He opened his arms to gather me in them. As I found my natural and comforting space against him, he said, "Thanks for telling me all of that."

"Thank you for giving me the time to tell you."

He rubbed my back for a little while before breaking the silence. "And, you know, I don't think there's any reason not to tell Little Bun the truth about our first time here … the first time we met." When I leaned back to look him in the eyes, he surged on with his reasoning. "The fact is, Mai, kids nowadays? They're like in preschool and practicing active shooter drills." When I scowled at that depressing mental image, he continued, "I know, but it's true. When we tell our kid our story, the most important part is that they'll know their momma is a kickass, brave woman who stands up for what is right and knows how to protect those around her."

I shook my head at his sentiment. "It helps having you by my side."

"You and me, Maya." He winked.

I started to rest my head back onto his chest, but

something halted my action. Slowly, I looked up to, once again, claim his eyes with mine. "Kickass?"

His eyebrows curled inward. "Of all the words I just said, that was the one you—?"

"I'll tell you who is kickass."

I placed his hand on my stomach. It wasn't gas. It was our baby. It was his or her first flutters. I had known it was about the time to expect it, but I wasn't thinking that way when I had first woken up. Yet, sitting there as close as I could to our little one's dad, I knew it was their first kick. It was their first time to officially tell us they were there. While I knew the babe growing inside me couldn't truly hear or certainly comprehend what was going on outside the womb, I wanted to believe she/he was letting us know that not only did it like the comfort of us bound in love, but it could also be brave and strong. I only hoped they wouldn't have to face too many challenges, like I had in my life, to prove it.

CHAPTER THREE

Less than a month into our marriage, and I was pretty sure I had the "wife look" down. It was a week before Christmas. Hawk and I had brought gifts over to the Murphy house for the kids but none for their parents, and I was embarrassed when Finn announced they had gifts for us. It was bad enough to be empty-handed, but when it was your boss, it seemed ten times worse.

I opened my eyes wide with a glare at my husband. "You told me not to get anything for them. You said you don't exchange gifts."

It was my first holiday season with the crew, but not Hawk's. He had been Finn's right-hand man for many years. He should have known. He shouldn't have argued when I had wanted to buy something for Finn and Lara, too.

"We don't," Hawk immediately protested my words and gave a suspicious, thanks-a lot-bro look at the country crooner.

"It's really mostly a wedding gift," he argued. "We were going to do something for—"

"Oh, really, we said not to do that." Although, practically everyone Hawk and I told of our nuptials had sent something, including his mom, Della, who was upset about not being a part of our big day. "We don't need anything," I concluded.

"You two really are perfect for each other." Finn shook his head at my statement, which I did recognize sounded a lot like what Hawk would have said.

"Chance and Arinn, come on, we're going for a ride," Lara called out to her little ones. When her son whined—clearly already enamored by one of the toys Hawk and I brought—Lara added, "You can bring it."

"We'll take my car." Finn put one hand on Hawk and the other on me.

"What? Where are we going?" I asked Finn but glanced at Hawk, who had the same bewildered look as I did.

"To get your present," our boss answered in a matter-of-fact way.

So, we were not only getting a gift, but we also had to drive somewhere to get it? What did that mean? I was not one for surprises, perhaps because so many dark moments in my life had happened completely out of the blue. At the same account, I needed to trust more. It was something Hawk was always encouraging me to do. With him I could. So when he agreed to the plan, I did, too.

As we entered the garage and started toward the Murphy Range Rover, Chance said the same thing I was thinking. "We can't all fit."

"Guess we leave the kiddos at home."

Finn was in a particularly lighthearted mood. It was nice to see. December was his downtime in his extremely fast-paced yearly schedule. He had more of a chance to spend time with family and compose. It was a complete contrast to his regular schedule of attending award shows, making TV appearances, and getting ready or actually being on the road.

"Daddy, no!" his mini-me cried out.

Finn tousled his son's hair. "Just kidding, bud. I would never leave you or your sister."

I knew that to be the truth, especially after the scare the

family had when Arinn was abducted. Even though that had happened prior to my arrival in their lives, I knew the story well because of the media coverage at the time and the Murphys recounting the tale to me. I held on to my stomach, thinking of how I was already in fierce, protective parental mode, and the babe wasn't even out of the womb yet.

"We can take out Chance's booster seat or … Maya, can you sit on Brawny's lap in the front?" I refocused on Finn's suggestion and playful tease of my husband's name. "It's not a far drive at all."

"Uh …"

"Mai, it's all right." Hawk went along with the suggestion when I hesitated. "I got you. We used to ride like that all the time growing up."

I took in a deep inhale. It was another instance when trust became a factor. I trusted Hawk. What I *didn't* trust were my memories.

After another breath, I tried to make light of the request. "It's not you I don't trust. He"—I pointed to our boss, who had drivers on tour and to special events—"doesn't drive a lot."

Lara burst out laughing. "Finn's a good driver, and I say that even knowing he makes fun of *my* driving!" She started hoisting Arinn into the car seat.

"Come on." Finn shook his head in my direction. "It really is pretty much around the corner."

"All right," I agreed. "Let's go. The suspense is killing me."

Because of how my dad died, whenever I was in a car, I was a rule follower—seatbelts before putting the car in drive, turn signals even when on a rural road with no other cars, and certainly an alert driver were on top of my list. Thankfully, I had all of that on our commute down a back road to the unknown. That is, if you counted Hawk's strong arms being my safety belt. And, luckily, it probably took longer to get the kids strapped in, start the engine, and close the garage and security gate than it took us to get to our destination.

It was when we once again stepped out of the car that Hawk understood my cause for apprehension. As Lara and Finn got the kids out and they immediately started to swarm the open field, Hawk whispered so only I could hear, "Sorry, sweetie, I wasn't thinking."

"You said you got me. I trusted you." I had, but I was also glad to be out of the car.

"Go ahead and open it." Finn was pointing at the large wrapped box—the only thing in the area besides grass.

I nodded to Hawk to do the task. I had absolutely no idea what could be inside something that appeared to be the size of a love seat. No. It was, actually, bigger. And why in the middle of an empty lot? I was afraid my face would give away any shock, disappointment, or alternate extreme feeling if I opened it. Better to get Hawk's reaction. He was definitely the stoic type.

When the wrapping came off, Chance and Arinn made their way back over to the four of us adults. "Can I ride it?" Chance asked.

"Dude," Hawk turned to Finn. "I am not your lawn boy. I'm not coming over to cut your grass."

His tactic of not understanding was to use sarcasm. It was a good choice, as a riding mower seemed like an odd gift since we lived in a townhome with a spot of grass not much bigger than the mower itself. I often joked that our yard could be cut with scissors. I was definitely glad I was not the one who had opened the gift.

"Not *my* grass. This …" The country singer swung his arm around the field-like area in which we were standing.

"What are you talking about?" Hawk's tone changed on the last word before he paused and glanced at the kids. "Hey, man, is this the place …?"

"Where we got her back," Finn answered in a serene manner.

I felt like the two men were talking in some kind of code.

Where were we? Who came back?

"It's where we knew she was safe and healthy and …" That time Finn stopped, and I knew it was because he was getting emotional. "Yeah. A year ago."

"It's been a year, huh?"

"It has."

While Finn answered Hawk's question, I put the pieces together. "Arinn."

"Yeah." To the outside world, Hawk could seem gruff, but to all of us in that field right then, we knew what a sentimental and steadfast man he was. His soft voice personified that, as he remembered a year before when the Murphys were reunited with their daughter on, from what I was gathering, the land on which we were standing.

Lara brushed her hand along Arinn's hair and looked at us. "You know when Finn bought it, the idea was to make sure to do something special … so that there are only good memories when we see it. And what else would be better than having our friends start their family here?"

"We're giving you the land to build your own house," Finn punctuated his wife's thoughts.

I pushed aside any other questions I had and sputtered out one that took precedence due to my pure astonishment. "You're giving us …?" I looked at Hawk, who was equally lost for words.

"Oh … uh …" he managed.

"Look how close you will be for my beck and call."

"Finn!" Lara verbally berated her husband's joke and then looked at me. "That's not the reason. But having you close by—almost neighbors—would be nice."

I was still too overwhelmed to react, other than reiterating the offer. "You're giving us the property?"

"And the mower."

"And the mower," I echoed Finn.

"It goes all the way back to a creek, which eventually leads to the river." Our boss pointed to a spot that seemed more of a horizon.

The gift was too much. It was unexpected. I'm sure it was phenomenal, but I couldn't even process.

"Geez, uh …"

"That's … It's a lot, man." Hawk vocalized what I couldn't.

"Look, do I have to make accepting gifts part of both your contracts?"

My husband rolled his eyes at our boss, but spoke to me. "You good with this, Mai?"

By the way he scanned the land then, as if he was already constructing a future in his head, I could tell *he* was. And since I had a minute or two to process, I was warming up to the idea. Our townhome contained only two bedrooms, and I didn't want to duke it out with my child on whether the second was my workspace or their room. Plus, the no-yard issue. The home wasn't really meant for a family. It was for what Hawk had first purchased it as years before—a bachelor pad.

"Uh … yeah. Yeah."

"I guess it's a 'yeah.'" Hawk confirmed my answer but immediately did a protective tease when I hugged Finn with a thanks. "Hey, what did I tell you about hands?"

I released those hands and instead playfully smacked Hawk with one. "I'll write out a formal thank-you card, okay?"

Hawk pecked me on the lips and stuck his hand out to shake Finn's. "This is seriously … Thank you. Yeah."

A place to build a house from scratch with room to roam for both us and our little one. It was a fresh start of our own. It almost seemed too good to be true.

***

Celebrating Christmas with Hawk's family in Oklahoma was put on hold until the end of January since it would be the only time everyone's schedules matched up. His younger brother, Liam, went out of town with his wife's family every year. His older brother, Jake, was still getting situated after being transferred to an army post in Virginia. Plus, his wife, Naomi, was spending a few weeks with her family in Japan. And Hawk's mother and her significant other, Elijah, were taking a holiday bus trip to Florida.

Having no close family left of my own, Hawk and I were invited to spend the holiday with Sophia—Jeff's sister—and their family in my home state of Maryland. But we declined, knowing it was time to make our own new traditions. That involved getting a little tree, putting up a few decorations, and binge-watching some Christmas films—with the age-old debate if *Die Hard* was one. Then we went shopping for our gifts to each other … our wedding rings. That was to be the highlight until we had received the unexpected and spectacular gift from Finn and Lara. So, also during the week of Christmas, Hawk and I researched and drew up a basic floorplan and wish list for our soon-to-be home.

Thanks again to Finn's connections, directly after the holiday, we met with an architect who agreed to make our dreams into a reality. Hawk and I both liked the country ranch feel. I imagined a stone sidewalk leading to the front porch where, alongside two rocking chairs, there would be a bench swing like the one at Della's, where Hawk first said "me, too." We decided on an open-concept, with no formal dining room or living room. Instead, there would be a center island with sink that separated the kitchen from the dining table and family room with stone fireplace. The house would have two wings off that central area. The first would host the garage, laundry, pantry, built-in desk for my work area, and master suite. The other wing would be home to two hall closets, a powder and full bathroom, and three bedrooms. One of those would be the nursery, of course. I still had the leather rocking chair my mom read to me in. So, I already imagined it in there. Another bedroom could be a playroom, and the third would be for guests. I didn't dare think about having another kid. I considered the one inside me a miracle. It was most definitely a surprise, since

I mistakenly thought I couldn't conceive. Besides, Hawk and I were both in our mid-to-upper thirties—biological clock and all that. On the architect's coaxing, we decided to add a partial second floor, which would be part attic/storage and part game room with a powder room, bar, and closet. It would make an ideal man cave for the boys in the band. But we would wait to finish that off until after we moved in. Necessities first.

Once the papers were signed, all we had to do was wait for the beginning of construction. Building a house was something neither of us had ever done. While some of it was nerve-racking, we felt a special bond to that ground and the new beginning it represented not only to us but the Murphys, too.

Both Hawk and I were back to work in January. I was helping promote the new single and also teasing the film soundtrack that Finn was involved with. Hawk was in the thick of helping plan and organize the multi-city, summer-long tour. There were so many details with venues, transportation, driver schedules, opening acts, catering, hotels, etcetera. It was one of the most stressful aspects of both Finn and Hawk's jobs. I was glad they had done it for a number of years so it was well-oiled. I was also thankful it was not part of my job description, and I learned to stay out of those conversations so that unwarranted stress wasn't thrown at me.

What I *was* looking forward to was having a date night. After spending an afternoon at the Murphy abode celebrating Chance's fifth birthday, Hawk and I were desperately seeking alone adult time, which did not involve any country music talk. While we didn't work directly on the same things for Finn, a lot of topics crisscrossed, and we had to remember to set them aside every so often.

"Hawk?" I called out, hoping for his assistance with a necklace's particularly hard clasp. "Hawk?" I tried again. Getting no reply, I decided to make my way out of the bedroom. I cleared my throat upon seeing him sitting on the living room sofa completely engrossed in whatever was on his phone. "Alex?" I raised my voice a little.

On my pronunciation of his formal name, he looked up. "Them fightin' words."

I walked over to him. "So is ignoring the mother of your unborn child."

"Sorry, sweetie. I was a little preoccupied."

"What's up? Sports scores? Is it NFC or AFC?" I was pretty sure I got those terms right.

I wasn't a football fan, or really any sports for that matter. In contrast, Hawk definitely was when he could be. His schedule didn't often allow him the luxury. He told me he made a point of it, though, for playoffs. Thank goodness hockey's were still months away.

"No." He placed his phone on the coffee table. "I … God, I just found out something."

"What? What is it?" I asked cautiously, knowing by his almost blank, distracted look and stumbling of words that it wasn't good.

"Naomi died." He didn't lose eye contact, but there were definitely a few blinks as he said the words.

"What?" I beseeched, having totally been taken off guard at the unexpected, devastating news regarding his brother's wife. "What? What happened?" I rested the necklace near his phone on the coffee table.

"I don't know." He patted the spot on the sofa next to him. "It was the middle of the night. They think it had something to do with her diabetes. Crap! I can't believe …"

I moved close to him on the sofa and touched his hand. "She was still in Japan when it happened?"

"Yeah. Shit! This … It sucks."

I remembered an even sadder fact. "Oh my God, they have a little boy."

"Not that little but, yeah, Raiden's thirteen."

"That's little. Too young to lose a mom." I understood that particular pain. I tilted my head onto Hawk's shoulder, which, thankfully, didn't have any long-lasting ill effects from a serious injury months before. "How'd you find out?"

He rested his chin on the top of my head. "Momma. It was her on the phone."

I gave us both a minute or two to simply absorb the tragedy before lifting my head back up to look at him. "When's the funeral?" My voice dipped momentarily, recalling days past. "What can we do?"

"From what I understand, everything is happening fairly quickly. They're having a small, private ceremony in Japan," he acknowledged not only where Naomi was from but also where she and Jake had met when he was stationed there. "She'll be cremated. Jake's gonna bring part of her ashes to be buried in our family plot. My mom wants to do a memorial service then, too. Nothing formal. More like a gathering of friends and family."

"When?"

"Next weekend when they were originally coming. Only now it's …"

Yeah. Sigh. It would be when we had planned on seeing them for January Christmas. Although I had met Della and Hawk's other brother before, it was to be my first time meeting Jake and his family. How could it be? No Christmas. No celebration. The family would still get together, but instead it would be a sad time of darkness and mourning.

"Geez, Hawk. God, I'm so sorry. I—" I bit my bottom lip. I wanted to sever it, as if it would symbolize ending the pain for the family, but I knew it wouldn't.

"I love you, Mai. I want to make sure you know that."

I don't remember a time when tears so instantly flowed down my face. I am sure my pregnancy hormones didn't help, but it was the unfiltered, pure honesty of his sudden words that filled me with emotion. The thing was, I *did* know what he said was true. He didn't say it all the time, nor did he need to—we actually said our *me, too* more. I cupped his face in my hands and kissed him through my tears.

We wouldn't go out on our date night. In fact, we didn't

leave the townhome at all. We forgot about necklaces and sports scores. Instead, we sat on the sofa in each other's arms, thinking about precious time and love … and how you can never have enough of either.

CHAPTER FOUR

Right before we opened the door, my feet swayed and I took in a deeper-than-usual breath. I knew it wasn't something anyone looked forward to, but I needed to be there for Hawk and his family. When he grasped my hand, I'm sure my husband would have said it was for me, but I knew—or at least hoped—it was a mutual sense of security and comfort. I was determined not to think of the last memorial I had attended but, instead, concentrate on his hand and the love attached with it.

As we entered, there was the immediate switch from outside to inside … from normal life to depressive state … from silence to a collective milling of grouped voices. I had to take Hawk's lead. I was unfamiliar with the majority of the attendees. But he was, even if it had been years since being face-to-face with some of them.

It was a trio of women gathered near the sofa that got my immediate attention. Only one was facing us. She had wispy hair that was perfectly highlighted. Although, I couldn't tell if the blonde or the copper shade was the natural hue. The expression on her face upon seeing Hawk was indescribable but definitely noted. There was a lot of emotions captured in those few seconds, making me look at my husband with query.

"My sister," he answered, and it made perfect sense, not only because of the unsaid interaction but also because of their matching hazel eyes.

I knew very little about Hawk's half-sister, Annie, besides that she was the youngest Brannigan sibling and the only one who was not Della's. His father married the "other" woman, aka Annie's mom. Because of that and the fact that their dad died at a fairly young age, the siblings had a distant, semi-strained relationship.

The same could most definitely be said when it came to Hawk and one of the other women I recognized among the three. "Is tha …?" I mentioned the short, curvy, dark-haired woman who was talking with Annie and Liam's wife, Keita. "It's Oaklee with them, right?"

"The one and only." His grumbled response confirmed the identification of his ex-wife, whom I had only met briefly once.

"What is she doing here?"

"God only knows." He shook his head.

From an opposite direction, another woman approached, drawing our attention away from the trio. "Oh, oh, Alex. I'm so glad you're here. Oh." Della tipped on her toes and hugged Hawk.

"Sorry, Momma. Sorry we couldn't get here sooner."

"Understood. I know it's a long drive." She turned to me. "Maya, how are you? How's the little one?"

I touched my blossoming belly. "All good reports."

I was being as careful as I could, especially with my mom's miscarriage and an uncle with autism. But, so far, the baby was doing fantastic. And in a few more weeks, I would be in my third trimester.

"Great. Something positive in our lives, huh?" Della squeezed her eyes with determination, but a drop or two still released. "Oh, my heart breaks for Jake and Raiden."

"Where are they?" Hawk craned his neck around the inside of the rustic, yet completely finished, barn.

Della didn't like the idea of a mournful gathering in her personal house. So, it was taking place in the second building on her property. The barn, which reminded me of a log cabin from the outside, wasn't used as a home for any kind of animals but, instead, as an extensive storage area, including hosting family room and dinette furnishings, area rugs, and a TV. Those had been in Elijah's place before he moved in with Della, and the couple didn't need double of everything. Hawk had teased that it was Elijah's own man cave if/when he got in the doghouse with Della.

"The kids are all in the house. Jake and Liam went to check on them." Hawk's mother was most likely speaking of Raiden, as well as Liam's grade-school-aged daughter and son. "I think it's more of a break from all of this, though. Jake doesn't like the attention and fuss. You two are peas in the pod like that."

I almost laughed. Della had nailed Hawk on that one. It was both an endearing and aggravating attribute of his.

"Well, I'm sorry we couldn't have gotten here sooner for Jake's sake but not so sorry that things are winding down and we missed most of the guests. Could have been spared one more." Hawk did a one-nod in Oaklee's direction.

In return, Della rolled her eyes. "Came with Phillip."

Hawk's ex-wife certainly didn't have a fan in his mom. That I had noted when I'd first met Della—before Hawk and I had known we were pregnant or moved in together. My own relationship with my mother-in-law had started off a little rocky, but the more I got to know her, the more I understood it was because of what a devoted and protective mom she was. I vowed to have the same mentality when it came to both Hawk and our baby.

"Well, *Phillip* I wouldn't mind seeing," he acknowledged with an obvious reference to not wanting to see someone else.

"I'll send him your way," she offered. "I'm gonna see if Eli can help bring some of the food back to the house." She pointed toward the extensive built-in workbench area, which had a spread of food and beverages.

"Momma, I can help."

"No. No. You had a long day and just got here, middle one. Talk with your friend. Be with your wife. Eli's happy to help."

While Della headed toward her beau, I purposefully turned so my back was to Oaklee. I wasn't ready for her. I knew it was probably inevitable that we would have to talk, but I wanted avoidance for at least a few more minutes. As I straightened Hawk's dark blazer, he filled me in on the fact that Phillip was Max's older brother, making him Oaklee's brother-in-law. The Brannigan and Dierks boys grew up together. Although, when Max married Oaklee after her divorce from Hawk, it was hard for the men to maintain a friendship. But, then again, besides family, Hawk pretty much left Oklahoma behind him years before, when he moved to Nashville and began his career.

After being on the road a good part of the day, my pregnant body needed a potty break. So, as Phillip started making his way over to Hawk, I headed toward the back of the barn where there was an additional bump-out area that hosted a rear door and a basic powder room. Almost immediately after leaving Hawk's side, though, I felt terribly exposed. It was like everyone was staring at me … although there were few people left. I knew it was because I was the outsider … the newcomer … the one who called their native boy something different.

But then I stopped at the easel set up for Naomi. Surrounded by a couple vases of the most beautiful soft-pink flowers that had to be out of season, were photos of the sister-in-law I would never meet. From those pictures and the stories Hawk told, I knew she had been happy, despite marrying into a family and culture completely different than hers. If *she* could do it, so could I. Damn, I wished I could have known her.

It was when I was coming back out of the restroom that I basically ran into Jake. Although we had never met, I knew it was him. The couple of photos I had seen helped, but it was really because of the military uniform he was wearing and his resemblance to Hawk. It was their similar noses and mouths, although the latter was a little more difficult to tell because Hawk sported facial hair and Jake was clean-shaven. Jake's eyes weren't hazel like Hawk's, though. They were darker and seemed to sadly reflect his current state of mind.

"Jake?" I went for the confirmation as we entered the main room together—he from the back door and I from the powder room. "I'm sor—"

"Thanks for coming." He spoke immediately and almost robotically.

The widower already had that look—the look of too much pity, the look of *I can't attempt to smile*, the look of the world being swept out from under you. I knew it. I knew it all too well.

"You're a friend of …?" He was attempting to make conversation but seemed to have little energy or will to do so, similar to how his feet were continuing to move forward but shuffling as they did.

"I'm Maya." What a sad way to meet one of the most important people in my husband's life.

"Oh, oh, Maya." He stopped and turned his eyes to actually meet mine. "Alex's Maya."

"Yeah," I agreed with a slight smile, liking that connection to Hawk.

"Sorry. I've heard a lot about you. Congratulations on everything. Alex … He … Yeah, he seems good."

"Thanks."

Our joy wasn't what we were supposed to be concentrating on, though. I remembered despising anyone who was happy around me when Jeff first died. It was unfair. It was not right that they could have joy and I couldn't. Worse yet, Jeff couldn't. It wasn't a healthy or kind thought, but I also don't think it is uncommon with those who are grieving. I wondered if Hawk's brother thought the same about me, despite the words coming from his mouth.

"I'm sorry we're meeting under these circumstances," I offered.

"Yeah," he agreed. "She was looking forward to meeting you." His eyes seemed to glaze over or wonder for a second before adding, "It was just so sudden."

I understood. Almost everyone who had passed away in my life had died suddenly—my dad, my mom, my mom's mom, Jeff. None had been easy. I wished in each of those cases to have had the moment to realize it was coming … to say something. Even though my dad's parents both died of basically old age, I didn't get to see their health deteriorate because they lived so far away in Canada. Therefore, their deaths also seemed sudden. Grandpa Charles was the only one I had been able to be with and comfort in the retirement facility he had moved into after my mom's mom passed away.

"Her parents said she'd had a headache and felt a little off, but she'd had a long day catching up with friends who were a few hours or so away from their hometown. She drove, and she said she just needed some sleep. She was always so good about managing her diabetes. I never thought …"

His comment reminded me of Jeff's career as a police officer. We both had known any given call could be the one, but naively never thought it would come to fruition. I knew I should say something to Jake … something comforting … something meaningful. But if my experience taught me anything, it was that there were no words that could meet that challenge.

"I'm sorry." It was the most generic response there was, but it was the truth, and I followed it up by trying to make a connection so, perhaps, he wouldn't feel so very alone. "I know what a loss it is. I know how … how it feels. How you—"

"You can't possibly know what he's going through."

Jake and I had been in such a solemn, intense conversation that I hadn't seen anyone approach. My complete concentration had been on him, which it should have, and not on the woman who was wearing too much makeup and a clingy, lacy, black dress that was more suitable for prom night than a memorial service. I wondered if she wore it specifically knowing she would see Hawk. Maybe it was because she was mentally stuck in her teenaged years. She sure seemed to act like it.

Regardless, I tried to be the more mature of the two of us and ignored her looks and verbal slaughter. "Unfortunately, I do. As a spouse and as a ch—"

"Didn't see this happening." Oaklee stopped my sentence with her own as she looked at the baby bump extruding from my muted gray dress. "Not the way he acted and what made our marriage implode. How did you manage that? I'm sure he is furious. He likes his freedom."

While his ex-wife was not a frequent—if hardly ever—conversation between the two of us, Hawk had told me enough about her and their relationship to understand. It was important and healthy for me to know, just as I had told him about Jeff and me. Oaklee came from a big family. She was the first born of seven, and all the siblings were close. Because it was what she had always known, she had wanted to start a family right away. Hawk had not, especially after just losing his father and only barely being out of high school.

As I silently prepared my retort, she abruptly censored herself and dove into Hawk, who had sided up to us. "Alex!" Oaklee couldn't see his stunned look at her sudden hold on him, but I could. "Oh God, it's so terrible." She was suddenly talking in a sickening sweet tone. "I can't believe it."

He pulled her swiftly yet kindly away. "Oaklee." His head did the smallest of nods to me as if checking to make sure I was all right.

I returned a reassuring one back as Jake said, "Glad you're here." I'm sure he meant being home in general, but I also think he was grateful Hawk's presence had interrupted the current catty conversation. "Appreciate it, brother." When the two men embraced momentarily, I brought my hand down to my belly, feeling a tiny flutter from our little one.

Oaklee's shrilly voice interrupted the brotherly bonding. "I'm so glad we are *all* able to be here for you." God help me, even with tears coming from her eyes, I wondered if she wasn't playing up the whole scene a little. "Remember that time Jake brought Naomi home, and we all—"

"That was a long time ago." Successfully cutting her off, my beautiful man then segued to me when speaking to his brother. "Maya and I came straight here from her doctor's appointment. Sorry we couldn't get here sooner for you and Rai." He took my hand.

"Do you need anything?" I offered, glad to have the opportunity to shift verbal gears.

"Neh. Really. I know you've had a long day," said the grieving man with obvious circles under his eyes. "Go. Go get unpacked or whatever. I'm gonna try to wrap up things here. Should only be family at the house. This, you know, isn't my thing."

Hawk clamped his strong hand onto his brother's shoulder. "Yeah, everyone should be leaving." I wondered if Oaklee noticed or even cared about Hawk's blatant eye roll toward her. "We're gonna grab some stuff from my truck, and then we'll meet you at the house."

"Sure thing," his brother agreed.

Hawk reclaimed my hand and then we thankfully, promptly, made our way outside. After a couple steps taking in the refreshing air, he stopped and turned to me. "What was Oaklee saying in there before I got to you?"

"Nothing." *Let it go*, I silently encouraged myself.

"Maya …"

I said the truth then, not only because I vowed to do so with my husband but also because I knew keeping things pent up wasn't good for the baby. It wasn't only about eating correctly and not drinking alcohol. It was about mentally being free, too.

"She pretty much accused me of getting pregnant on purpose."

"That bitch. She has no right." His hand immediately became tighter on mine. "She only thinks that because she is the master manipulator herself."

It was my turn to reassure. "I know. But, seriously, what is wrong with her? We're at a memorial for goodness sakes, and she's a married woman practically hitting on you!"

Hawk rubbed his hands down his face and along his jawline in obvious frustration. "There's something you should know." He paused for a second. "Something I just found out from Phillip."

"Um, okay. More small-town Oklahoma gossip?" I was trying to keep my wits about me, and I could tell Hawk appreciated it with his half-hearted chuckle.

That time he rubbed my hand. "I guess her marriage isn't so sound. Oaklee was giving the excuse that Max didn't come tonight because he wasn't feeling well. But, in reality, they're separating." My *huh* must have been more vocal than I thought because he said, "Phillip's trying to get them to work through it for the kids' sake."

"It's especially hard when there's kids involved."

"Yep." Hawk seemed reflective, surely thinking of his own childhood consisting of three siblings with parents who separated. "Believe me, Mai, she's a little b—"

The creak of the door opening behind us halted Hawk's thought, which was probably for the best. Enough bad Oaklee juju. Annie emerged, swinging her thick blue coat onto her spaghetti-strap black dress. As she strung her arms through, I nudged Hawk. If days/events like the one we were in told us anything, it was to say things while you could, especially if it involved family. Hawk didn't have that chance very often with his sister, and I encouraged him to take it.

"Annie." After a semi-awkward hug, Hawk took the opportunity to introduce us.

"So nice to meet you," I offered and then admitted, "I

know this is a weird thing to say right now, but I adore your hair."

She let out a soft chuckle. "Oh, thanks. The blonde is more for the job. Otherwise, it's similar to ..." She gave a nod at Hawk's dark mahogany hair and then said to him, "You look happy."

"I am." He kissed my temple as punctuation. "It was good of you to come, Annie."

"Yeah, I'm glad Keita called. It was nice of your mom to include me, too. She's always gracious." Annie spoke kindly of Della, which I knew had to be an awkward relationship for sure, considering the circumstances.

"We're just getting our stuff from the truck. Are you gonna—?"

Annie cut me off before I had a chance to say *stay*, and I wondered if it was because she thought I was going to say the opposite ... like she was another outsider like me who wasn't considered core family. "I've gotta go. I have an early rise tomorrow."

"Yeah." Hawk's one word was stoic, not letting me decipher if he was relieved or disappointed by her answer.

"I saw Liam, but I didn't see Jake again to say good night. Tell him, you know, to take care." She took a breath and then looked Hawk straight on. "And you, too."

"Will do," Hawk agreed.

"It was nice to meet you, Maya."

"Same," I acknowledged, and then we watched her walk past the old wooden picket fence to her car. "You did good." I smiled at Hawk.

"Hmmf. It wasn't so bad." And before he could give me any more sentiment when it came to his sister, he acknowledged the make of her vehicle. "Punch bug yellow, by the way, and it's a classic." According to our personal punch bug game rules, he was going to throw two punches my way.

"But it's still parked."

That rule—the parked rule—overrode the others and

was the best of all. It meant we kissed. And, boy, with the other events of the day, I sure needed that right then.

CHAPTER FIVE

It could have been a number of things that woke me that night—a different mattress, memories on my mind, or a dream I couldn't remember. At least the reoccurring one of Percy had gone away after talking with Hawk about it. No matter which, though, I couldn't get back to sleep.

Not wanting to disturb Hawk with my tossing and turning, I decided to venture downstairs and see if Della had some kind of decaf tea to soothe my sleeplessness. Walking past Raiden asleep on the sofa, I made my way into the kitchen. That's when I discovered I wasn't the only one living a nocturnal life. I was surprised—although, I guess I shouldn't have been—to find Jake, donning shorts and a simple long-sleeved shirt, sitting at the farmhouse-style table with a mug in his hand. What was in it, I did not know. Perhaps another form of liquid that might ease one's brain … one that a pregnant me could not partake in but could have definitely used.

"I didn't realize anyone was up." I pulled at the strings around the bust of my green smock nightgown, feeling a little exposed in front of a brother-in-law I had just met. "I can leave you to yourself," I offered as an apology for interrupting what was surely a much-needed moment to himself.

But Jake was up. Not only awake, but he *stood* up. After he walked around the table, he scooted a chair out for me. He did it without a word, but the invitation to join him was understood.

"So gentlemanly," I said essentially just for something to say. While I had talked with Hawk's brother before we all went to sleep, it had been alongside the immediate family. We hadn't had any true solo time together, and I recognized it could be awkward with me being the newbie to the family group.

As I sat, Jake reclaimed his own seat. "Alex doesn't pull out a chair for you?"

"He does sometimes," I acknowledged. "But he doesn't need to. Since the moment we met, he knows I can take care of myself. It doesn't stop him from being over protective, though. I'm starting to realize it's a Brannigan trait." I gave credit to all the brothers.

"Hmmm." Modesty was one, too, as he flipped the narrative to another protector. "I imagine your late husband was, also. A cop, right?"

"Yeah." Any reference to Jeff always brought an instant solemn overcast to my inner core. I wondered when—or if—that would ever change. "My grandma was thrilled that I was taking a self-defense class. I think it had something to do with one of my mom's boyfriends before meeting my dad, but she never directly told me. Anyway, Jeff was the instructor. It was how we met." And before I went any further down my personal melancholy lane, I prompted with a lighthearted query, "So, you couldn't sleep, or just trying to sneak an extra piece of Della's pie?"

"The first, but the latter sure sounds like a bonus. Can I get you some?" Again, with the family taught and/or military manners, he began to stand.

"No. No." I put my hand up in denial. "Already had too much. Eating for two doesn't take in account for heartburn."

"True enough." The way he said it made me think he was recalling his wife's own pregnancy.

After a moment of silence between us, I offered, "Nighttime is the worst. It's too quiet. Too many thoughts creep in."

His slow blink let me know he understood that I was no longer talking about acid reflux but the sad bond we had between us of losing a spouse. "On top of that, I'm not a good sleeper. Momma says I've been that way since birth. It's the thing that bothers me the most about when Naomi died. If I had been in Japan with her, I would have known she had gotten up and wasn't feeling well and needed something. I would have been able to help." My shoulders sunk upon witnessing his depressed eyes and knowing he was reliving that pain and wondering what could have been. "How'd you make it through, Maya? How were you able to keep going on?"

I appreciated the fact that such a strong man was being vulnerable enough to ask. Maybe it was because it was the middle of the night. Or maybe it was because he felt comfortable with someone who was more of a stranger. I knew I hadn't wanted to talk with anyone close to me when Jeff first died. Logically, it should have been the opposite. They were the people you were supposed to lean on. But, in a weird way, that made it all too real. Strangers created a façade that I was talking about a whole other sad woman who had lost her husband suddenly and violently.

Regardless of the reason, I answered Hawk's brother with the same vulnerability. "Honestly, I don't know. For a while, a lot of it was a blur. There was so much going on because of how he died—the press, the charges, and the trial. I had to wake up and be present every day. And then when it was over, I kind of crashed, and then slowly … slowly"—I made a point to reiterate—"I made my way back up. Not that I will ever be the same," I added because no one can be the same person they were after losing someone they love. "There are still things …" As if to confirm my thought, my chest sucked in an involuntary breath similar to one of my minor claustrophobic moments. It was enough to make me slightly change the direction of my dialogue. "But where you're at now? I get it. You don't want to hear one more 'I'm sorry' or 'How are you,' or you'll lose it."

"Amen."

"That's why when I first met you and started to say something similar you clipped me off."

"Yeah. Sorry."

"No problem. Really." I smiled, even if it was a melancholy one. "You know, I wonder how people would have reacted if I answered with blunt honesty how I was actually feeling back then."

"Probably not well. It makes *them* feel bad."

"Still, they're only trying their best to help." And after a second, I added, "If you can, let them."

"Never has been in my nature."

I instantly shook my head. "You and Hawk really *are* two peas in a pod," I quoted Della.

"I hear that a lot. Still amazed by all of this, by the way." He nodded to me and, in particularly, my belly.

"*I* hear *that* a lot." I did a slight chuckle, glad to hear it from someone who said it in a kind way … not out of jealousy or spite.

Likely also thinking of Hawk's time with the black-laced vixen, Jake reinforced his meaning. "He's so happy after such a long time."

"We both are." I wanted to confirm, not only in case he had any doubts about my role in his brother's life but also that you can be happy again after the throes of grief.

"That's good. I already miss tha—" He stopped himself, and I understood. He was ending his time with his wife, while Hawk's was only beginning.

"Your brother—"

"Wants to know what this little late-night meeting of the minds is about." I caught a glimpse of Hawk's sleepy smile before he kissed the top of my head. Of course he was awake. He didn't sleep well either, especially if he knew I was up.

When he sat, I answered his query with a white lie. "Della's pie."

He didn't blink with his response, despite obviously seeing there wasn't any pie or even plates or silverware out. "Worthy." Hawk raised his chin up toward his brother. "How you doing?"

Jake and I instantaneously caught each other's eyes. He rolled his as I shook my head. And then we both laughed briefly at my poor husband's expense.

"What?" Bewildered, Hawk looked from me to his brother.

"If you really want to know how I am …" Jake took a breath, glanced at me for a nod of encouragement, and then, with pure sincerity, spoke his truth. "I … I feel paralyzed. No." He rubbed the top of his head. "It's worse. It's like a part of me has been amputated … without anesthesia."

Thank God Hawk didn't hesitate, and he didn't try to say something soothing or, unknowingly, condescending. His reply back was just as honest. "Shit … yeah."

Silence settled in the room, and I suspect we were all in our own thoughts regarding loss. I gave it a moment or two before I took the lead to change the subject. "Hawk?"

"Yeah?" Still in a mellow mood, he turned to look at me.

"I was thinking that I'd like to go to the musical with your mom and Elijah."

I got the response I expected from my husband—a grumble. "What? Really?"

Della had told us that part of the proceeds for the following night's event were going to benefit one of her best travel clients who had been diagnosed with stage-four cancer. She didn't want to miss supporting her but was hesitant to leave with the loss of Naomi. But her sons had encouraged her and Elijah to go. A live performance of a classic tale was far removed from Hawk's wheelhouse, Liam had a prior commitment, and Jake was obviously not up to it, especially since the burial of the ashes were to take place during the day.

"Yeah." I nodded.

"Aw..." In an obvious display of disgruntlement, he started to roll his eyes at Jake but then aborted quickly, I'm sure realizing he was lucky to have a wife to do something with. "Okay, we can go if you really want."

I did, but it was only part of my ultimate plan. "I didn't say *we* had to go. Why don't you stay with Jake and Raiden and have a boys' night?" By observing their sibling bond, I realized a chance to simply be with each other and let loose would probably be good for both of them.

"You sure?" I think he tried to disguise it, but my husband seemed instantly relieved.

"Bro code and all that," I teased the newest Finn Murphy song and then added a sarcastic, yet truthful, scenario. "Hawk, I don't want my experience of the play to be interrupted by yelling at you to get off your phone or wondering exactly how long it takes for you to use the restroom or get snacks."

When Jake spit out a single burst of laughter, it allowed Hawk to laugh a little, too. "Whatever." He turned more definitively toward his brother. "You game?"

"*I* will let you check your phone and you *have* to get the snacks."

"I think I'm down with that," Hawk answered Jake before putting his hands on the table as if he was getting ready to stand. "Speaking of, is anyone actually going to have a piece of pie?"

"No. All yours, brother. I need to get some sleep." Jake actually stood. "See ya in the morning or, you know, in a few hours." And he exited.

I ran my fingertips along the top of Hawk's arm. "I should try to sleep, too."

"Okay." He stood and gave me a hand in doing the same. Again, it wasn't something he needed to do, but it was sweet. The same could be said about his fluttering of kisses on my lips right then. And then he smiled, almost like a little boy getting caught raiding the liquor closet. "I am seriously hungry for pie now. I'll be up in a minute."

***

I only made it to intermission. That was no fault of the production. The storyline and acting were amazing … actually much better than I expected for local theater. It was simply because I was wearing out. Between the stress and not sleeping well the night before, I knew my limitations. It was why I had driven separately from Elijah and Della. I didn't want to fall asleep during the play, and I wanted to be awake enough to drive back to Della's. It was very important to me.

Even though the front door was unlocked when I arrived back at the house, no one appeared to be home. Hawk, Jake, and Raiden were supposed to be there, having their boys' night. I called out a couple times and searched the residence. But no luck.

Sitting on the family room sofa, I took off my strappy black flats and wiggled my slightly swelled feet around. As I did, I looked at the rug, and a flashback of Della's dinner-time conversation with Jake and Hawk seared through my head. In true momma fashion—despite her boys being grown men and having families of their own—she had jokingly warned them to behave while we were out. She told them to stay put if they were drinking and to not spill anything on her new area rug.

It made me think. Maybe they took her warning seriously and went outside or even to the barn. I wouldn't interrupt, but I wanted to at least tell Hawk I was back and see how the three were.

With that in mind, I decided to forgo the shoes. My feet felt so free without the confinement. Besides, it was Oklahoma. It seemed like a barefoot kind of place—tons of long, dry grass and neighbors far enough away that you couldn't make out any details. It was, in fact, similar to the lot where we were building our new home. I walked out front to where I had parked Hawk's truck and then started along the side of the house toward the back, where the barn was so many yards away.

That's when I saw it. And heard it. God, I even smelled it. The barn wasn't totally engulfed, but it was definitely on fire. I had to get in there. I had to find Hawk. Shoes or not, I took off running.

When I went for the barn's main door, I could feel heat near the handle, but it didn't burn my skin. As soon as I opened it, though, I could tell that clear sight was pretty much going to be futile. Smoke was on the rise and, seemingly, worse than the flames, which appeared to be mostly at the south end.

After my initial assessment and a few more steps inside, a sense of the walls closing in started. I was hoping it was simply my claustrophobia kicking in, and the actual, physical walls weren't deteriorating. But it didn't matter. I couldn't let it. I had a mission. I had to make sure Hawk was okay. I had to make sure he wasn't in there.

If it was hard to see, it was equally hard to breathe. I wanted to cover my mouth and nose, but I had to call out his name. I had to find Hawk. I couldn't … I couldn't … No, it couldn't happen again.

"Hawk! Hawk!" Each time I yelled, I inhaled. Each time I inhaled, I coughed. Yet … "Hawk! God, where are you? Hawk!" As I continued into the barn, I heard nothing in response except for the crackling of fire and possibly timber. I knew I shouldn't be in there. I knew it wasn't safe. I also knew I had to try again … just a few more steps, even though I could hardly see. "Hawk! God, please. Hawk! Where—?"

In the midst of the coughing that ensued, I thought I heard something that wasn't a natural element. It might have been a voice. I strained to concentrate. It could have been Hawk. It might have been Raiden. I didn't know the thirteen-year-old well—even less than Jake—because he, with due right, had been very quiet and sullen since we had arrived.

"Raiden? Hawk? Jake?" Cough, cough, cough.

"Maya! Maya!" That time the voice was clearer. The voice was beautiful. The voice was my husband's.

"Hawk, where are you?" Even though I heard him, I couldn't see him.

"Shit, Maya."

"I can't …" I felt a singeing sensation in my nose. "I can't breathe."

Oh my God. Never mind the smoke, my claustrophobia was hitting an extreme. I had no idea where I was. Panic was setting in. And with the smoke, I couldn't breathe, which was the thing I needed to do the most when I started with one of my claustrophobic attacks.

"Make a beeping sound. I need to figure out where you are."

He sounded semi-calm, even though I knew he couldn't be. He had to be panicked. But I was, too. And he knew me well enough—well, better than that—to know I needed him to be as calm as he could be right then.

"What? Make a what?" A pull on my arm halted my speech.

Hawk was close enough to me then that I could see him, even if it was hazy. His non-descript shirt was pulled up over his face to protect himself from the smoky surroundings—a smart, but confining, idea. "Crap!" He pulled at me again, that time both in a forward and downward motion. "Get down low. Come on."

Hawk's massive body seemed to envelop mine as he firmly, yet carefully, managed to cover and guide us. It seemed like it took forever, but I'm sure it was only a matter of minutes or even seconds when—among some swearing and dodging of flying flicks of fire, which I felt prick my exposed forearm—we were out of the burning barn. After walking a few steps from the immediate danger, Hawk patted my top-covered left shoulder, and I wondered if there had been a straggling spark there. But besides it being on the back side, I couldn't see it because my eyes were burning and a little foggy.

As I started blinking and went to rub them, Hawk pried my hands from my face. "Let me see. Let me see. Are you all right?"

Inventory of my wellbeing was instant. My back ached. My eyes and lungs stung. My body was hot. But the worst part was, I still couldn't seem to get enough air. Despite being outside, I couldn't catch my breath properly. To say I was panicking would be an understatement. I was going absolutely insane, and the strange part was, it was only increasing since escaping to safety.

"Breathe. Breathe, Maya. God, sweetie, breathe."

I tried. I felt his hands grasping mine and heard his words encouraging me. Yet, it was hard to release my panic about not only having been inside the barn but also not knowing if he had been, too. Or, his brother and nephew.

"Hawk, are you okay?" The words seemed to sputter out. But before he could answer, my head spun from him to someone approaching. "Jake, is that you? Where's Raiden?"

"Raiden!" Jake's eyes were wildly open. "Is he—" He stopped himself as all three of us saw the teen coming from the wooded area beyond the barn. "Raiden … God. You weren't in there, were you?"

"No." Thank goodness my nephew hadn't been in the barn. "I … I followed the fence down to—"

"Get the hose. Get the hose, Raiden! It's right there on the side …" After his demanding request, Jake's voice changed a little, and I could focus enough to realize it was because he was on his phone. "Yeah, yeah." He began giving Della's address as he walked in the direction of where Raiden was wrangling the hose.

"Hawk." My husband's name came out a bit raspy, but at least I could see him a little more clearly. "Are you all right?"

"Me? Shit! It's you. What happened? Can you try to take some deep breaths? Or at least stand still so I can hold you?"

It was only my husband's words and the bobbing of his hands on my arms that made me realize I was jittering. I was bouncing around like I had little red ants crawling all over me. I hadn't been that upset since the time I was trapped inside the damn storm cellar so many feet away. Well, that time might have, actually, been better. *That* time, I had only been upset about me. Worrying about Hawk being in the barn pushed everything to a higher extreme.

"Were you in there?" I was trying to be calm, but it wasn't easy.

"The barn? No, Maya. Why … why were *you* in there?"

"I thought you—"

I tried to explain to Hawk, but he cut me off, obviously emotional himself. "Jake and I were on a quick beer run. When we returned, I saw my truck was back and I went to look for you. That's when I saw the barn. What happened? What started the fire?"

"The fire department is on their way." Jake was by our sides again. "Good job, Rai. We need to douse. Maya, are you all right?" When Hawk's brother touched my arm, I nodded more than gave a verbal response. "Okay. Alex, we can't let this hit the grass and take off. Alex!"

Hawk wasn't concerned about hoses, the property, or the barn, though. "Medics, too?" He asked his brother, but his eyes remained on me.

"Yeah, they're all coming," Jake acknowledged before scurrying away, calling out for Raiden to give him the hose.

Encouraging me to breathe, Hawk guided me to sit on a stump, which I wondered if it was from a tree that had come down during a tornado. God knows, there were plenty of them in the state. I was trying to do as he asked—breathe—when the ambulance arrived. Hawk waved his hand so they would come in my direction.

"Alex, we need help!" Jake called out. "We have to get

this under control. I know the department is on their way, but—"

The paramedics reassured Hawk that they would tend to me, and he reluctantly went to aid his brother. Still seated on the tree stump, I was bombarded by a series of questions as blood pressure cuffs were placed on my arm: Was there anyone else in the barn … How long was I in the smoke … How far along was I in my pregnancy … Any other medical concerns they needed to be aware of? The sound of the police and fire department arriving simultaneously made it difficult to hear the medical professionals ask the question about why I was in the barn in the first place. But when the sirens were cut and the two emergency services went to help the Brannigan boys with the blaze, it was much easier to hear my explanation.

That's when Hawk, suddenly once again at my side, interrupted with clear anger. "You don't ever, ever do that again. Ever," he reiterated as if a stern schoolmaster.

With my heightened anxiety and realizing how I absolutely could not have survived Hawk dying, I yelled right back, "I thought you were in there. You could have died. Of course I was going in to find you." A cough strangled my speech on the last word.

"Then you let me die, Maya. You let me die. Don't you ever do something like that again. Never. Don't put your life at risk like that."

I needed an extensive gulp in order to get air into my lungs. It wasn't only due to the smoke intake and my claustrophobia. His ridiculous proclamation was making me beyond upset.

"I am not going to let you die. God …" I needed to pause. Every time I spoke, it irritated my lungs.

"Listen to me—"

"I hear you. Damn it, Hawk, I love you. I am not going to watch you die. I am not going to have that happen again. Not another—" Cough. Cough. I couldn't sit anymore. I don't know what my BP had read—probably not good—

but it had to have skyrocketed even further at that point. I could feel it. I needed to stand. It would help me think or breathe or … just be. "I … God … I …" I was trying not to cough because it agitated everything, but I couldn't help it.

"Maya … Mai, don't get up."

I did, though. "I would go into that barn five thousand more times to make sure you were okay. Let … let …" I was so mad knowing he would belittle my feelings and that he thought I would not fight for him.

"Maya, sit! Come back here. Don't b—"

As I started walking or pacing or something that allowed movement from feeling confined—despite being outside—it occurred to me that I couldn't feel my blood pressure any longer. But immediately after, I realized that probably wasn't a good thing. I wasn't feeling *anything*. It was almost a numbness. Well, besides the consistent irritation in my lungs.

I had to bend over. The coughing episode that ensued was too much—too much on my chest and even my ability to catch my breath. I lost all manners and didn't even attempt to cover my mouth. Instead, I had one hand on my upper torso and the other on my baby bump.

"Maya! Shit!" As Hawk swooped me up in his arms, he beckoned out to the EMTs, "Get me the damn stretcher," and all I could think was, *Please make this stop.*

CHAPTER SIX

The flashing lights … the hurried voices … the crackling material … the heat from the nearby barn—there was so much chaos. But it was nothing compared to the madness that overcame me when I was being lifted into the ambulance and the paramedics attempted to place the suction cup around my mouth. The instant I smelled and then felt the plastic close to my lips, I swatted it away like it was acid. I used one hand initially, and then the other joined in when the medical personal persisted. But I was determined. Nothing was going to be a vacuum around the part of my body that allowed me to breathe. Even though, logically, I knew that was exactly what it was being placed there for. I didn't care if I was making a spectacle of myself. I couldn't handle the suffocation feeling I knew would come with what they wanted to do.

I seemed to be winning the battle of wills. And that was really saying something, since it was two healthy medics versus a weak me. But my fuel was pure fright and adrenaline, which not only gave me strength but most likely also made me look possessed.

"Maya, we want to help you, but you need to let us. We can't be injured doing it," said the one medical personnel, who seemed ready to give up, while the other tried holding my hand.

Then the weight of the whole vehicle seemed to shift as I felt more than saw Hawk get into the ambulance with us. "Maya, you have to. You've got to do it. It's gonna help you breathe."

"No! I don't want it!" My swatting was like the windshield wipers on the tour bus when we would travel beyond the speed limit through a T-storm.

"Maya!" His voice rose even more. "I will hold you down if I have to."

The combination of Hawk's blunt words, his hand on one of my forearms, and the pleading in his eyes had me give in. It took a couple attempts—I wasn't one to go down without a fight—but I conceded. The breathing mask was on.

I immediately started taking big breaths while trying to focus on Hawk in order to mentally gain his strength. He switched his grasp from my arm to my hand. He still looked worried but at least gave a reassuring, closed smile. No … not a smile. Maybe just a less tense facial expression.

"Maya," the no-nonsense EMT began talking a lot calmer, probably because she knew she won our tug-of-war. "We're taking you to the hospital. They'll do a more thorough exam."

I shook my head. No. I didn't think I needed to do that. I cooperated … sort of. I was getting the air. A few more puffs or whatever and I'd be good to go. I pulled at the mask to verbalize my discontent, but the instant it was removed, I started to cough.

"God. Let's go then." My. Husband.

The same EMT placed the mask once again around my mouth and then started to exit the ambulance. "You're going to have to follow in your car, sir," she instructed.

"But I—"

The second EMT interrupted Hawk. "It's the rules."

What? I had to go to the hospital, I still had a horrific

suction cup over my main source of natural air, *and* they were sending Hawk away? There was no way I could do it. Oh, shit. *Breathe. Breathe, Maya,* I kept chanting internally to myself.

"That's ludicrous. She should have someone with her," my husband seemed to actually verbalize my thoughts. "She can't breathe. She needs a familiar—"

"I got her."

They were on either side of the stretcher talking about me as if I wasn't even there. I may as well not have been since I couldn't speak up for myself. I didn't dare take the mask off a second time. I needed it to do its magic. I needed to breathe without coughing.

"We'll be there in no time. Follow right behind us if you want," the EMT suggested.

Breathe. Big. Deep. Breathe. Dear God.

I tried to be brave and nod to my husband that it was okay. It wasn't. But it had to be. I needed to be smart … if not for me, then for the baby. We needed to get checked out, despite my fears.

"Okay." Hawk gave in. "Okay." He pressed my hand up to his lips and then, doing as told, exited the vehicle.

The back doors consequently shutting were not helpful when it came to my claustrophobia. It wasn't like we were in Hawk's truck and I could press a button and let the window down. Not only could I not open the ones in the back of the ambulance, but I also couldn't even see through them, since I was stretched out flat. I decided to close my eyes and imagine happy thoughts.

Because so much of the ride was me doing that and concentrating on breathing, I really didn't remember the details. I do know the medic repeated her reassurance that everything was going to be okay and that the hospital transport was precautionary more than anything. They didn't even have any lights or sirens on. Although, I wished they had so we could have gotten to the hospital's bigger, open space that much sooner.

Once we did arrive, everything happened rather quickly. I was shuffled off for tests and was told Hawk had to fill out some preliminary information regarding my admittance. Because, even though I was not a sports fan, I did know the basic three-strikes-and-you're-out baseball rule. And that applied to me and my medical scenario. High blood pressure—strike one. Smoke inhalation—strike two. Tail end of a second-trimester pregnancy—strike three. Except, I wasn't *out.* I was *in.* The combination led me to an overnight stay for observation and then to see about any other results that would come in later.

Adorning ever-so-lovely standardized hospital pajamas and sitting in the bed that was to be mine for the night, I took in a couple breaths, glad to no longer have a mask covering my mouth. There was a little burn when I inhaled too deep, and if I tried to resist a cough, it only made it worse. I looked out the window to the dreary nighttime sky and then at the even more depressing IV dripping into my arm. I wasn't exactly sure what was in it, but I knew it was nothing serious and was safe. Everything the medical personnel did, they took both me and the baby into consideration.

With time to think in the solitude of my one-patient room, I started feeling bad about the events of the evening and what had led up to me being there. Especially because, purposefully or not, I knew it was my doing—from my entering the barn, to reacting poorly, to my husband's fear. I was still a little upset with Hawk, despite rationally understanding why he had said what he had about wanting me to leave him die. If I thought about it, I wouldn't want him risking his life for me, either. But, regardless, we both would. That's what we signed up for when we fell in love.

It was in that moment when the man himself walked in. God, was I glad to finally see him, as we had been separated since they started my tests. Without a word, he closed his eyes and shook his head before looking again and walking toward me.

As he did, I asked, "Are you all right? Did you get checked out?"

He had been in the barn, too. Granted, not for as long as I'd been. Plus, from what the medical personnel told me during my exam, women take bigger and deeper breaths when pregnant. That and my panic caused more inhalation. My heart and lungs were working harder and longer in that atmosphere than Hawk's. Still, I was concerned about him.

"Yes. I'm not the one being admitted, though." Surely realizing his response came across a tad rough, Hawk took a calming breath. Scooting a chair against my bed, he sat before resting his hand on mine and then spoke in a softer tone. "If something would have happened to you …"

When he didn't—or couldn't—finish his thought, I did so in our special way. "Me, too." On his blip of a smile, I continued, noticing my voice had grown hoarse, "So, you asking me not to help you is like asking me not to breathe." Before he could interject, I gave him credit. "I forgot to stay low like you taught me, but I remembered to touch the door with the back of my hand to feel for heat." Not that it would have stopped me from entering and trying to find him.

A volunteer firefighter, Hawk's father had bestowed a lot of fire safety wisdom on his kids and, therefore, Hawk had also with me. One rule I personally struggled with, however, was keeping the bedroom door shut when we were sleeping. It was claustrophobia versus burning in your sleep. In my eyes, up until that night, I would have rather burned.

"You somehow missed the lesson about getting out, staying out, and calling 9-1-1."

Before we got in another argument essentially about loving each other, I slightly changed the subject. "Jake. How's Jake?"

His eyebrows came together in a confused crinkle. "What? You know he and Raiden are okay. They weren't even in the barn."

"No. Yeah." My attempt to clear my throat didn't help

the raspy sound the smoke irritation had caused. "He had to have seen me, though. He had to have seen me on the stretcher and the ambulance pulling out. He had to be thinking about …"

The realization seemed to streak across Hawk's face. "Naomi. Oh." It wasn't that he didn't care for his brother. It was that his sole focus had been on my welfare. He handed me the bedside water bottle, hoping it would help the roughness of my voice. "I texted them. They know you're … okay."

Noting the slight hesitation before his final word, I reinforced what the doctors had. "I am. And the baby, too." As I placed his hand on my belly, I commented on his clothing. "You got some new attire?"

"Guess mine smelled too much of smoke. They're running them through the laundry service with yours. At least I got some decent sweats." He touched his plain gray sweatpants and then the patterned top that was similar to the one I was wearing, except mine was more of a gown. "I'm not taking a cutesy, matching family photo with you, though."

He was joking, but it made me emotional. Relief was starting to sink in—relief that we were all okay. That didn't always happen. I knew that all too well.

"Hey …" He noticed a straggling tear on my cheek and touched it.

Trying my hand in being stoic, I redirected. "Did you talk with your mom?"

"Yeah," he answered but immediately came back to his concern about me. "You okay?" Although he loved being my defender, Hawk knew I was tough. So, the rare tear was obviously putting him even more on alert.

"Yeah, yeah. Tell me about your mom," I insisted.

And, thankfully, Hawk went along with my request. "Eli got the call about the barn during the play. He and Momma were pulling in as you were going out."

It made sense. Elijah was a firefighter. I couldn't imagine

how he felt getting the call about their own personal residence.

"The barn?" I questioned cautiously, with the fear that I already knew the answer.

"There's nothing left." Seeing my face scrunch in sadness, he added something positive. "But at least it was contained to that. Momma wants to come here, but visiting hours are over."

"You know what I'm starting to not be fond of? Your mom's place." I tried to say it in jest, but there was a boatload of truth with it. "What's the deal with her property and me?"

A small nose breath and nod told me he was also remembering when Mother Nature had me trapped alone in Della's storm cellar months before. "Yeah, that wasn't the best welcome to Oklahoma. And today, most definitely, was not a good one."

His statement gave me the opening to say something I knew I should have from the start of the day. It was, for sure, another reason I had been up in the middle of the night on a "search for pie." But with all the other sadness already in the house, I hadn't felt a need to add to it. Right then, though, in the hospital room with so many emotions, I knew I needed to. I needed to be honest about the day and why the significance of it only added to my adamancy regarding entering the burning barn.

"I have to tell you something." His silence and steady look in my eyes told me to proceed. "I already hated today." I took another sip of water. "It's like a curse … giving me a reminder of all I've lost and that I didn't deserve to be happy."

"What?"

"Jeff died two years ago today."

There. I said it out loud. The day that haunted me on the calendar. The year before had been extraordinarily rough, slicing at a wound that hadn't yet healed. Back then, I had still been in a state of some disbelief that I was actually living the life of a widow. Acceptance had been swinging in and out. But another year later? I had come to terms with Jeff's fate but harbored some guilt. Guilt for being happy, despite knowing it was what Jeff would have wished for me. Guilt for living a life we both wanted and he didn't live to see. And guilt for realizing if Jeff hadn't died two years before, Hawk would have never been in my life. And that was impossible to imagine.

"Today?" Hawk and I hadn't even met on the first anniversary.

"Yeah, I texted Sophia and her parents earlier. I wasn't going to tell you."

"Geez, Maya, of course you should have told me. Share those things with me. I want to help you through that. We all have those days."

"I know." I did. We had shared some of our stories of loss, but ten months of knowing each other and eight months into our relationship, no matter how solid we were, I was still learning how not to feel like I was burdening him with them.

"I'm sorry. I'm sorry that any of this happened. I'm sorry it happened today. I—"

"I apologize, sir, but all visitors were supposed to have left. Or, are you another patient?"

Hawk lifted his hand from mine and turned toward the scrubs-clothed gentleman who was walking in. "Hey, yeah, I j—" I saw the recognition in Hawk's face as he aborted his comment and instead spoke the man's name. "Vincenzo?"

"Uh, I am. Who a—?" And then the stranger seemed to identify Hawk. "Alex?"

"Yeah." Hawk stood.

"Hey, long time." He looked at the tablet he was holding and seemed to read from it. "Brannigan. Huh. Yeah. Maya? You related to this chum?" Luckily, his playful jab on Hawk's bicep told me he was joking.

"Afraid so," I teased back.

"Thanks, Mai." Hawk shook his head and then did the introductions. "This is my wife, Maya. Vincenzo and Liam were college roommates for a couple years. Although, I thought you moved out of town when you went to med school."

"Yep, but moved back. Boxes aren't even all unpacked. Got a great offer here and wanted to be close to family. Didn't realize you were back, too."

"No. Not. Just visiting," Hawk corrected and insisted immediately. Besides his family, Hawk seemed to detest his Oklahoma roots. I wasn't sure if that was because of the memories or if he simply preferred seeing the world.

"Well, I'd probably go with a ball game, barbecue, or the fried pie place on Main … not the hospital."

"Funny." Hawk rolled his eyes at the doctor's tease.

"Maya, looks like everything is okay. Yeah?" Vincenzo was once again glancing at his tablet. "Just keeping you at our fine establishment overnight for observation. Anything you need?"

"No. I—"

In the seconds it took me to try to clear my hoarse throat, Hawk came up with a request of his own. "Listen, man, there's no way, you know, I can stay the night, huh? It's already late, and she's not from this area." When there was a slight hesitation from the doctor, Hawk added, "I mean, what's the difference if I'm in here or in the lounge down the hall, because I'm not leaving."

"Still stubborn, I see."

"What?" Hawk denied the doctor's character diagnosis—one I definitely knew as the truth. "I am not."

"Like the time you and Liam refused to take any money or anything for helping with my parents' yard the summer my dad was so sick."

That definitely sounded like Hawk. Sometimes stubborn was a good thing. Sometimes stubborn was the way you showed you cared. I knew I could be that, too.

Hawk also didn't like the spotlight. "Your dad took

priority."

"And it seems you are falling in that category, too." He looked at my baby bump. "Is this your first?"

"Yeah." We both smiled our answer together.

"All right, pull the curtain so you don't draw any attention to our bending the rules. The chair you were in actually reclines and is semi-comfortable to sleep in. I know. I've had to catch a few winks here and there."

"Thank you." Hawk shook Vincenzo's hand with strength and gratitude. "It is so good to see you, man."

The doctor turned to me. "Rest you and your voice. Try not to do this." He put his hand up to his throat and demonstrated the gargling I was attempting to do when speaking. "Lots of fluids. Feel better." And with that being his final word, he pivoted and left.

"You weren't kidding when you told me it was like Mayberry around here."

"Sometimes it has its advantages," said the hometown boy as he reclaimed his seat.

"You know you don't have to stay," I offered an out but knew the thought of him being there did make me feel more secure.

His non-verbal response was to test out how far back the cushioned chair reclined. "If you're not using that blanket on the end of the bed, I might just feel like I'm tucking myself into the Ritz."

I scoffed. "All yours." I had plenty of covers already. As he claimed the said blue blanket, I shifted a little, resisted the throat gargle, and admitted, "I am tired. That's why I initially came back to Della's early. Besides a little jump start in between …" It was Hawk's turn to grumble as I continued, "I am ready to get some sleep."

"Good. You know I can't go to sleep before you." It was another of our truths.

I held my hands out to his lightly bearded face. On my touch, he leaned in and kissed me. Maybe there was one good thing about the day, after all.

CHAPTER SEVEN

"He what? What?"

Besides a couple coughs here and there, and when the nurse had come in the middle of the night to take out the IV, I had slept rather peacefully in the hospital bed. Pure exhaustion could do that. But what I was awoken to the next morning was far from restful or calming. It was Hawk's voice, and its volume was rising with each word. Once I stretched my back and rubbed my eyes, I realized my husband was no longer next to me. The blue blanket was on the chair, but Hawk was at the doorway all the way across the room.

The muscles in his arms flexed at the constraints of the hospital shirt. "And no, I'm not gonna calm down. He … Damn it! Did you know about that?"

I couldn't see who was the receiver of the wrath since Hawk's body was blocking my view, but I knew as soon as the other person spoke. He wasn't as loud, but it was definitely Jake. "We … I … No."

"Oh my God. I can't believe—"

Jake interrupted his brother with some intense volume of his own. "He just lost his mom!"

Hawk was equally as adamant. "My kid almost did, too

… *and* their own life!"

I had to stop the siblings, not only for their sake but also for any hospital witnesses who surely had greater concerns than whatever the brothers were arguing about … which seemed to be me. "Hawk?" I began shifting my hips to get out of bed.

"Maya." He turned from the archway of the door and started toward me. The tightness of his jawline portrayed his tension, but his voice attempted to mask it. "Sweetie, I'm sorry. I didn't mean to wake you."

I nixed saying the sarcastic thought that popped in my head about him probably being able to wake those in a coma. It wasn't the time. It most certainly wasn't the place.

"What's going on? What's the matter?" My legs felt good dangling off the bed after laying down for so long.

"I'll tell you later." Hawk took a step toward me. "Go back to sleep."

"I'm pretty awake." I cleared my throat more than coughed, but if felt like I could eventually get something out of my lungs. "Tell me now."

He blew out a tremendous gust of air. I knew my throat irritation had triggered the right emotional button in him. Hawk did not like me to be in any kind of pain—physical or emotional. So he knew in order to avoid that, he needed to do as I requested.

Still, he had to get in a demand of his own. "Stay. Don't get up. I'll come to you." He got to the edge of the bed and sat next to me. When I searched his eyes for some answers, he turned toward Jake, who was making his way farther into the room. "We found out how the fire started."

"Yeah?"

And … nothing. Nothing in reply to my prompting for details. I looked from Hawk to Jake, and the three of us then did a kind of merry-go-round view of all our faces. There were definitely some accusatory vibes, but caution seemed to be mixed in, too.

"What?" I asked again.

And then it dawned on me. Me. They were looking at me. Was it me?

"Oh God, did I do something somehow? Did I …?" I was mentally going over the previous night, even before leaving with Della and Eli to go to the play. No, I hadn't been anywhere near the barn. With that mental recollection, a sturdy cough left my mouth.

"You didn't do anything. You are the victim." My husband caressed my hand and then glared at his brother.

"God, Hawk, then what's wrong?" I tilted my face toward his and used a more hushed tone. "What happened? It wasn't an arsonist, was it?"

"It was me. I caused the fire."

It wasn't Hawk who said those words. It wasn't Jake, either. It was someone else who had entered the room without me knowing. And by Hawk's quick reaction of getting to his feet and starting toward his nephew, he hadn't either.

Both Jake and Della—who came in with her grandson—became instant barriers between uncle and nephew. "Alex, geez, he's a kid."

Della echoed a similar sentiment toward her middle child. "Hey, I know you're upset. You have a right to be, but you need to listen." She put an arm around Raiden's back.

"He better get out of my sight. I mean it." Hawk's pointer finger swiveled from his nephew to his brother. "You, too."

I didn't care what Hawk wanted. I wasn't going to sit anymore. I had to be at his side. I needed to calm him down so the whole situation wouldn't blow up any further. The destruction of a physical building was enough. I couldn't bear to see their family in shreds, also. There was already too much sadness. Everyone needed to do what I struggled with in closed-off areas—breathe.

I rubbed my hand against his upper arm. "Hawk …" Crap, there was that stuff in my lungs again.

"I'm sorry, Uncle Alex. Really. Really. You don't know how much."

Taking a step away from his grandmother, I had to give the thirteen-year-old credit—he manned up and without any immediate prompting. And to take Hawk on in the mood he was in? That was gutsy … uncle or not.

The dark-haired youth's eyes, which had dipped down in the middle of his apology, did a slight blip back up when he then spoke directly to me. "I'm so sorry."

"What happened?" I weaved my fingers in between my husband's as the hoarse words came out.

Hawk held on tight, all the while shaking his head. "You need to leave, Raiden. I don't want her upset."

"Seeing you mad and not understanding what happened is what's upsetting me." I looked the slight distance up to my husband. "I want to know."

"Raiden …" Jake verbally nudged his son in a firm-but-not-yelling way—something which seemed to both warrant respect and show authority.

The younger Brannigan nodded in fast, small motions to me. "I'm sorry, Miss Maya. I … I was smoking." On his admission, which I gathered everyone in the room knew besides me, I felt Hawk's hand tighten even more on mine. "I was at the back of the barn while Dad and Uncle Alex went out. I didn't want the smoke smell to be in the house." He looked with a flash of guilt at Della, and I couldn't help but think the house and property, ironically, still probably reeked of smoke. "One of my friends hit me up on my phone. He wanted to video chat. So, I put the cig out." His eyes dipped again. "You know, so there wasn't any video proof. I started walking the property. I didn't know … I didn't know. I thought the butt was out when I walked away." I didn't know Raiden well at all, but with the softness and ache in his voice, he did seem remorseful.

"What is a thirteen-year-old doing smoking?"

"Like we didn't try some shit at his age," was Jake's reply to his brother before turning to his son to confirm his fatherly stance on smoking. "But he's not doing it again."

As an affirmation, Raiden slowly blinked once and then began apologizing again. "I'm sorry, Uncle Alex … Gram … Miss Maya. I—"

"You're all right, right?" That was the only thing that mattered to me. Everyone being safe had been my solo concern from the beginning of the entire barn ordeal.

"*He* is fine." Hawk dropped my hand in what I believe was a pure reflex of frustration.

"I'm gonna be fine, too," I reassured and looked to Della for backup from the other "injured" party. "And …?"

"It's just a barn. And I have insurance. The only important thing—the photos—were copies. Everything is saved online."

My mouth gaped open at Della's statement, as I connected some dots. The only photos that were in the barn were of Naomi. They were on the easel toward the back of the barn. That was where Raiden had been when the fire started. Damn, that poor kid. I looked at him and nodded slowly, hoping he knew that I understood but didn't need to call it to anyone's attention. I got it. I remember after my mom passed, a five-year-old me taking one of her photos and looking at it every night as I fell asleep, right after my grandma closed the door to my new room at her house. I didn't want her to know. I didn't want her to be more sad. But what I did want was time with my mom to myself, even believing somehow that looking at her photo long enough would make her come back. But, of course, she didn't.

"And, you know, we have the framed paintings of the barn in the family room." She smiled, as I recalled Hawk telling me Liam had commissioned an artist to do a few seasonal paintings of the property. "That old, beat-up sofa of Eli's and that tiny TV? They needed to go. Should have sold or donated them instead of moving them." She shook her head and changed topics. "Maya, I'm glad you're okay. I know Alex said you're going to be released, but I had to come by and see you for myself … and I brought these."

From the tote bag on her shoulder, she pulled out the black flats I had left near the sofa when starting out for the barn the night before.

"Oh, thank you. I was going to have to wear these slipper things home." I wiggled my toes covered in the hospital stockings.

As my mother-in-law handed me my shoes, Jake tagged on, "And we came because Raiden needed to own up to his wrongdoing as soon as possible because he's going right back and starting on cleanup."

"Yes, sir."

On the teen's acceptance of his fate, Della purposefully took a second or two to look at Jake and then at Hawk before she nodded slowly. "Enough then. It's over. Done." Her hands spread from in front of her belly out to opposite sides.

I might have laughed at how the two macho, grown men seemed to go mute and didn't dispute their momma, even though they had been out of her house for as long as they had lived in it. I had a lot to learn from Della. In a lot of ways, she reminded me of how strong my grandma had been.

"Come on. We'll get going. When you are released"—she looked at me and then to Hawk—"go straight to Liam and Keita's. We're all bunking there for at least the night until the air seems good enough. Elijah is bringing your stuff over right now."

"Uh …" Hawk seemed to circle the people in the room with some hesitation in his eyes. But when I rubbed his hand, he replied to his mother, "Okay. We'll see you there."

Jake took a step closer to me. "I'm sure glad—so very glad—you are all right." His eyes—which had been solidly on mine—closed for a second or two, imagining, I'm sure, another Brannigan wife who wasn't so lucky. "Yeah," he said softly after reopening them. Then he dipped his head in a quick nod to his brother. "Alex." The one word was solid, punctual, and holding on to some tension. And with that, he turned and followed Della and Raiden out the door.

I waited until the three left before I grabbed a tissue and spewed out a little junk from my lungs. "Oh, geez, that feels better."

Shaking his head, Hawk silently coaxed me back onto the bed and stroked my hair, which desperately needed a good shampoo, conditioner, and comb-through. He certainly wasn't playing beautician right then, though. He was doing it as a soothing technique. He would one hundred percent claim it was to calm *me*, but I knew he needed the moment to find his own center, too. "I'm sorry."

I was a bit shocked by the offering. "I'll take it, but why?"

"For losing it right now. You're supposed to be relaxed. Also, for yelling when we were at the barn. I was just scared. And, Maya, I'm not used to that. But since you came into my life, it seems to happen a lot." I appreciated not only his apology but also his softer tone.

"The person you really need to say you're sorry to is Raiden."

And with that, his agitation started to flair again. "What? No. For what?"

"Hawk, you said he's always been a good kid. He made a questionable decision and got caught up with his friends. He didn't mean for—"

"It to almost kill someone?"

I continued the statement as I was going to, despite his interruption. "An accident to happen. Talk with Raiden. He needs support right now. He's mourning. He needs to know someone has his back and understands."

"Maya …"

"What if our little one does something like—?"

"They won't," he said with the upmost confidence.

"Oh, geez …" My laugh, unfortunately, came out staggered, but I persisted with my tease. "With us as parents? Mischief and not thinking is going to be a regular occurrence."

"So, you're admitting you weren't thinking when you went into the barn."

"No." I clicked my tongue and shook my head. "I was actually talking about you. I may have been half out of my mind last night, but I heard you say you were on a beer run. Why were you driving when you had to have already been drinking? And then you drove to the hospital, too?"

I expected him to look at least a little guilty, but he did not. "I'd only had one beer before we left. Jake had a couple. We didn't want to suck down all of Elijah's stash, and it wasn't the kind we preferred. And …" He raised his finger. "We had been playing a video game with Raiden for a while. Perfectly fine to drive. But, Maya, shit, I would have sobered up pretty damn quickly seeing you like you were if I already hadn't been."

"Okay. Sorry I *tsked* you."

He smiled softly. "You're gonna make a phenomenal mom."

"I still sometimes can't believe I'm getting the chance to try."

There was the slightest of pauses before he added, "I'll talk with Raiden."

"Thank y—"

"How are we doing in here?" One of the hospital workers strolled into the room looking at a tablet similar to the one Vincenzo had the night before.

"Uh, I think we're okay." I assumed the plural form of the question meant me and the baby.

"Let me take a little listen and check some boxes so we can get you out of here. What do you say?" As the doctor prepped his stethoscope, Hawk reclaimed the chair he had slept in.

I did as instructed, taking breaths in and out as the doctor found different parts of the front and back of my torso to examine. When he asked me to breathe in deeper, the damn persistent phlegmy cough erupted. Dr. Frederick—as I read his name on his coat—told me it was to be expected.

The older practitioner put his hand on my belly and, as if on cue, the baby kicked. "Well, an active tyke is a good tyke."

"Until it's thirteen."

"Hawk …" I rolled my eyes at Hawk's jab at Raiden, and he smiled—a good doctor's report could only improve my husband's demeanor.

And then came the *not* so good news. "Your blood pressure, though. It's still a little disconcerting."

Funny how my eyes went to Hawk. A little of that was because I was afraid of his reaction, but a part was also for his reassurance. Although, I was pretty sure the two most likely would not match up.

"White coat syndrome," Hawk offered as a sarcastic answer, but I could tell by the slowness in his words that he was thinking otherwise and worrying.

"Or *husband* syndrome." I gave an alternative but immediately regretted it. I didn't want Hawk to take any blame on himself if my BP or anxiety was high. "I'm kidding. I truly don't like the constriction on my arm when you're pumping the blood pressure gadget. I think it's part of my claustrophobia—the feeling of constraint. But if you say the baby is okay, I can already feel it subsiding."

"I'm sure that will help. We'll need to keep your OBGYN abreast of your write-up here."

"Of course," I answered Dr. Frederick.

"Then you are free to go."

CHAPTER EIGHT

"Are you sure you're okay to drive the whole way?"

Hawk had heard me ask that question so many times in our relationship, I wondered if he even heard it anymore. At least he learned not to take it personally. He knew what it was based on. He understood my issues from childhood and, unlike the night before, it had nothing to do about drinking.

"That hospital chair could not have been the most comfortable of sleeping arrangements last night," I tagged on regarding his probable lack of sleep.

"Wasn't," he admitted. "But it was next to you, so it was where I needed to be." He did a quick peek at me in the passenger seat. "I'm fine."

"Okay."

"We'll be home soon enough."

"It's still hours!" We were only midway through our commute.

The original plan had been to leave the next day, but between a rare wintery storm due to arrive overnight and limited space at Liam's, we decided not to stay at his place and instead head out after dinner. At least the day had provided an opportunity for the family to come to a better place than that morning in the hospital. Everything just needed a little healing—whether that was physically with my breathing and the barn's rebuild or emotionally by grieving a loved one and forgiving a juvenile's mistake. When the brothers and uncle/nephew gave one another macho hugs before we'd climbed into our truck for the trip back to Nashville, I had hope it would all eventually happen.

"Come on, Mai, it's you and me. Being on the road is basically our life. We're—"

Hawk's phone rang through the speakers of the truck. We both swiveled our heads to the dash. Seeing it was Finn, Hawk didn't hesitate to pick up via the connect button.

"Hey, what's up, Chief?" Hawk used his nickname for the crooner.

"Sorry, I know it's getting late and you're with family," the singer apologized.

"Not as many as you might think. Just Maya and me. We're, actually, on the road on our way back to Nashville."

"Oh. Thought you were coming in tomorrow."

"Change of plans," Hawk gave an abbreviated answer to Finn's comment. "I'll fill you in later."

"Okay. You're both listening?"

"Yeah," I confirmed.

"Well, speaking of change, the reason I'm calling is, Danny has a scheduling conflict." I assumed Finn was speaking about Danny Roth, who was one of his country music counterparts. "He can't play the gig at the All-Star Game."

"Tell me they asked you." My husband's enthusiasm was evident by the slightly higher pitch in his voice and how he glanced at the dash as if he could see Finn's face.

"They did," he confirmed, with I believe similar zeal.

"Nice. What are the deets?" Hawk interrupted himself, though. "Wait … When is that? Is it this coming weekend?"

"Yeah, it's Saturday. But we'd go up early Friday and leave either after the game on Saturday or Sunday. Want to make sure you're on board. Have to make flight reservations and need to know how many. Not bringing the band, and I'll use the equipment at the facility. Thought it could be a family thing. I think Chance will love it. Maya … Reese pretty much has the publicity covered, especially with Roger's contacts," he referenced Reese's sports agent husband. "But if you came along, it would be nice. I just wasn't sure how you felt about going …"

The way Finn trailed that sentence and the fact that it was a current sport in early February made me realize. "It's hockey, isn't it? The NHL?"

"Yeah, sweetie, it is."

"And in DC," Finn tagged on with the double whammy. "The Capitals—"

"Oh, shit. I forgot that's where it is this year." Hawk held out his hand for mine as he continued talking to our boss. "You know what, man? Mai's been through a lot these past couple days. She, actually, needs a follow-up with her doctor on Thursday afternoon." He mentioned the OBGYN appointment I had managed to get for three days later.

I hated that my thoughts on the sport and the ramifications of the fire were taking the joy out of my husband so quickly. I wasn't a person who let circumstances get the better of me. I was tougher than that. Losing my parents at such a young age and being a widower of a cop had groomed me to be so.

"I—" A cough bounced me in my seat, but I prevailed in what I was going to say. "We should go."

"Maya, are you all right?" Finn asked at the same time Hawk's eyes momentarily left the windshield to look at me.

"Yeah," I cleared my throat and kept on topic. "I think it's time I see inside the new arena."

Placing a calming hand on my stomach, I was well aware that decades old wasn't exactly new. But the only Capitals rink I had been to was as a child. And at that time, the site had been in Landover, not DC … back when I thought hockey was the best thing ever … back when my dad was one of the star players in that rink … back when he was alive and my childhood and family were still intact.

Both men knowing my history, let the slightly inaccurate statement slide. Hawk simply prompted a confirmation, "You sure, Mai?"

"Yeah, maybe I can catch up with Sophia and Juanita, too." I smiled, thinking of a reunion with my former sister-in-law and good friend who both lived in a nearby area of Maryland.

"There's not exactly a backstage, but I can see about getting them passes." Finn was obviously recalling the first time us three gals met him.

"You know …" I was still wrapping my mind around the idea that I not only would be returning to my hometown but also to hockey. "No. Thanks, though. I think I'd like to do the rink part solo. I mean, obviously, with you guys, but …" I squeezed Hawk's hand, feeling the emotions already preemptively bubbling inside me. Could I do it? I knew I wanted to. I wasn't sure if it was the sentiment of those past few days or knowing I had that secure hand and his heart, but I knew it was time. "And, you know, if Reese has the PR, I'll completely take care of socials. I'll even do a blog."

I got another look from Hawk with a subtle smile and a slight nod. "I think we're in, Chief."

"Great. I'm glad. Let me work on booking everything, and we can touch base tomorrow?"

"Sure thing," Hawk agreed with our boss. "Hey, and Jake appreciated the money you donated in Naomi's memory. That was cool and unnecessary, but thanks."

"Can't imagine … can't." Finn's voice dipped in emotion. "Going to hug my wife now."

"Yep." Hawk clicked the disconnect button and reclaimed my hand. "Maya …"

"Me, too."

***

Once we were back in Nashville, Hawk and I dove

directly into our regular routine … as much as regular and routine as we had. He met with Finn and some execs about boring sales and revenue things, as well as the details of the All-Star performance, while I decided to pen a blog. Since the tour ended, I didn't post as regularly—only when there was fun or noteworthy content. Some weeks that was a couple days in a row and more than a few times a week. While other times, there was a longer space in between posts. The topic I decided on was a reflection of both our experience in Oklahoma and also something I knew the country crooner believed in wholeheartedly himself. Finn wanting to take Chance and the family with him to the All-Star event was just the latest example. It was about family being first—before fame, before fortune, before anything.

On our way to the doctor's that Thursday, we made a pitstop at our new home site. It was coming along beautifully, and I likened it to the baby growing inside me—both were building strength and ready to meet the world in a few months. The house already had its foundation set, complete with a storm shelter inside the residence. That was on the Oklahoma boy's insistence but one part of the home I hoped to never use. And we had written our names on the beams for good luck before the walls had started taking place. Imagining the books on the future bookshelf, the baby's toys scattered on the floor, and the sunlight beaming through the magnificent windows, I had to pinch myself for dreams coming true.

And the doctor's appointment started the same way. Since she wanted to do a thorough exam, considering the incident in Oklahoma, I got another ultrasound. Luckily, it was with good results. The baby even seemed to open its eyes momentarily.

"Practicing your squint," I teased Hawk on how his eyes narrowed when in deep thought.

He gave me a smile but then seemed to do the beforementioned eye motion as the doctor made some other observations. "I'm going to have you self-monitor your blood pressure at home. Record everything—numbers, headaches, pain, whatever, and I'll see you next week." She had been sitting at the desk, typing as she talked. With an additional press on the keyboard, a paper started coming out of the printer.

"Next week?" I straightened my clothes, knowing it was almost time to leave. "I thought since I'm here now, this one would take the place of my regularly scheduled appointment next week."

"No. I still want to see you. It's important. I'm concerned about your blood pressure, especially with the accompanying headache."

"I mean, yeah, but everyone has headaches," I tried to rationalize.

"Yes, but we need to get the BP down, Maya. And I'm trusting the fluid in your lungs is on its way out, too … hopefully just residuals of the fire." She handed me the paper.

"What—" Hawk started to ask.

"We're just monitoring, okay?" She sounded reassuring … I think. "I'll see you next week."

I slid off the exam table with Hawk's help. "Well, you'll see *me*. He's—"

"You'll see both of us." He looked from the doctor to me.

"You can't. You got the radio gig with—"

Hawk and I were doing a good job of interrupting each other. "Family first, Maya. I'll be here, Doc." He shook her hand.

I smiled, knowing with that comment that he had read my blog. It was something he had done since we were first getting to know each other. Back then, I had thought it was either part of his job or as a means of wooing me. But it was, actually, neither. It was simply Hawk, being one hundred percent invested in the things that mattered to him, and I had no doubt one was me.

***

Having just come out of the soothing shower after a yoga workout, I was feeling relaxed. Probably more so since we first set off for Oklahoma. That feeling didn't last, though. From beyond the walls and down the hall, my husband's angered voice was the culprit as to why not.

"I said, what do you want?" There was only a slight pause before, "No, there's no reason to." I couldn't hear the other person, but it was obvious Hawk was responding to someone else. "Look, we've managed to be okay with each other for many years. Don't change that." As the one-sided conversation continued, I got dressed. "Well, maybe that's why." Another moment of silence from my husband happened as I started to make my way out of the room, hoping I looked half decent if we had company. "Great, and thanks for paying your respects, but that's it. You—" He seemed to be cut off. "Of course she was there with me." His temper flared even more with that reply. I gathered he was talking about me, but who was he talking *with*? "Ah, you know what, Oaklee? God. She could have been killed in that fire and you're—"

I took a few more steps to see Hawk standing alone in the living room and facing the large windows, confirming what I had begun to suspect. The other person was on the phone. I was especially glad of that fact, having found out it was Oaklee.

Instead of joining him, I went into the nearby kitchen to start making dinner. With the doctor's not-as-good-as-I-hoped report earlier, I was seeking comfort … and that included food. So, I started making an easy gnocchi and sausage soup recipe my grandmother, who loved Italian cooking, used to make. I thought we might pair it with a baked potato.

"You better drop it. I don't appreciate at all what you said to her at the memorial." Almost immediately, he followed with, "No. No. Don't deny it. You'll just be digging in deeper." The rattling of the kitchen equipment must have alerted Hawk of my proximity because he then said, "I'm gonna go help her now. You need to concentrate on *your* marriage and kids—not me, not Maya—*your* family. That's who you should be talking wi—" I'm not sure if she cut him off or if he did so himself. Regardless, he finished up with a verbal bang. "So help me, don't f-ing call again." I knew for sure he had hung up because of the Neanderthal like "Ahhh!"

I waited. I breathed. I let him walk. Because even though I had yet to see him, I could hear that Hawk was pacing. And after a few minutes, I put my food items aside and went into the living room.

He had his laced hands on the back of his head as he went from one side of the room to the other. When he saw me, he closed his eyes. "Mai …" He said it almost as if a warning to let him be.

"I guess I shouldn't take *your* blood pressure right now."

Hawk shook his head and reopened his eyes, managing a glimpse at me. I didn't think he would laugh, even though I had said it, of course, to lighten his mood. But at least he seemed to take in a breath or two.

"She is ridiculous."

"I thought you two didn't talk." I tried to pull my words off as a casual, inquisitive comment and not those of a jealous wife over an ex, but there was definitely some of that.

"We don't. I'm not sure how she even got the number. You know when we've talked?" Hawk was still speaking rapidly and with a slightly raised voice. "You know the only time we've talked in any form over the past how many years? You have been witness to them. Both times in Oklahoma and … and now. That's why we've managed to be decent with each other."

I don't know why I even entertained the thought of jealousy. If it was on anyone's part, it was Oaklee's. It was obvious she couldn't handle seeing Hawk happy. She seemed like the type of woman who only went after what she couldn't have. That doubled up with her own marital woes was not a good combination.

Even though I had basically internally answered my own question, I outwardly asked, "So, why did she call? Just to bitch?"

That riled him up more. "I don't know!" And then slightly less abrasive, "Apparently."

"Okay." I remained calm. "Hawk, I'm gonna put my arms around you, all right?" Placing my lips on his chest, I could feel his strained muscles through his shirt. "She's not worth it."

As the beating of his heart started to subside to a more regular pace, he pulled me slightly away. "I absolutely agree, but I don't like her attacking you. You have enough on your plate."

"Hey, listen, I know you're anxious about the doctor." Of course he hadn't said anything directly, but I knew. "And about what this weekend means for me. But Hawk, I can do it. I can do it because I know you're here. What I don't need is worrying about you and your anger. Because I believe I heard a saying once. Correct me if I'm wrong." I was amused before even relaying it. "If it has to do with you, then it has to do with me. If it's you … it's me."

On me reciting back what he had told me, his headshake was more on the genial side. "I like how you manage to use that at your convenience."

"Thought you'd like to know that I listen when you talk." I looped my hand with his and swung them together with a smile. "I could use some help chopping the onions, and I'm thinking you might need to hammer out some aggression."

"Love to." But he stopped our forward movement and first encouraged me into his embrace before lovingly feathering his lips on mine.

CHAPTER NINE

Arinn and I were soul potty sisters. She was in the midst of potty-training and went frequently to try, and my pregnancy had me doing the same. When Lara joined us in the restroom prior to boarding the airplane, we had a chance to get some just-girl talk in. A partner in distaste of aviation, I didn't know much of Lara's background, but I knew she was a survivor, and that was just another reason why she and I hit it off as friends.

"He was so mad after the fire," I related Hawk's fury to Lara. "One day, he's telling me how brave and kickass—his exact word—I am, and then practically the next, he's yelling at me to never do something like that again." I rolled my eyes and shook my head.

Helping Arinn dry her hands, Lara looked at me. "You know when Finn and I knew Hawk loved you?" I blinked repeatedly, not expecting her to go so serious. "We first, of course, saw the beginning attraction. He would talk about how independent you were and could take care of yourself."

"Exactly!"

"He liked that. He's the same way. A protector." On my nod, recalling my conversation with Jake and how I seemed to be drawn to those types myself, she continued, "But as he got to know and like you, he didn't want to see you be put in those positions, where you had to be brave and take care of everything." Lara pushed the door open with her elbow, and we walked out of the restroom. "He didn't want you to be harmed physically or emotionally." She paused her feet and made sure to look more directly at me. "When Hawk stuck up for you when Finn was upset about what you wrote on Father's Day … that's when we started to see it turn into something more for him."

I closed my eyes. We had disagreed on that day, too. It had really been our first. Hmmm …

"And then after what happened the first time you went to Oklahoma?"

"That's when *I* knew," I admitted to when I truly realized I was in love with Hawk. "I only got in that dang coffin-like space because he wanted me to."

"He didn't need you to be brave. He needed you to be safe."

"Yeah," I spoke more softly, making all kinds of connections. "I can't be a weak damsel in distress, though."

She did a light chuckle and watched as Arinn ran to Finn, standing with Hawk and Chance so many feet away. "No, he certainly doesn't want that. It's just that loving someone ramps up the worry factor."

I thought about how Hawk had said since meeting me he seemed to be more scared than ever in his life, and I smiled. It wasn't that I wanted him stressed, but I understood what Lara was saying. I understood because I felt the same. As we approached the men in our traveling group, I stood directly in front of my husband, tipped up on my toes, and gave him a sweet kiss.

"Uh, not that I'm complaining, but what was that about?"

"Just … me, too," I replied to the protector's question. Me, too, with all of it.

***

I was glad the red-carpet event didn't take place at the ice arena. It gave me a chance to ease into the whole hockey thing. Fans stood a couple rows deep to watch the players dressed in suits strut the red carpet. Finn—with Chance at his side—was also a part of it, while Lara and Arinn stayed at the hotel for nap time. Hawk acted as a bodyguard following along with the Murphy boys, and I was granted a spot along the long stretch to take photos and capture video clips of all the participants. There were plenty of legit reporters, too, and, similar to the Oscars or any big musical awards ceremony, there were obligatory stops to chat and answer questions. I found it amusing that they were just as nonsensical as any other red carpet: Who are you most excited to see … How did it feel to be chosen … What are you wearing? For Finn's part, he was dressed in classic black slacks and a white shirt, which only close observers could see had a hockey puck and stick pattern. He was prepared for that question and knew it would be a great conversation piece. Chance looked adorable in a blue suit. Hawk? He simply tried to blend in, security lanyard and all.

Although I'm pretty sure my husband spotted me first, it was Chance who said something when the trio reached my perch. "Maya! It's Maya!" As if he didn't know I was in town and even sat next to me on the plane—much to Hawk's chagrin, as the five-year-old didn't stop talking the entire time. We all had noticed how Chance had been coming out of his shell during that past year, and it was good to see, except for maybe a couple-hour plane ride with nowhere to roam.

"Hey, bud." Finn chuckled. "Do you think Maya has a question for us?"

"No!" Chance answered incredulously. "She knows all the answers to us!"

I had to laugh, and with it came a cough, which, of course, even with the noise of the crowd, Hawk heard and furled his eyebrows at me. The fluid in my lungs really had dissipated over the week. There were only minor ones when I laughed. Being in good humor seemed worth it, though.

Finn caught Hawk's look and bent down to Chance. "Well, *I* have a question for you. How about you head back to the hotel with Maya now? You need a little break before your time with Mommy and Arinn tonight."

That had been the plan all along, but it wasn't supposed to happen for a half hour or so. Helping with the kids had always been a part of my job—just more so when we were on tour. Hawk and Finn were going to stay at the hockey facilities for the evening activities, and I was to take Chance back to Lara.

"No. I like the red carpet," the younger Murphy denied his father's request.

"Oh, boy," Finn sighed. "Not exactly reassuring when trying to raise a kid properly." Finn was notoriously famous for keeping his kids out of the spotlight. So, in addition to the Maryland event being huge for *me*, it was also for him to have Chance be a part of it. "Family before fame, Little Man." Finn looked at me as he stood. He not only read every one of my blogs, but he also had to approve them before being posted.

"Chance, you want to know the truth?" I took my turn to bend to the little boy's level. "These two"—I swung my index finger out to Hawk and Finn—"are just worried about me. They want *me* to go back and rest, and they know they need a big kid to help me." I peered up at the guys who looked anywhere but at me. Guilty! "You want to know something else?" I lowered my voice a tad so he thought it was a secret, but I knew the men could hear. Well, maybe not Finn, who was busy signing stuff behind me, but I knew Hawk was alert.

"What?" The five-year-old definitely liked thinking he was in the know.

"I've seen the end of this line." I nodded toward the rest of the red carpet walk. "There's not much." Kind of a lie. "We'll fool your dad and Hawk. We'll go back and have more fun than them because, you know what? I bet you didn't think of this yet, but it's a hotel. That means we need to make a … a what?"

"A fort!"

Hawk's eyes didn't leave Finn as he signed someone's hat, but I saw his belly roll in silent laughter upon Chance's declaration. The original blanket fort almost a year before was not intended to be something for Hawk and me. I had only met my future husband and the kids moments before that creation. It had been built for the kids as a way to keep them safe, quiet, and distracted as the danger outside the hotel door surrounded us.

"We can use my new hockey stick to hold it up," Chance continued while pointing to Hawk, who was holding a stick filled with a number of autographs.

I gave the young Murphy a thumbs-up. "Great thinking." And then I stood up a little more properly. My back was already hurting a little from standing so long, and crouching wasn't helping. "Tell your dad we're leaving. Forts before fame."

That time Hawk broke his personal code of protocol and legitimately laughed. I gave myself an internal high-five. My comment had been pretty quick-witted.

As Finn was telling his mini-me to behave and that he'd see him later, I took the stick from Hawk. "I am okay, by the way."

"Keep the fort up then." He spoke softly and gave me his alluring smile. "We might use it tonight."

I pushed the sexy boundaries a little further. "Don't drink too much at the rink later so *you* can keep something else up."

"Maya!" Hawk said my name but glanced at Finn and Chance, surely to see if they had heard my comment.

"Me, you, and hotel rooms, what can I say? It does something to me." It was true about hotels, but also my hormones were seesawing again. The pregnancy had me going from unattractive morning sickness, to elated with life, to not feeling sexy, to desperately wanting my man. I had a feeling being vulnerable in Maryland had me not only wanting him but needing him, too.

"I'll get him back in good shape for you." Finn smirked, as Chance was looking at the people calling out his dad's name.

"Geez, Maya, really!" Embarrassed that Finn heard, Hawk shook his head. "That way." He pointed in the direction for Chance and me to go. "And see ya later."

***

While Hawk and Finn finished the red carpet and then went to the rink to do a walk-through and rehearsal for the next day's performance, Chance and I *did* build a pillow and blanket fort, but it was in the Murphy's suite, and Lara and Arinn assisted. Well, they actually did most of the construction. I was busy posting photos of the red carpet to the different social sites. Even though before the event started I had cleared it with Finn that I could use Chance's image, I double-checked—and triple-checked if you counted Lara—before hitting send. And, of course, the photos with Chance were the ones that seemed to have the most hits, likes, and comments … overwhelmingly positive. While Finn's followers were due to his music, adding a personal morsal every so often made them swoon even more, like they were getting some kind of precious insider trading. When truth be told, celebrities are just like the rest of us, with their own stories of heartbreak, loss, and love.

Lara and the kids joined me as I met up for dinner with my two bests pals—Juanita and Sophia. Juanita was hosting at her apartment, which worked out beautifully because she lived fairly close to the hotel, and Chance and Arinn wouldn't have to sit still at a restaurant table. Instead, they played with their toys and ate some packed food in the family room while us ladies had a fondue feast of different sauces and dippers in the adjacent dining area.

The main topic of conversation seemed to be about me and the baby. I would have preferred not to be the center of attention but understood my role since I was the element that tied the women together. Juanita and Sophia only knew each other because of me, and the two times they had met Lara were at Finn's concerts when they had been practically fawning over her husband and his talent—albeit innocently, as Sophia was married and Juanita was in a serious relationship.

By the time the pound cake with chocolate sauce and strawberries was served for dessert, everyone was more comfortable with one another. That, I guess, included Chance, who decided he was going to involve Arinn in a mock red-carpet act. Even though he was the interviewer, he also often answered the questions for Arinn, who did not seem overly amused by her brother's directorial debut. Us gals were, though.

When the song "Roxanne" belted out of Lara's phone, I knew it was Finn calling or texting. I had come to recognize that was their song. Why? I didn't know, especially since it wasn't one of Finn's. The country music star's wife stepped away from the girl gathering, read the message, smiled, and then told Chance and Arinn that it was time to clean up.

"Yeah, we should go," I agreed, although sad to see our night with my friends end.

"Maya, we can always get a cab." At the same time Lara was talking, she was dribbling chocolate onto her finger. She took a photo of it and appeared to send it to her husband, who I knew was with mine in a private lounge watching the All-Star Skills event. Lara turned to Juanita. "You have no idea how perfect this dessert is. Instead of football, we just made a hockey bet."

Before I could question, a text from my own spouse came through on my phone. I looked to see an image of Hawk with a few bottles in front of him. They were all sparkling water. I practically spit out the similar beverage in my mouth. I knew the underlying message—it was his photographic response to my earlier tease about not drinking and the implied act of what would happen once he returned to the hotel.

An idea came into my head immediately. "I'll be right back, but I am definitely going to the hotel with you guys."

I promptly made my way down the hall. I'm sure everyone thought I was going to use the bathroom, but I wasn't. I went in Juanita's bedroom, laid down on her bed with the pillow propped under my head, and did a close-up selfie of me looking tired. I then sent it to Hawk with the accompanying text, *Already asleep. You may as well drink.*

I was laughing to myself as I plopped the pillow back under the covers and made my way into the main living area. I could imagine Hawk's disappointment and wondered how he would reply. When he didn't right away, it dawned on me that maybe he wasn't going to at all because he didn't want to disturb me. He really was a sweet guy, and he was already worried about me. Perhaps it hadn't been the right joke, because he didn't even get that it *was* a joke.

The kids, Lara, and I had said our goodbyes to my friends and were in the rental car when my phone rang. Since I was driving, I asked Lara if she could accept Hawk's call and hit the speaker button. When she did, I called out, "Hey."

"And where exactly are you sleeping, Goldilocks?" I couldn't tell by the tone of his voice if he was kidding or not.

"Huh?" That's all I had.

"The photo you sent is not from the hotel. It's not the same headboard."

"Oh … oh!" I exclaimed. "You and your da—ng"—at the last minute, I amended my word for the kids in the car—"Hawk eyes. It was a joke, and I was at Juanita's. On our way back to the hotel now."

"Good, because I *am* having a real drink, and I *am* going to be very ready."

Oh … *Damn.* I could say the word because it was internal

that time. If my hormones weren't already on high alert, they were then. Lara's eyes kind of widened alongside the sly grin on her face. She knew what he was referencing.

Backseat Chance, of course, did not. "Hawk, are you ready for hockey?"

"Geez, Mai, are we on speaker?" After hearing Lara's and my laughter, he sounded exasperated. "Not funny."

"It has to be on speaker because I'm driving!" I exclaimed and then a little more softly, "And I am very awake. See you when you get there."

"Hey, yeah, Chief …" It was obvious my husband was talking to our boss then but wanted to make sure I heard, too. "We're gonna need to leave … like soon."

***

When he walked into the hotel room later that night, there was a look on Hawk's face that I'm not sure I'd ever quite experienced. It seemed to be a mix of so much … said so much. And when I thought about it in conjunction with the talk I'd had with Lara at the airport, it was because Hawk *was* so much. He was complex. I think he had always been that way, but I had a feeling our relationship, especially as it continued to grow, made him even more so. It wasn't a bad thing. It was almost like he was coming into a new self.

That look he gave me was relief. It was exhaustion. It was worry. It was passion. It was heart. It was security. It was happiness. It was … it was everything.

For all the looks it was, there was no sound. He took his hands to his feet to first remove his shoes. And then he went north to do the same with his jacket and red, long-sleeved shirt. He seemed to do it all without missing a blink of his eyes as he watched me. I was sitting on the bed, legs crisscrossed, laptop on thighs, monitoring the socials. But when he started to walk toward me, I quickly shut the device and slid it onto the nightstand. Still without a word, he crawled on the bed and bracketed his large hands on my face.

His kiss was powerful yet caring. It tasted of mint, which I assumed was a coverup to the alcohol he had partaken in. I didn't begrudge him that. It was something neither he nor Finn did in excess. If anything, I was jealous that because of the pregnancy, I couldn't have a glass of wine or beer or any other form of alcohol myself.

He paused and looked at me, our faces mere inches away. "How are you?"

"Good, especially with each one of those." I brought our lips together again. We continued mating for a minute or so before I took my turn. "How about you? Everything go okay at the rink?"

"Mmmm-hmmm." It was *my* loose, long, white shirt he was taking off that time. "No fort," he acknowledged, as he tossed the garment aside, leaving me only in my panties.

"It's in Chance and Arinn's room. Would you prefer we go there?"

His headshake was slight alongside the diminutive, amused curve of his mouth. But his eyes—those hazel eyes—were locked in on me. He was focused. Hawk was never one of many words, but when concentrating, even less. And it was me he was focusing on—him and me … us. Between his look, touch, and those smooth yet electrifying kisses, I don't know how the remainder of our clothing was removed, but it was. Then the world disappeared—the lingering mental flashes from the fire, the thoughts of confronting the past via a hockey rink, and even the not-so-good blood pressure reading taken prior to Hawk's arrival. All that was left was us, our love, and that hotel room.

CHAPTER TEN

Since so much of the weekend was about hockey and, therefore, memories of my dad, I focused on my mom for our Saturday mid-morning jaunt. A short drive led Hawk and me to the quaint Maryland town that had been part of my personal history. After getting out of the car, the two of us peered in the building's windows to see a barre wrapped around the room, a few school-aged ballerinas balancing on toes, and a woman standing near what I knew was the office in the back corner. I remembered only vaguely going there with my mom before she passed away. Back then, it had been the art gallery her and her friend, Shalee, had owned. I was also there when Shalee shut the doors for good, selling it so she could retire and move away. If not an art studio, I think my mom would have appreciated that the space was being used for dance because dancing seemed to have had a special place in her heart.

Hawk and I then walked around the surrounding business neighborhood, taking photos of the church tower, library, stores, and restaurants. But before leaving, I made sure to pick up some pastries at a family-owned café, which had been there for about fifty years. Any time I would visit the area, I always made sure to stop by. I had an undeniable, unexplainable pull toward it. I felt hope and love there ... definitely love. Maybe because it was French, and it reminded me of my dad's French-Canadian heritage. Or maybe it was their divine chocolate mousse crepe cake. Regardless, the combination was hard for me to deny for sure.

And then we had just enough time to go back to the hotel. We needed to freshen up and change outfits before heading over to the rink. While Lara and the kids were going later, Finn, Hawk, and I needed to arrive a few hours prior to the doors opening for guests.

I was glad to be immediately thrown into work when we arrived. It didn't allow me time to overthink where I was and what it meant to my life's story. Saying your parents don't shape who you are is a complete farse. Even if they didn't raise you, that itself creates a significant squiggle in the outline of the person you are. It may not be and doesn't have to be the complete picture, but it definitely starts the shape.

Conveniently positioned next to a store full of T-shirts and sports caps, one of the first places we took note of was where Finn would see fans who paid extra for a signature and a few words. Next, we were shown past the concessions and into a private box. Finn and Hawk already knew it, of course, since that was where they sat the night before. But it was new to me.

Then we ventured to the center of attention—the ice. Seeing the rink was the part I dreaded the most. Maybe, though, because I had been answering questions, planning media points, and listening about where Finn would perform, being in a place I had pretty much avoided my entire life didn't immediately physically or figuratively knock me down to its slippery surface when we got there. The fact was, I was standing tall, and the chilly atmosphere almost felt warm and welcoming.

I looked at the banners hanging high from the ceiling, listing the years of the various championships—divisional, conference, and, of course, the biggest one of all. I stared at that Stanley Cup banner for a good solid minute, feeling such a mix of emotions. It was my dad's greatest professional achievement, yet it was the last thing he had known.

Hawk brought me back to the present when he spoke to Finn. "Since we have a few minutes, if you're good, I'd like to take Maya to see the … you know."

"Sure," Finn agreed and looked at me before seeing another NHL rep approaching, most likely wanting something else from the singer.

Not being a part of whatever secret language Hawk and Finn seemed to be in the midst of, I furled my eyebrows and made a joke of it. "Yeah, can't wait to see the 'you know.'"

The only reaction I got, though, wasn't anywhere close to a reveal or an answer. It wasn't even a joking jab back. It was Hawk resting his lips on the top of my head and taking my hand. He led us away from Finn and toward one of the rink's hallways I had not yet been in.

I started to question, but Hawk interrupted. "How you doing?"

"Yeah. Okay." It was true, especially with him beside me.

As if gauging my legitimacy, he squinted at me as we turned down another hall. We were going farther away from the signs that directed fans to the sections for seats. It was seemingly a more restricted area, but because we were wearing lanyard passes and the gates weren't yet open, we had free reign to the quiet and empty area.

When Hawk started walking a little slower, it caused me to question him. "Where are we going? What do I need to see?"

"We're here."

I'm not sure I actually heard his last word, though, because it was then that I did see. I saw it. I saw him. I saw Noah Collins.

Of course, it wasn't really my dad. But behind one of the

hall's display cases was what would most likely be akin as a memorial to him. Hawk came to a stop alongside me and rubbed our connecting hands with his thumb. I didn't look at him, though. I was too busy looking at the number eighty-five red jersey with Collins written across it. I was too busy looking at my dad's accolades: the defenseman's Norris Trophy, the Stanley Cup, and the All-Star selections. And I was too busy looking at the photos. They were the most entrancing. There was one of him with his funny '80s hairstyle shaking hands with a man in a suit. I was pretty sure it was when he first joined the team, since I recalled seeing a similar photo that my grandparents had sent me alongside some of his other boyhood things. Another picture in the display case showed my dad in hockey action. He had a serious look on his face, the stick was down, one leg bent, and the other as if in mid-sprint. And then there was the photo with the Stanley Cup. A rare, bearded version of my dad was kneeling on the ice while embracing a four-year-old me as we held the trophy. At the same time, he was kissing my mom.

Damn. Damn. Just damn.

As if he could hear my internal flood of emotions, Hawk wrapped his arms around me from behind and rested his chin on one of my shoulders. He didn't need to say anything. The embrace was perfect, even through the bulkiness of the jersey I had packed last minute and actually had the guts to put on when we had changed at the hotel. I think I knew then—maybe even when the trip first came up—that I was ready for the challenge. I was ready to be in the hockey part of Maryland … to honor and remember my dad.

"He was happy." I stared at the photo of my grinning parents. "They were happy."

"You also looked pretty happy."

I turned around on Hawk's words, and he touched the one corner of my mouth that rose when I smiled—just like my dad's. "To clarify, I am now, too." I leaned onto his chest and looked at the display again. "Thanks for taking me to see the 'you know.'" I said it in jest but felt actual tears welling.

It was in that moment when I saw someone approaching. I swiped at the new wetness on my face and left Hawk's embrace. It was one thing to be emotional around my husband, but to strangers, Hawk and I were there to work an event representing Finn Murphy. I would not be unprofessional.

"That." The man with strawberry-blond locks pointed to my oversized top. "It look like authentic jersey. Collins." He glanced from the display in front of the three of us to the name across the back of my jersey. "Orange with stars. It legit All-Star jersey from back in day?"

Back in the day. Yeah. Back then. Legit. But I just shrugged.

"Where you get it?"

"My dad," I replied to the stranger that time.

"Where did he? I no think eBay has those." I was guessing the man with broken English was similarly aged as Hawk. He seemed in good shape, but most likely too old to be a hockey player himself.

"It was my dad's," I repeated, although with the slightest of word changes.

He looked again at the display and then at me … more specifically that time at my name. Not the one stretched across the back of the jersey but at my first name on my all-access pass. I was attempting to do the same with his, trying to figure out who he was. But *his* lanyard, unfortunately, was flipped backward, and all I saw was a blank white card.

"Maya? You little Maya? Maya Collins?"

Hawk started to correct him by stating *Brannigan* as my last name—he really did like men knowing I was his. It was sweet, in a caveman kind of way. I interrupted, though, wanting to better understand what this man in front of us meant by *little*. It certainly wasn't my age or weight as I touched my baby belly. He said it in a more familiar way.

I decided on simplicity. "I am."

"Oh, golly. Golly." He looked to the photo of me with the Stanley Cup and then back again.

"And who are you?" Hawk was getting in protective mode.

The stranger didn't answer directly, though. Instead, he further confirmed my identity, seemingly getting more genuinely excited as he did. "Little Maya. We knew each other, ya? Our pappas … they play together. The Caps, ya? Until the Cup and …"

And. Yeah, when my days of smiles had ended for a long while. Still … who was this guy in front of us?

"You and your mamma and pappa live near us. We at each other homes. My parents Victor and Fa—"

"Famke," I finished for him. "The Swedes." I then understood his accent. "My dad called your dad the Swede."

Yes, I remembered. There were glimpses of my life back then, which were stored ever so faintly in my brain. Some were legit and some from tales retold over and over again. But the ones he was talking about were definitely fond memories. Even after my dad died, the Swedes made a point to keep in touch with me, until Victor was traded to another team.

Gustav laughed. Yes, that was his name. His name was Gustav, and he had a younger sister a couple years older than me. "And my pappa called—still calls—the great Noah Collins *rookie*."

It was my turn to laugh, although it was more of a smile. I knew it was because it was one of those moments you wished there were more of. "How are they … your parents?"

"They good. Good. Back in Sweden. So is Agnetha and her family." He reminded me of his sister's name. "How 'bout you?" He didn't give me a chance to answer. "Oh, my pappa will be over moon to know I talk to you. He said your dad best teammate eva. He talk about good ole days with Uncle Noah all the time."

It warmed my heart to hear my dad referred to so affectionately. And I knew it was true. He had been a phenomenal hockey player and, somehow, an even better son, husband, and father. But I blamed the sports world—all the others who adored him—for taking him away. It was because I associated the day he died with hockey. What I forgot to remember, though, was how happy he had been. He'd been playing his best and getting the rewards of that. He got to share that joy with his fans during the Stanley Cup victory parade, but he also wanted to do so with his family in Canada. It had been his choice to drive that distance with limited sleep that very same night. And it was a mistake that cost him everything. But standing there in front of the tribute to him, I knew I needed to focus on remembering the happiness and love … not the grief.

"What are you doing here, Gus?" I claimed Hawk's hand. His was another love I definitely treasured.

"Coach. Ya. Assistant for the Canucks."

"You played defense for them for a number of years, right?" I should have figured Hawk would know that. He had a good hockey knowledge base. He was just respectful most of the time not to tell me a lot of it.

"Ya," Gus confirmed. "Injuries got best of me. Now coach."

"Sorry, this is my husband Hawk."

"Nice to meet you." Hawk shook hands with my childhood friend.

"Here for game. Need to pick up players. Running late. I … I can't wait to tell my pappa."

"Here." I pulled my business card out of my purse. "Have them contact me. I'd love to, you know, reminisce."

"Thank you, Maya." Gustav gave me a hug.

As he did, I was facing the display case. I saw my parents smiling. I know it wasn't real or possible, but for a second, I believed it wasn't about the silver trophy in the image. It was them smiling at a grown me. It was them seeing me come full circle—seeing me reconnect with Gustav, seeing me in Hawk's loving arms, and seeing me about to have a baby of my own. It was them knowing I was happy again.

***

Even though it was early when we arrived back at the hotel, we were all pretty tired from the busy day or two. So, we decided to stay in for the evening instead of going out. Since Chance begged and had been good during the games, Finn and Lara agreed to take the two kids to the hotel's arcade area for a little bit. Finn was hoping to blend in by wearing a Capitals hat and glasses because, as much as he adored his fans, he also wanted to live a "normal" life where his kids could do things with both their parents and not be holed up like prisoners. In contrast, Hawk and I wanted exactly that. We were content staying in the room and eating the pastries we had gotten from the French café earlier.

While Hawk talked with Jake on the phone, I cut the pastries in half so we each had a sampling, changed from my jersey into pajamas, and checked my blood pressure. The numbers were still high, but I blamed it on the emotional roller coaster of a day. I felt fine, after all—maybe even better than fine. Just tired. I did know, for sure, the coughing had almost completely ceased, which was a good sign.

"How are Jake and Raiden?" I questioned Hawk once he finished his conversation with his brother.

"Managing. He asked about you."

"Did you tell him I am fine?"

Hawk didn't answer directly. "I saw your eyes when you read the BP."

I wasn't going to lie, but I truly believed what I said. "It's a little high. Once we chill here, it'll go down."

I thought he would argue or debate in his protective way, but, instead, he proceeded on stripping out of his hockey day attire and getting into a pair of beige sweat pants. "All right, what do we have here?" He eyed up the delicacies as he stretched alongside me on the king-sized bed. "What should I have first?" He picked up the raspberry tart as I went straight for pure chocolate with a brownie.

"How did Raiden get his name?" I asked as I sunk my teeth into the sweetness.

Not seeming fazed by my new topic of conversation, he gave a prompt answer. "Japanese for thunder and lightning. They wanted a strong name and for it to represent Naomi's heritage. But it also sounded American … like Aiden."

"Hmmm …" My semi-verbal reply was for both the brownie and understanding the multi-purpose of my new nephew's name. "I like that it has meaning."

"You thinking about names for Little Bun?" He knew me well.

"Yeah, especially because I don't want Little Bun to stick." I partially chuckled at the name Hawk was so fond of using for our unborn child.

"Already have it registered—Little Bun Brannigan," he teased, and I was glad to hear it.

We were both more stress-free than we had been in over a week. Hawk loved working for Finn, but because he took his job so seriously, events were sometimes on the tense side. The All-Star appearance wasn't on a grand scale, so that helped.

I laughed. "Might have worked for a girl but definitely not a boy."

"Are you still okay that we found out?"

"Too late now if I'm not."

Hawk and I had originally chosen not to find out the gender of the baby, but after the fire, we both decided to have the doctor—no, not a big reveal event—tell us the sex. I wanted to cheer on and know the baby more than ever. I believed us being able to talk with it, knowing what gender it was, and coming up with a name created even more of a bond.

"*I* definitely am." Hawk grew up with brothers, and I saw the connection he had with Chance. He was absolutely going to be a great boy dad. Although, a little girl with Hawk as a father would have been the most protected creature on Earth if that had been the case.

"I am, too. I want him to have a name like Raiden's. Something that has meaning for both of us."

"Mmmm-hmmm." Hawk had moved onto the chocolate tart, while I was considering which donut to partake.

"We could do a variation of your name." It was definitely something I had been thinking of.

"How do you do a variation of Hawk? Uh, I don't think so."

I pushed on his arm in a light manner. "No—your given name. Xander or Zan with an X or Z. Or even Alec."

"Sweetie, no. You know I don't like my name. I don't want to pass it on to a child."

My lips vibrated against each other when I let the breath out. I had expected as much. Although I did like the thought of a father-son name connection.

"Come on." He sounded exasperated, but I knew it wasn't at full force. "It's like saying the baby is due on your May fifth birthday, so we name it after you but Mayo."

"No!"

"Exactly." He gave me a wink.

"What do you think the likeliness is that we will be able to pick a name before I fall asleep?"

"Pretty good. Not gonna take too long. Won't even have all these desserts done."

"I like your confidence," I verbally applauded. "What's *your* thought then?"

"You want something with meaning?" His question took on a more serious tone, and it made me wonder if he had already been thinking of names, too. My husband—macho but magnificently thoughtful. "Something maybe to represent family?"

"Yeah."

"Then, we're already done."

"What?" My face scrunched with doubt. "What are you talking about?"

"Collin," he proclaimed with precision in his voice and an all-composing gaze on my eyes.

"Coll—"

I couldn't finish. Emotional, I needed to shift to get a more direct look at him. I hadn't even considered the name, but of course it had meaning. And of course it was perfect, especially because Hawk was the one who brought it up. With his immediate reply and confidence in saying it, I knew he had definitely been thinking of names for our future little tyke.

"Really?"

That time he smiled a large closed grin. "Yeah, especially after this weekend. By the way, I'm so proud of you, sweetie. I know it was hard."

Second to seeing the display for my dad, watching the men first take the ice had been the most emotional part for me. It transformed me back to watching him play and even faint memories of my tiny self being on the ice with him. Strong and steady he had helped me glide. I hoped someday I could try on skates again and do that with …

"Collin." I leaned over and gave Hawk a sweet kiss. "Collin is perfect. I love it." Then I went into sass mode so I didn't get weepy. "What about the middle name? I guess I'm not getting Xander for that, huh?" I was going to try an Alexander version however I could.

But … "Nope."

"Do you have the middle name picked out, too?" I teased but kinda hoped he did, as boy names were tough.

"Maya, I can't do all the work around here." And he threw in another wink.

"Insufferable." I shook my head and thought for a moment.

He went back to take another bite of the raspberry tart. "I like this one better."

"Well, great, but don't eat too fast. I have a feeling the

middle name is going to be quite a debate." On his headshake, I started trying to lay out our baby boy's full name. "So, we have *my* last name and *your* last name. Now, we need a name to bring the two families together … something about us."

"Don't kids sometimes have the name of where they were conceived? Like Paris … or Vegas … or Memphis?"

"We don't really know where, though." Afterall, we were on tour traveling from city to city the summer the baby took seed.

"Collin Backseat Brannigan?"

"What? No!" I gave him another love tap/hit for his tease. "I don't really like the idea, anyway, but …" I offered up an alternative. "What about where we met?"

"Uh … okay. The Keys." But we both kinda scrunched our noses—it didn't seem like a name. "March for the month we met?" he suggested.

"Maybe," I said but wasn't completely on board. "Keep going."

After a couple seconds and bites of our food, Hawk smirked and looked to the hotel amenity we had filled together when first coming back to the room. "Ice for the bucket you were carrying." Collin Ice Brannigan did seem a little badass, but then Hawk started laughing and busted out, "He could be the 'Ice, Ice Baby.'"

And I laughed, too. Nope. Crossing that one out.

"Okay, what else?" I prompted.

"Hotel."

"No."

"All right, give me a chance. I'm just tossing stuff out."

But flashes of the first time we met at the hotel filled my mind. And then I recalled our honeymoon at the same place. It really was special.

"Miles!" I exclaimed, probably a bit too loud … but that was it. "Miles," I said a little softer but with the same enthusiasm. "It's called the Miles Hotel *and* the name could also represent all the miles we have been through together.

You even said it in your vows! How do you feel about Miles?"

"Love it." The man who went by Hawk rather than his given name would be completely on board with that rationalization. "So … Collin Miles?"

"Uh …" I picked at the coconut cinnamon donut. "Yeah, I … I think. Yeah?"

Had we just chosen our baby's name? It made it so real. Not that the ballooning belly in front of me didn't already do that.

"Well, *I* think"—he poked me in the arm—"you're still awake, and we already have the full name. Told ya."

CHAPTER ELEVEN

Preeclampsia. It was the word I didn't want to hear. It was the word I'd feared when doing some online research after the doctor appointment prior to the Maryland trip. Of course my OBGYN had advised not to do that, but it was in my nature. Heck, it was a part of my profession. And even though I had done everything to relax and keep my blood pressure low, it did not work. I think even if Hawk and I had been whisked off to a beautiful island and there was no more violence, financial concerns, or anger in the world, it wouldn't have mattered. The pregnancy disorder was already set, and there was no carefree solution to stop or reverse it.

Preeclampsia. I let out a breath. Okay. I thought I had accepted it, knowing it was going to be a strong possibility, but actually hearing the word from the doctor's mouth that next week? That needed a breath. Or two.

I thought Hawk was going to soldier on since he knew of the possibility, too. And he did … somewhat … in a way. He was brave for me but still wanted to place blame. "It's because of the fire … the smoke. That's what did this, right?"

I cringed. I didn't believe that at all. If the fire had a part in it, it was small. I knew there had to be more pieces in the preeclampsia puzzle. It did no good for me, Hawk, or his nephew to think that was the reason. I worried that Raiden could not handle the guilt on top of his grief and, geez, simply being a teenager. Youth drug use and suicide rates were skyrocketing, and that was just a normal kid simply trying to live in the world. How could Raiden survive with all three factors bombarding at one time? Della had told Hawk she was making plans to fly out to be with Raiden and Jake for a while. It would hopefully help Raiden and alleviate some of Jake's worry about his son, while also dealing with his own grief.

I decided it didn't matter what the doctor's response was. I wouldn't let Hawk go down the rabbit hole of blaming his nephew again. What was done was done.

Luckily, her answer backed me up. "There's no way to tell if it is an underlying factor. Or if by it happening, you got to a medical facility faster than you would have with our appointments, which alerted us sooner to the warning signs like blood pressure. In that case, a weird blessing in disguise."

Before I could reply, Hawk denied what he thought I would be thinking. "No, don't. You still shouldn't have gone in the barn."

Most likely feeling the twinge of tension between Hawk and me, the doctor continued with an encouraging fact. "Good news is … Maya, your lungs sound better."

"They are." I nodded.

"The headaches are sporadic but not bad, is that right?" The dark-haired doctor leaned forward a bit, and behind her spectacles seemed to peer into my eyes as if she could see the pain behind them.

"Yeah," I agreed but thought my pain tolerance was pretty good, though. "They don't really last," I offered, hoping it was the right answer.

"But the BP is too high, and the urine sample reading is another indicator. You've put on some weight. But, you know, women tend to do that with pregnancies. We're going to keep monitoring the hands, feet, ankles, etcetera for swelling." She softly patted my hand. "I know preeclampsia is not what you wanted to hear, but be reassured you've done everything correctly, and I think with your mother's history, we need to err on the side of caution."

My mom had a miscarriage when my dad died, and a year later she had an aneurysm and passed away. I don't know which of her medical concerns Dr. Edgewood was referring to. Regardless, neither sounded good to me.

"What are we looking at here, doc? What specifically should we be doing?" I grasped Hawk's hand as he said those words.

"With preeclampsia, we will keep monitoring, and even though it is not the term they are using nowadays … *bed rest.*"

My face immediately pinched. "I have to stay in the hospital?" Images of bedpans and raised limbs flashed through my brain.

"No," she answered immediately, and I felt Hawk's hand in mine relax a tiny bit. "If you go into a work situation, I want it modified so you schedule in a couple hours of rest during the day. That can be in bed, your sofa, the bathtub …"

"So, stay put," Hawk condensed what he thought the doctor was saying.

"Not exactly. Maya, you'll still need to get up and move. The point is to relax." Papers were once again coming from her printer. "I'll be seeing you more often, too." She gave a sarcastic smile. "I know … lucky you. Now, do I need to write out a get-out-of-work pass for your employer?"

I liked how she was able to joke yet kept things professional. Dr. Edgewood knew what I did for a living and who I was employed by. Lara had been the one who referred me to her, as a matter of fact.

"The guy runs a tight ship. I'm thinking we may need union representation." At least Hawk could tease about it.

Although, I feared his sarcasm was a mask to cover his fear over our news.

"No, I don't think it's necessary," I more directly answered the doctor.

Hawk returned to his serious persona. "And what happens if the preeclampsia gets worse?"

"Let's not have that happen," she replied.

My husband was persistent, though. He was a details guy. He needed all the facts so he could evaluate and strategize. "But ...?"

"Could lead to complete bed rest to prevent miscarriage or having to give birth early. Again, we're not there. No reason to think the worst." Dr. Edgewood stapled two sheets of paper together.

"But be prepared."

"Instead of my employer, you might want to write a note for my husband, reminding him I am allowed to actually move. You know ... walk, breathe, laugh, get up, etcetera," I teased as I accepted the papers from the doctor. "I'm already expecting propped cushions everywhere I dare roam."

"Does she need certain pillows?" Hawk looked at the doctor, and I wasn't sure if he was speaking in earnest or not, until he squeezed my hand and smiled.

"Let him pamper you. That's always nice."

"It is." I admitted to something I was already a recipient of. "So, nothing really has changed then." I let him help me down from the table. "Just lightening the load a little and monitoring."

"Eliminate stress," she reiterated.

"You got it."

I wasn't sure how my husband could sound so confident with his response. Had he not lived our life that past almost year? No stress? Ha! Yeah. No problem. As if.

***

For me, the next couple of weeks really were fairly carefree. It wasn't a busy time for Finn as far as promoting went. The first wave of the summer tour arrangements had been made and ticket sales were coming in. So, he had some time to sit back and concentrate on writing and recording—all which took place in Nashville. I, of course, continued to monitor and post on social media, and Hawk helped Finn with any nitty-gritty details.

The most exciting happening was our house. The two of us were constantly going over there for check-ins and confirming things with the crew. By Valentine's Day, from the outside, you would have thought it was done. It wasn't. The inside was basically still a shell. We would need to pick out paint colors, bathroom fixtures, and much more so the rest could be completed. There was a roof and basic walls with insulation, though. Therefore, we decided to celebrate the romantic holiday there. We had talked about going to a luxury hotel—it was our thing, after all—but decided since we had just been away twice in a row, to create our own oasis.

As day was turning to night, we took a stroll around our new property. While Hawk and I followed the slightly overgrown path to the creek bank, I was thinking how much I loved that our new home was on the outskirts of town. It had such a sense of calm that you didn't find in the urban setting of our townhome.

Looking out to the water, Hawk stood behind me and wrapped his arms around to support the bottom of my belly. Gosh, did that feel good. It was like he was not only cradling the baby but lifting away some of the weight and, therefore, pressure on my back.

We watched as the red hues of the setting sun turned the sky an odd purple shade, and a few stars started to peek out. We both had our phones silenced for the evening, but I pulled mine out to capture the beauty of the scene. When I looked at the image on the screen, I instantly saw a connection between it and a photo my parents used to have hanging in their bedroom. Although theirs had been black and white, it still had the same striking sky and country path feel. I believe my mom had been the photographer of theirs and it had something to do with how they met. But, sadly, I didn't remember, and all who might have known were gone.

When the cooler wind started to increase, we knew it was time to get in the house—both because of the chill and the lack of light at night. With those two things in mind, once inside the main living area, we spread pillows and blankets over the hard, unfinished floors. Then, while I lit a half dozen candles and placed them on some turned-over, yellow construction buckets, Hawk made sure the generator was working so we could use an indoor firepit.

I had packed silverware, glasses, nonalcoholic wine, plates, bowls, napkins, and a couple trays to go with our picnic-like theme. The food itself was inspired by Juanita's girls' night. Using a potluck of what we had on hand in the townhome, I made a charcuterie board with a few types of crackers and cheeses, strawberries, apple slices, blueberries, a couple meats, mixed nuts, mustard, jelly, and honey. There was also some heart-shaped candy.

Hawk went the traditional route with his gift-giving. The first was jewelry. I was stunned by the gorgeous silver and diamond curved earrings. They closely matched his cufflinks. In addition to the gift was the promise that we would get to wear them at an awards show in the future—something I had, regretfully, missed in November.

The second gift was also something that initially seemed traditional. Alongside a box of chocolates, he got me a bouquet of romantic lilies and red roses, identical to the one when he'd asked me to move into the townhome with him. It was the container that the flowers came in that was unique, however.

"Is this a—?"

"It is." He had an amused and gratified look on his face. "Check out the inscri—"

But before he could finish his thought, I saw what he

was referring to. The ice bucket had my name on one side and his on the other. "That's so funny. I love it!"

I gave Hawk a kiss and then handed my gifts to him. Mine were all custom decorations for our new home. The first was a map, highlighting all the places we had been. We reminisced about those and the locations we still wanted to see together. The second was a front doormat that read *The Brannigans* and *Welcome to Our Home.* It had three hearts in one corner and a separate heart with the year in another. It was done in gray and Tennessee orange hues. I was afraid he would think it was too cheesy, but his immediate placement at the front door told me otherwise. The third gift was *definitely* cheesy but also appreciated. A neon sign stating *Bro Code* after Finn's "Boys' Weekend" song, it would go in the man cave area of our new house.

Between nibbles of food and in the serene solitude of our isolated home, Hawk and I spent the evening talking about our dreams—for the house itself and what we would like to accomplish in the future. We also reminisced about our wedding day—looking at the photos and recalling our vows. And then we finished by giving each other massages, making love, and snuggling ever so close under the blankets.

***

I would have to hold on to that warmth and love as February turned its page to March. My bump was definitely protruding more, and the little one inside me couldn't seem to make up his mind if he was going to try out for gymnastics with an abundance of leg cycling and hand swats or if he would lay dormant for such a long time that I felt a need to eat something sugary to make sure everything was still okay. Of course, that was always on my mind—fretting that everything was all right with the pregnancy. I'm sure most mommas-to-be were that way, but the preeclampsia certainly kicked my worry up a notch.

Hawk tried his best to alleviate some of that. In his

typical nonchalant way, he either made a joke to blow off my anxiety or insisted that there was nothing to fret about. He also tried the art of distraction. The sexy ones worked, depending on my waves of pregnancy nausea. But when he offered to see a local theater production with me—he even found it and brought it to my attention—I knew he was desperate.

"Seriously," he countered when I laughed. "It's *The Outsiders*. I liked that story."

"You read that?" I'm not sure I ever saw Hawk read anything other than articles online. In fact, the bookshelf at his place was bare of any of the items it was named for until I moved in and brought some of my own.

"The movie," he answered, as if I was being ridiculous. Then he added, "It was filmed in Oklahoma."

I took an extra second to look at him before answering. I could, indeed, see him liking a story that involved fighting for brothers, both biological and through friendship. But … "You know they're going to be singing and dancing."

He momentarily closed his eyes, as if taking in a sudden headache. "I know. But at least it's not Finn for a change." He smiled and then nudged me. "Come on, one-time offer."

"I love you. I'll take it."

Unfortunately, all of Hawk's attempts at deescalating my worry—including the musical, which he said wasn't as bad as he expected—were temporary reliefs. That's because the prenatal doctor appointments weren't all too reassuring … at least on my end. The baby was small but meeting the milestones. Me, though? Despite all the tricks of the trade, my blood pressure wasn't any better. I continued to experience a few headaches, in addition to some difficulty breathing, heartburn, and weight gain/bloating, especially around my feet and ankles. While all those things may come with a normal pregnancy, Dr. Edgewood said she wanted me to limit even more of my activities. I was still encouraged to be active but minimize how much per day and week. I was already not sleeping soundly. How was I supposed to rest and not have my blood pressure go up after hearing that?

But I had to. I had to. I was plucky and strong. I was determined. I would keep going. I could do it. I would do anything for the baby. Anything.

CHAPTER TWELVE

I continued to try to concentrate on the good stuff of the pregnancy as the end of March came into view. One of those was making sure everything was set for the babe's arrival. I packed my hospital bag for starters. It was early for sure, since the baby wasn't due until the beginning of May, but it was something I could actually accomplish.

We weren't doing much with Collin's room/my office—no baby decorations or change of paint color—because he wouldn't live at the townhome that long before we moved. The house was to be completed around the beginning of September—conveniently around the time the summer tour ended. And then we would move in shortly after. But we would definitely need the bassinet and changing table prior to that.

"Happy Anniversary, by the way." I handed Hawk the screwdriver once he had the top part of the changing table in place.

"Huh?" His face pinched as he directed his look at me. "Are we doing some kind of month thing I already missed? It's not a year. It's not even the right ..." He seemed to think for a second. "No, it's not even the right date."

"Well, I'm glad you know that," I teased. "Not our

wedding anniversary. The anniversary of when we met."

"Ah! Yeah? Really?" He went back to his manual labor task.

"Glad it was so memorable." I shook my head.

"Sweetie, you know there is no way I will ever forget meeting you or how we met. Probably next to the day we get to meet junior here, it will be the most memorable." I smiled as he quickly brushed his hand along my stomach. "I don't think I was paying much attention to the specific date on the calendar that day, though."

"Who would have thought a year later we would be putting together a baby room?" I held the table top as he tightened it.

"Certainly not me." He chuckled and grunted on the final twist. "I was counting down the minutes to hand off the two little ones I had with me."

"Awww, come on, you adore Chance and Arinn."

"Still . . ." He gave the changing table a little shake to test its sturdiness.

"Well, all *I* wanted was to be left alone."

"And now?" His smile was so damn irresistible.

"I can't stand the quiet when you're not here."

It was true. In a time when I should have been my happiest, I was depressed and feeling increasingly trapped. While certainly not as severe as claustrophobia, I didn't like being cooped up. I needed socialization ... and not just saying hello to a couple neighbors strolling by with a baby or dog. How ironic that it was the exact opposite of how I had felt the very first time I met Hawk. I had wanted to avoid even the smallest interaction that day in the hotel hallway.

It didn't help that my husband's schedule was starting to ramp up and mine wasn't. He and Finn took a quick trip to Manhattan for the country star to make a TV talk show appearance. Reese handled any PR since she lived in New York.

While they were away, Lara brought the kids and lunch

over, but even food was depressing. I had to limit salt, couldn't partake in lattes, and other foods no longer agreed. Besides checking up on me, her main motive was to go over the details of a small, intimate baby shower she was hosting in my honor. It was more like an evening of appetizers and desserts with the band-family ladies. I had known very little of it because she didn't want me to have to plan anything. And although normally I would have hated the attention, the thought of being with gals and celebrating the baby instead of worrying about it was, at least, something to look forward to.

***

I was one day into my thirty-fifth week of pregnancy when I thought I was absolutely, for sure, going to completely lose it. I remembered Sophia complaining during her last pregnancy. Her second son had been due at the end of September, and by mid-August, she had just about had it between the miserably hot heat and having a bulky belly while watching other women wear bikinis. She had been ready for the baby to be born. "Get him out of here," she had said a number of times. Well, I was definitely feeling that way, too. Although, for completely different reasons. I was ready to rejoin the living of doing everyday things.

Hawk, unfortunately, was facing the brunt of my frustration that day. He was getting set to head over to the studio, and I didn't want him to go. More than ever, I coveted talk and companionship. I was already sensing the emptiness that would come with his departure. Instead of saying so, though, I found a task for him to do—a way to keep him home, even if for only a few more minutes.

"Before you go, we should get the car seat in the back of my car."

"What?" He had his tablet in one hand and his car keys in the other. "We can do it later. We have plenty of time."

"It's just sitting there. May as well get it in. And you'll be tired when you get back." Because I hadn't been, he wasn't sleeping well either.

"Maya, I'll get it. It's not a big deal."

"You know what? Fine. I'll do it." I started toward the steps where I knew the car seat sat near the front door.

"No, you won't. Don't touch it. It's too bulky and heavy. What the hell, Maya? Why is everything suddenly so …?"

As he either aborted his fury on purpose or was just so frustrated he didn't know how to conclude the thought, I took a deep breath. "I don't know." I admitted to the honest feeling of simply being overwhelmed with life. "I'm bored. I'm anxious. I want something to do. I'm going a little bit nutzo."

"A little?" He tried light humor, shook his head, and then spoke earnestly. "I wish I could do this for you … carry the baby."

"If only," I sighed, thinking pregnancy should be a fifty-fifty deal just like conception.

"I'll put the car seat in on my way out, okay? I already watched the video on it. It'll only take a couple minutes. All right? Anything else?"

"Can we talk about the birth plan?"

"The what?" His head jerked back a bit.

"Don't act like you didn't hear me." Man, I was one naggy bitch. I could hear it and feel it but couldn't do a damn thing to change it, just like my beast of a headache, which seemed to be going in waves.

"I heard you. I guess I don't understand. There's a plan? I mean, I thought you had contractions or your water breaks or whatever, we see doctors at the hospital, there's some pushing, and you yell at me … kinda like what you are doing right now."

I rolled my eyes at his attempt at humor. And then I breathed. It was as much of an apology as he was going to get.

Hawk tried an alternative but again with a touch of

comedy. "What kind of plan can there be? Can you say I'd like a five-minute push and ice cream after?"

I tried my best to go with his lighthearted effort. "I wish. A birth plan states my preferences for labor, like who and what I want in the room. It's drugs. It's the umbilical cord and the atmosphere in the room. And then there's how to feed the baby, where he'll be, circumcision—"

"Okay, okay." I'm not sure if he cut me off—no pun intended—because of the manly part of that last decision to be made, but he did get my point of needing to talk about a lot. "Listen, sweetie"—he countered my anxiety with a little calmness—"whatever you want, I got you. Write that stuff down so I have it, okay? We'll be fine. We can talk about it tonight. Now, I need to get to the studio. You'll conference with us later, right?"

"Oh, yeah, shoot! I almost forgot about that." Was pregnancy brain legit, or was I just losing my mind completely? "I'm gonna do a little yoga and then take a shower before I meet with all of you. What an exciting day," I added with sarcasm.

He ignored it. "I love you, Mai."

"I don't know why," I mumbled and immediately apologized for dismissing his sweetness. "Sorry. See you on the boring screen in an hour or so." Thanks to preeclampsia and Dr. Edgewood, no more in-person meetings if I could sit and join online.

"You got it." He lightly brushed his hand along my blossoming belly. "Keep your mom in line, Collin."

I swatted Hawk away and toward the stairs with a slight chuckle. He didn't talk to the baby as much as I had started to. He wasn't quite convinced that a child could hear and recognize voices in utero. Plus, he had the reputation of being a man of little words. I guess he thought his directive to our son was an important message right then, though. But he should have known his request was a very tall task.

***

"All right, Maya. I think we look good on your end, right?"

"Yeah," I answered Finn. "I'm set. Got something to work on."

I had spent over a half hour on the video conference with Finn, Reese, and Hawk. It was funny—I knew my husband intellectually understood, but he didn't truly realize how different talking in that format, rather than with everyone in the same room, was. His facial expressions would not go as unnoticed as they normally did. For one, his frustrated, protruded jaw was magnified when we were discussing how I would not be able to head out with them on the tour's fantastical months-long journey of music and friendship. It made me sad, too, but there was no way for it to happen with the baby's due date only a couple weeks before the first show. But besides meeting up with them when some of the stops were close enough to drive to from our home, I wasn't going to be a part of it. A tour bus full of bunks and people was not conducive for a newborn, crib, and smelly diapers. That was for sure. Instead, during the summer, I would work from home, with Collin by my side.

The other quite noticeable Hawk expression came at the conclusion of our meeting. He winked right as I said I was going to sign off. I guess I should have been glad his focus was solely on me, but he somehow forgot that everyone else could see his flirty gesture, too.

"I'd wink back at you, hot stuff, but I'm afraid your wife might catch on." That was a teasing Finn.

"Awww, I thought that was for me," Reese chimed in from New York, as we all witnessed Finn going a little sideways from a hand shoving him … a hand that had my husband's wedding ring on it.

As laughter erupted from our boss, one last look of exasperation filled Hawk's box on the screen. "I'll see you in a couple hours or so, Mai."

"I won't tell your wife," I teased and threw in a wink of

my own before disconnecting.

The irony of my statement was not lost on me a little later that afternoon. I had managed to keep my demeanor light after the conference call, partly because of the positive energy the three of them had exuded and partly because I had decided to bake. I hadn't really done much of that since Jeff died. Subliminally, I suppose it seemed to me like a domestic wife or mom thing to do. And, besides, cooking was more my skill level than baking. But, somehow, there I was—married and in my third trimester with a longing to suddenly bake. And we had the standard ingredients to make cookies, so why not?

As I put them on the cooling rack, I hoped the chocolate chip/walnut cookies would taste as good as they smelled. Even if I should resist, they would be a nice sorry-for-my-pissy-attitude-earlier/thanks-for-putting-up-with-me treat for Hawk when he got home. We could even turn off our devices and have a date night in, something we hadn't truly done in a while. With that in mind, I was thinking of what to make for dinner when the phone rang … and with it went my good attitude.

Having a landline was something we were still debating about when it came to the new home. We weren't going to get one, but seeing the Oklahoma area code pop up made me reconsider. If Hawk's family—or any of our friends—needed to reach us and our phones weren't for whatever reason accessible … Well, sadly, we both knew the importance of contacts and emergencies.

Not recognizing the exact number on the caller ID, though, I answered generically. "Hello?"

There seemed to be a hesitation before the female responded. "I'd like to speak with Alex."

Needing a stretch, I wiggled my lower back around. "He's not here. This is his wife." I was thankful the grumble I got in response didn't seem to signify any urgency but, at the same account, didn't sound friendly. "Who's this?" I tried. "Can I—"

"It's his *other* wife."

"His …" It took me only a second, and then *I* wanted to do more than grumble. "Oaklee."

"I'd like to talk with him. He lets you pick up his cell?" Her voice was nasally, punctuated, and condescending.

Regardless, I tried not to counter with the same harshness. "This is our landline." I wanted to grab a piece of paper and write down *absolutely no landline in new house.* But, instead, I remained stationary, hoping to draw the conversation to a quick end. "And, you know, he wouldn't have a problem with me answering if it *was* his cell."

Although it was the truth and vice versa with mine, it didn't happen all too often, and I confess … I told her that just to make a dig. Oaklee really rubbed me the wrong way. It's a shame because it hadn't been that way with Jeff's ex-girlfriends. There had been one we seemed to run into sometimes when we'd been out and about, and it had been cordial. Another worked at his nephew's school and was happily married. None were like the spiteful hornet's nest named Oaklee.

"He wouldn't like it if—" She started again, as if she knew him.

I interjected and tried to keep my cool when doing so. "Oaklee, he's not the same guy. He's not twenty-year-old Alex. He's changed. I'm sure you have, too."

Then again, maybe she hadn't. It was probably why they were divorced and she was most likely going through another one. She hadn't changed at all. "Well, aren't you all high and mighty? You didn't know him then. You probably don't even really know him now."

No sense in continuing the ridiculous conversation. "Listen, do you need something specific? Hawk told you he didn't want you calling."

"Hawk … That's not—"

"Hawk," I reiterated with determination as I paced a little in the living room area.

"He didn't tell me not to call."

"Oaklee," I bellowed. I think I was starting to actually physically feel the blood pressure rise in my arms. "I was standing right there when he said it. Oh, you know … this isn't good."

"Can't handle talking the truth?"

"No. No! This isn't good for the baby. I'm gonna—"

"That baby … Is he still saying he's on board with it? I'm sure he's just—"

"Goodbye, Oaklee." Forget manners or civility … I hung up. And when I did, I reconsidered the landline debate again, because there definitely was a phenomenal feeling you got when slamming a landline phone down that you didn't get with a cell.

I let out a deep breath before I actually screamed. That infuriating woman. It really did astonish me how Hawk had ever been attracted to her. Was it a time in his life when he needed to cling to something and she was the closest in proximity? I understood immaturity when you are, indeed, not old enough to know who you are going to be, but, God, most human beings develop, grow, and learn to be, well, decent. Hawk certainly had. Oaklee? Not so much.

Ugh! I screamed again. I knew I shouldn't let her get under my skin … that I had nothing to fear. Oaklee should, actually, be the one to be pitied. But everything was getting to me. I didn't need one more aggravation in my life. What I needed was calm, peace, good health … and more winks.

I did a few additional laps around the main floor, stretching out my neck and back as I did. I could feel the pulse in my swollen feet getting faster and faster. Knowing I needed a bigger space to walk out my aggression, I thought of doing one of my short walks around the neighborhood, but it was looking overcast and had already rained earlier that morning. As I wrung my hands through the ends of my hair, I realized a destination. Although I had settled on a regular beauty salon since moving to Nashville, I couldn't simply pop in there without an advanced appointment. But I could go to a walk-in place since I simply needed my hair trimmed, especially my bangs. More, though, what I really needed was to have someone massage my head and talk about nonsensical stuff like their kid's school, the weather, upcoming vacations, or house repairs. Who cared? Just so it wasn't past lives and wives. I took a healthy gulp of water from the fridge, put my phone in my purse, grabbed my keys, and walked out.

CHAPTER THIRTEEN

Deja vu definitely had a hand in magnifying my panic. Even though I couldn't truly recall the first time it happened, I did subconsciously. It was absolutely a part of my makeup … my very being … really, the thing that made me the person I was. And there I was experiencing a very similar horror all over again.

If I had one thing going for me, it was that I had the power to do something about it. Whereas in the past, as a child and the lack of technology, I had been helpless. Even though I couldn't reach it, I could use my voice to connect to my phone.

"I know. I'm sorry," Hawk answered with an immediate admission. "There was a shitload to figure out with the—"

"Hawk?"

I reached up to my head. The ache was getting worse. That, plus the sudden downpour of rain was exactly why I was in the predicament I was in.

Oblivious to my plight, he continued with another round of apology. "I'm in my truck. I'm on my way home. Really. If you need to eat dinner without me—"

"Hawk!" That time my response wasn't a question, and it wasn't as calm. My upper right side was feeling a little odd, too, and I was sure it was due to my damn blood pressure.

"What?"

"I … I had an accident."

Maybe it wasn't my BP. Maybe it was the claustrophobic setting. That would completely make sense, since the initial onset of my having the fear of closed-in spaces was traced back to me being stuck in the car all those years ago. Or … maybe it was a combo. That was probably the worst-case-scenario truth.

"What?" His voice initially sounded like there was fret seeping in, but then it just as suddenly changed. "Oh, yeah, ha, ha, Maya. April Fool's. Not funny. Something a little less—"

I started to bawl. I couldn't handle any more. I couldn't handle the pain, the fear, and the fact that it was the stupid, made-up holiday, which I had completely forgotten about.

And with that, Hawk knew for sure I wasn't playing a prank. "Mai! God, what happened? What do you mean? What kind of accident? Did you fall?"

"No," I managed to answer immediately, knowing what happened to Lara during one of her pregnancies had produced an almost obsessive fear in my husband when it came to mine. "The car … it slid." Wiping at my eyes, I managed to stop crying. "I—"

"What?" With every reply, he sounded more and more alarmed and agitated. "You're driving? Why are you driving? Where—?"

"I'm sorry."

I was allowed to drive. But we had agreed he would know and I would stay local. So … fifty-fifty.

"Now's not the time." I was afraid he'd only be further upset if he knew I went to do something he'd think was frivolous like get my hair done—which I'm sure had become a complete unruly mess with the accident. And the alternative of telling him how Oaklee had upset me was even worse. "I can't get out, Hawk. I can't. The car is stuck, and I … I … God, I'm starting to panic, and I don't feel well."

"Shit! Shit!" I'm pretty sure that panicky feeling was hitting him then, too.

"I …"

It was getting harder or weirder or something to breathe. I felt weird all over, in fact. I was trying all the techniques I had learned for my claustrophobia. The problem was, nothing was working.

"Hold on. Give me a sec." Hawk grew quiet for a moment and then seemed to make a nondescript sound, similar to when he was trying to figure out something and had a mound of paperwork spread out in front of him. "Mai, is anyone there with you?"

"No." My heart felt like it was beating a mile a minute. "I'm all alone."

I turned to look out the back for any approaching vehicles, but all I saw was the car seat securely in place. With that, I felt a new tear roll down my face. It wasn't only for arguing about it that morning with Hawk, but it was also about the past. I had been that kid. I was the kid in the car seat stuck all those years ago, not able to get out … watching my dad take his last breath in the front. There was no one else then. There was no one else. I couldn't … I couldn't. I tugged at my driver's door again, but it was up against the tree. Thank God I hadn't hit it. I really didn't think I'd hit anything at all, besides some branches scratching alongside the car. But I couldn't get out, and the car wouldn't move because of the angle we were at … never mind the mud, which spun around on the tires.

"There's no one around," I reiterated. "I can't get out." Just saying that made me need to take an extensive breath, which proceeded on piercing my headache further.

"Did you call 9-1-1?"

"No. No. I can't breathe. I needed to talk with you."

That was the truth. Of all the breathing techniques I had acquired throughout my lifetime, talking with Hawk was probably the best. Even if I knew he was anxious himself, simply knowing he was there and we were connected helped.

And he proved that to me right then with his reassuring words. "You *are* breathing, Mai. You're breathing. You're talking. Okay? What else? Something hurt?"

"I don't know. Uh … Yeah. My head, my side … everything. I could maybe be, you know, panicking. I should have called 9-1-1. I wasn't thinking. I …"

I had been rattling off a response, and it was momentarily keeping me from thinking about needing to breathe, but then I did, and it was a massive inhale. How stupid was I? Why hadn't I called 9-1-1? Good God. I wasn't thinking straight. I was in panic mode. I needed to act like a mother, not a scared woman with trauma.

"Talk with me. Talk with me, Maya. I need you to keep talking. You did the right thing, okay?" He seemed to know what I needed to hear, despite not even seeing me. "I'm almost there."

"What? How?" I hadn't told him where I was. I didn't say what road I found myself stuck on—a damn back, deserted one. Or *had* I told him? I was really losing it. "I … Oooh!" My head, once again, made me aware it was in competition with my breathing. Plus, the pain in my side was more than the heartburn I seemed to usually reserve for nighttime.

"What?"

"I don't feel good."

"Shit, Mai. What were you doing driving? I told you—"

Nope, I couldn't listen to that right then. "Don't yell at me."

"I … I'm not. I'm trying to understand." Both his version and mine were true.

"I can't stand being cooped up. I needed to get out."

I wanted so bad to reveal the Oaklee part of the tale. Doing so would surely help me get some aggravation out, but it would also infuriate Hawk. I needed him as calm as he possibly could be, though, considering I was in my last trimester of a preeclampsia pregnancy and wedged on the side of the road.

"Mai … Maya!" His voice sounded different on the second proclamation of my name, almost as if he had hung up.

God, he had. He had hung up. But it was because he was standing there, tapping on my car window in the pouring rain. At first, I jumped, having not seen him approach in my panicked state. And then I breathed a real breath for the first time since I felt the car go out of control.

"Hawk …" I expelled as I opened the window.

"Maya …" He reached in for my hand and gave it a solid but comforting squeeze.

"Oh God."

"All right. All right. I'm here." His voice was his taking-charge one. "The airbag didn't deploy?"

"No. I didn't hit anything. It just slid and came to a stop, but now I'm stuck."

"Good. At least you're not hurt."

But was I? Despite knowing he was there and my breathing getting a little more stable, I still didn't feel right. It wasn't accident-related. It had started prior … at the tail end of my haircut. It was the increasing pain in my head. It was the nausea I had attributed to needing something to eat. It was the weird feeling in my midriff.

"Damn it," Hawk cursed after trying the door and seeing there was no way it would open with the towering tree pretty much propped against it. "All right. So, I know I can tow you out." His extended cab pickup was definitely heavy enough and capable of the job. "It might take a while." He shook his head, and beads of water splashed with it. "You can maybe stay put instead of trying to climb upward out the passenger."

I knew that was my alternative, and had Hawk taken any longer, I would have tried it myself. It was just that I needed to hear him first. It would be a challenge since the car was slightly slanted with the passenger side up. Plus, there was the gear shift and compartment box in between the seats …

and I was very pregnant. But not liking the trapped feeling, I would have gone for it.

"You okay with staying inside?" When I didn't answer, he prompted again. "Mai?"

"Truth?"

"Yeah. Yeah, sweetie. I need to know the truth. I need to know so I can best assess what to do."

"Hawk?" I grimaced when I said his name, not sure which of the ailments attacked me right then. "I really don't feel good. There seems to be pain everywhere, and the baby … it was more than a kick. Something is pressing and—" I cringed again. "I think I need to go to a doctor."

"What?" Even with the rain between us, I could see the fear in his eyes. "Oh, crap. Okay. Okay. Forget towing you. I'll get you out the passenger. Hold on." As he turned, I saw him slide a little in the mud and most likely curse, but I was already getting the window back up.

In those few seconds or so that it took Hawk to cycle around to the other side of the car, I felt another wave of panic set in. It wasn't about the coffin-like atmosphere that time, though. It was a whole other fear. It was for the baby. It was realizing what I had just said and knowing the possibilities of what it meant.

I cried the moment Hawk opened the other door. "I shouldn't have … Oh God."

"It's okay. It'll be okay." Hawk had gotten partially in the car. "You sure it's the baby?"

"I … I don't know, but there's pain, and I need to get out."

After he reached over to put on the parking brake, he grabbed the keys from the consol and then my hand. "Maya …" He took the second to rest his eyes on mine and spoke with confidence. "I got you."

As we worked together to guide my body over the middle of the car, it felt more like trying to manipulate a heavy chest-of-drawers down a split staircase. "He … the baby … I can't have anything happen. Not after all we—"

"God help me. It's okay. How are you doing? You all right? You're almost out."

"Yeah." I hoped that to be the truth.

"Hey …" Hawk brought me into his embrace the second I was free. "Hey …" Even though all I wanted was air, the compression of his hug felt so, so good.

I quickly swiped at my eyes and the few stray tears cascading from them. "How'd you find me?" That question had been momentarily set aside with the need to concentrate on everything else.

"I …" He started leading me out of the slanted area and away from the car. "The shared location feature we now have on our phones." He then quickly added, "You know I never use it, but it's there in cases like … well, like this."

"Oh. Good. I'm glad." I was thinking and appreciating my husband's overwhelming desire to protect those he cared for when my mind backtracked to the hows of it. "My phone!" I exclaimed. "My purse is in the car. It fell to the floor of the passenger side. I'll need it to call the doctor."

"I'll get it. Anything else?"

"No." A swish of all over pain filtered through my body. "Just, God, for the baby to be okay."

"Yeah." He squeezed my hand and quickly brushed my lips with his. "Let me get the purse."

As I watched him scurry—with a few minor slides—back to the car, I prayed the weird sensations circulating through my body would stop like, thankfully, the rain seemed to be. If only it had a little earlier, maybe the road wouldn't have been so slick. But I knew there had been other factors, too—the pain searing my head and the anger I still felt about Oaklee's call.

After Hawk helped me into his truck and we started to pull out, I called the doctor's office. They said we could meet with her as soon as we got there. Oh, and not to worry.

That I could not do. When I hung up the phone, I couldn't stop repeating what seemed to be my newfound mantra. "I'm sorry. I'm sorry. I'm so s—"

"Sweetie, please. It's okay. There's nothing to be … Everything's all right." He reached over and grasped fiercely onto my hand. "Concentrate on good things. It's simply another drive down a road for us, right?"

I tried to take a deep breath. "I love you, Hawk."

"Maya …" When his voice hitched and his head swiveled toward me, I knew he could sense my desperation … my need to tell him those words. And that more than anything else since he arrived on the scene seemed to cause him distress. "I can't—"

"I don't feel good." The feelings of both pain and anxiety were not going away, which, of course, did not help my breathing.

"I know. We're almost there. Damn it!"

I closed my eyes, held on to my belly, and tried to will myself to feel better. But as we got closer to the hospital, my headache was so fierce it was affecting my vision. I'd never had migraines, but I knew that was one of the main symptoms. And my breathing was becoming erratic, which I knew had nothing to do with claustrophobia. The truck windows were down, there was plenty of breeze, and it was cool outside. No, it was definitely something else.

"Mai! Maya! … Mai!"

"Huh?"

"You … you, like, zoned out or something. Give me your phone."

He didn't wait, though. He reached across to where it rested next to me on the passenger seat and immediately redialed the last number. After Hawk relayed my symptoms to the doctor's office, the plan was amended. We were heading straight to the maternity emergency area.

CHAPTER FOURTEEN

By Hawk's agitation, you would have thought everything was happening at a snail's pace once we arrived at the hospital. Because I was being poked, prodded, and answering an abundance of questions, I felt the exact opposite. Everything seemed to be going in a maddening rush. But at least I was feeling a little better. Throwing up and knowing I had medical experts nearby helped for sure.

The part *I* thought was long was after all the procedures and tests were completed … when Hawk and I were left alone in the cubby of a room with no answers yet. Not knowing anything was the torturous part and absolutely was not the date night I had imagined. He was making calls to get my car back home, and I was reading Lara's text regarding some last-minute baby shower preparations. I thought of texting her back to tell her things might need to be put on hold, but I didn't want to. I wanted to ignore that thought. I wanted to pretend everything was all right.

It wasn't, though. It was far from it. It was absolutely crushing.

"Damn …" Hawk expelled and stood to walk a couple steps after Dr. Edgewood had re-entered the room and told us the prognosis. His hands on his hips mirrored his irritation. "How could this happen? She was being monitored pretty much constantly."

I closed my eyes. I didn't need his combativeness, even if I understood it was out of his own fear. I needed him to be my ears and listen while the doctor explained how we were going to fix it. Because upon hearing her diagnosis, I was entering a type of mental fogginess, and I was hoping I wasn't going to start struggling to breathe again due to my increasing anxiety. Feeling closed in and confined wasn't always physical.

"Mr. Brannigan ..."

Hawk let out a grumble. It was an especially frustrated one. That was most likely for a multitude of reasons ... a) he hated being called *Mr. Brannigan* as much as *Alex,* b) we all knew she said it in the leading way to try to pacify him, and Hawk was not one for those types of tactics, and c) he wanted an answer but knew, no matter what, it wasn't going to be something either of us were going to like.

Dr. Edgewood tried again. "It was always a possibility, even though we were doing everything to prevent it." She pulled a rolling chair over, sat on it, and came closer to where I was sitting.

I reached out my hand for Hawk, standing so stiff on the other side. When he finally accepted it, I tried a question. "What can we do?"

"Let's talk about that." The fact that Dr. Edgewood hesitated and looked to Hawk and then me, gave me pause that it wasn't going to be good. "The best option to control the severity of the preeclampsia is to deliver the baby."

I was waiting for more, but when her face was so still, I understood. "You mean now? I'm not in labor." That had been the good news.

"No, you're not. But, yes, Maya—today. The baby is already in position." She swiped and glanced at the tablet in her hand as she continued to talk. "We should ind—"

My response that time was immediate. "No! It's too early. Why? Why would we do that? No."

When I felt the doctor touch my left hand, I realized my right one had been released from Hawk's. I looked over at him. He was moving—more like pacing—in the small space. But his enlarged eyes were on me.

"You already had a seizure."

"No, I didn't," I denied the doctor.

"What your husband described happened to you in the ride over here? That's an absence seizure."

"A what? You mean when I blanked out for like a second or two?" I was trying to comprehend so very much that was being thrown at me.

"He seems to think there was maybe a tic, too."

My breathing. My breathing was getting bad again. I held my head.

"Maya." Her voice was calm but directive. "Your blood pressure isn't good. There's a lot going on, and it's best if we get the ba—"

"No!" I refuted again. "It's too early for the baby."

"He's measuring at four pounds fourteen ounces," she countered as if that was to be reassuring.

I thought the exact opposite. "That's too little. It's even smaller than we were projecting, right?" I had been listening to the doctor. I had been looking online. I knew the facts.

"We're in one of the best hospitals for this. We have a full team of staff who have experience with late preterm babies." Why did she basically keep telling me the same thing? "There's a ninety-five percent survival rate." I'm sure she found that reassuring.

I did not. "What's the alternative?" There had to be a plan B, right?

"We admit you, try some meds, and wait."

"But that's not what you'd recommend?" Hawk stopped his strut and lived up to his name, zeroing his eyes in on the doctor.

"No. I'm not convinced medication at this point will work, and there are the effects on the baby to con—"

"Like what?"

At least Dr. Edgewood was straightforward with her response to me. "This isn't the beginning of your pregnancy so probably no physical abnormalities, but there may be birth defects and/or developmental and learning difficulties."

Wasn't that the same as a premature birth? I had read up on enough of that. Again … too much time on my hands. I had to figure out a better alternative than those two solutions.

"From what I think you're saying … after the baby is born, does the risk of me having seizures go away?" I was trying to remain as analytical as possible, but it was hard.

"You have no history of epilepsy or seizures of any kind. It's due to the preeclampsia escalating. Yes, the highest risk should end within the week after giving birth, but we'll monitor for four to six."

"Then, no. I don't want to deliver early. And no to the meds. They're both too risky. It's that simple. We wait it out. He needs to grow, and we don't even know if I am going to have a seizure." I then bookended my statement as double confirmation of my wishes. "No. No meds. No early inducing. No."

"Maya! Maya, what? Nothing? No!" Hawk started pacing again. "A seizure isn't good. She's not saying a blip like in the car. I'm pretty sure she's talking about a massive … God." Hawk turned to the doctor then. "What happens if she has a full-blown seizure when pregnant?"

"There's a chance of delivering early, but the studies on babies are good. I already told you that Collin is fine after your episode in the car. There's more of a risk to the mother. Preeclampsia isn't only seizures. It can cause stroke, heart failure, and other things." Dr. Edgewood seemed to be strangely siding with Hawk … not a good time for that.

It didn't dissuade me, though. In fact, I was getting even more determined. I was getting in kickass mode. "The baby needs to grow. The baby needs time yet. I'm not even at thirty-six weeks. Hawk, please …" I said with a plead. "I have to think of Collin. I need you to, too. You said you would support my birth plan." The one that we were supposed to discuss that night over dinner. The one that seemed to be going straight to hell. Tears were coming then, both from the pain in my head and the reality of what the conversation was all about. I waited too long for this miracle of a baby. I was pregnant because he was meant to be. I had to give Collin a fighting chance.

"Maya! God! This is like the damn fire all over again. You *are* thinking of Collin by being around to take care of him. You need to think of yourself. The doctor said they are prepared to care for Collin if you deliver early."

"It *is* like the fire," I threw the words back at him. "Remember what you said to me? Let me die. It's my life. It's my decision."

"It's—"

"Okay, listen. We all … Everyone needs to take a breath. Right now, the most important part is trying to be as calm and relaxed as possible." Even though Dr. Edgewood was more than a foot shorter than Hawk, she took charge by putting up a finger in his direction. "I know. I have already arranged to get Maya into a room … a real one. Because no matter what, she's staying." She said that to Hawk and then reiterated it to me in the same authoritarian voice. "We're admitting you. Close monitoring is essential for whatever … decision." I noted her hesitation and closed my eyes. "Mr. Brannigan—" The doctor seemed to know to correct the name that time. "Hawk … it might be best if you take a break. Maya will need some things from home—toiletries and stuff like that. How about if you go get those while we get her settled into her room? What do you think?"

He didn't answer, which might have been good. It meant he wasn't yelling. He kept staring straight at me, though, and taking some breaths. It was almost as if we were having a momentary reversal of symptoms.

"My labor bag is already packed," I offered. "And I'll need my laptop."

"Perfect," Dr. Edgewood agreed.

"Maya …" He blew out some air and then redirected his comment to the doctor. "She'll be all right until I get back?"

"She'll have a chance to relax." Code for: *anxious, protective husband needs a breather so his wife doesn't emulate the stress.*

He wasn't one to give up easily, though. "I don't want to leave her."

"Hawk." It was my turn to try to get him to do as the doctor wanted, and, somehow, I managed to do it with a sense of calm … at least externally. "I need you to do this for me." I wanted him by my side. But I also needed him to be *him*—the kind of man he'd always been … the one I could rely on … the one with an abundance of strength … the only one I trusted. In order to be that, I knew he had to take a break and regroup. "Hawk, me, too, okay?" I reassured. "Me, too."

I noticed his eyes. They were weary, but they were full of love. "I'll be back soon … so soon."

"Just be careful," was my automatic response.

Hawk brushed a powerful, emotional kiss on my lips and touched my balloon of a belly. "Relax. Think. Please." He turned to Dr. Edgewood. "Doc, you have my number, right?"

"Yes, sir. And here is mine." She handed him her card.

I watched his body turn and disappear through the doorway, and I felt a tear slide down my face. This wasn't how it was supposed to be. We were supposed to have weeks yet to meet our precious little one. I vehemently regretted my thoughts earlier that morning, comparing my pregnancy to Sophia's. I didn't want Collin out. I wanted him safe. There shouldn't be a precarious health decision to be made, especially one that caused Hawk and me to be at odds with each other. Hadn't we gone through enough in our lives? Why were we being thrown this, too?

***

The way my husband entered my private room in the high-risk ward wasn't much different than the way he had left the previous one. He did so slowly and with worry drawn on his face. "I'm going on record that I don't agree with this." He placed the bags on the counter as he approached my bed. "But, Maya, you know I will support you. I told you that. You know you have that … no matter what. You have to understand I'm worried, though."

I pursed out a breath. At least my breathing had truly regulated since I had last seen him. Given time to absorb everything and talking further with Dr. Edgewood had helped.

I greatly appreciated my husband's honest vulnerability … something he was very selective in showing others. "I do. I do understand. So am I."

"But you're still …" On my confirmation nod that my mind hadn't changed, he physically shook his head to stop himself from, I'm sure, arguing his point again. "Okay."

Grateful to change the subject, I noted the three bags. "Thanks for bringing my duffel and laptop. What's with the backpack? Did you add more stuff for the long haul?"

As it stood, I was in the hospital until I gave birth. It had been what I'd been dreading on that first mention of bed rest so many weeks before. That was until the alternatives were worse.

"Sort of. It's mine." He pulled the reclining chair a little closer to my bed.

"Yours?"

"I'm not leaving," he said matter-of-factly while sitting.

"Hawk …" His name wasn't so much a word as it was a breathy exasperation. "This isn't Oklahoma. You can't 'good ole boy' the staff here," I recalled my hospital overnight in his hometown. "Besides, who do you know in a women's hospital?"

"You underestimate my charm."

"I hope I don't." I pierced my eyes at his tease.

He momentarily got up and kissed me quickly on the cheek. "I talked with Dr. Edgewood. She said it was okay."

"She was the one kicking you out not too long ago," I proclaimed with shock.

"Because I was going to lose my shit over what you're doing? Yeah. I had a right to be upset." The fury was still obviously simmering underneath his words, but he also said it in a way in which I knew he conceded to what was happening.

I tried to keep the conversation on topic. "So, she gave you permission to stay?"

"She said considering the situation, yes. At least for tonight while we see how you do." He closed his eyes for a second. "Maya, I'd almost rather she'd said *no.* I don't like that she thinks I might need to be near."

"Oh, Hawk, I—"

He wouldn't let me see any more vulnerability, though. He plowed right into his protective, analytical mode. "How's your headache? Blood pressure? What about the other pains?"

He was looking at me as if watching the last ticking seconds of a hockey game. With a win, the team would go to the playoffs. But a loss? It was the end of the dream. Yes, I still remembered that feeling deep down.

"Um … you know, the pain is still there. Not as bad, though. Definitely not like before the accident or coming over here. I got some basic pain meds." Those I had agreed to.

The fact was, I was starting to feel okay. So much so that I was beginning to wonder why there was such a fuss. Shouldn't I be able to go home or at least not have a damn extended bed rest in the hospital? But there was the seizure—the seizure they'd said I'd already had. That was the proverbial nail.

"Did the doctor tell you anything more? Like, what triggered this? You seemed, you know, fairly okay before I left for the studio today." I noted how he emphasized the word *fairly*. "Agitated, but … It wasn't because of the car seat or birth plan, was it?"

"Oh God, Hawk … no," I denied instantly, not realizing he felt guilt over something that was not even remotely his fault. "No."

"Why'd you leave home in the first place? Were you expecting to be gone long? There were cookies all over the counter."

"Oh! Oh, shoot! I forgot I was cooling them."

"Yeah, since when did you become a baker?"

Since I've been bored out of my mind, I wanted to say. Instead, "I'm not, and I'm sure they're not even in the same hemisphere as your mom's." Della, I thought, was baker extraordinaire.

"Don't underestimate yourself. I had a couple before putting them away. They're pretty good."

"You were starving," I countered, knowing we had bypassed dinner with a detour to the hospital.

"True," he acknowledged, and retraced back to his original question. "So, why'd you leave?"

"Can we not talk about it, please?" I was feeling my agitation start to rev back up, and with that, I knew my blood pressure would, too. I didn't need that. And I certainly couldn't tell him about Oaklee—that would rile *him* up. "I needed to get out," I offered and then decided to try to lighten the mood. "Maybe I was all hot and bothered because a certain brawny guy winked at me online."

Knowing my reference immediately, he rolled his eyes and *tsked*. "Speaking of, I have to call Finn and tell him what's going on. The team is meeting tomorrow to run through what the plan is for the benefit concert. He'll have to do it himself. I didn't know how long the birthing class we had scheduled would take, anyway. Are we still on for that since it's here in the hospital?" On my nod, he continued, "And I'll tell him you won't be able to—"

"First of all, I can talk with Finn myself."

Hawk's hands went up in surrender mode immediately.

We had gotten in a couple verbal tumbles in the past regarding him defending me with our boss. I was adamant he shouldn't. I needed to do it on my own. I wanted our professional and personal roles to be as separate as possible, as unlikely as it seemed.

"And, second, I can still work." Before he started to argue, I clarified. "No, not tonight, but if I am going to be laid up here in a waiting mode, I want to do something. We should call both Finn and Lara, though. I've been putting off telling her to cancel the shower, but it's time."

"Oh, crap, the girl gig." He had obviously mentally misplaced that event with everything else bombarding us.

"Diapers, books, appetizers, and gifts aren't what's important." Yet, I felt a tear make way to the corner of my eye. "Call them. We can talk together, okay?"

"Yeah."

Before he dialed, though, he carefully started to make his way onto the bed with me. I didn't question it. I knew what he was doing, and I loved the idea. I wanted to be as close to him as possible. Luckily, the maternity hospital bed was much more accommodating than the one in Oklahoma. I wondered if it was made bigger on purpose—to either accommodate the extra space a pregnant torso takes or for something similar as to what Hawk was doing … having the coach be behind the mom during labor. I had seen that in a number of movies. I wondered if it was what the next morning's class would suggest, or if like seemingly everything else when having a baby, it would be an in-the-moment preference—a wing and a prayer.

Listening to the phone ring as I leaned my head back onto Hawk's taut chest, I smiled as he placed the phone on my protruding stomach … more and more a shelf as the baby grew. It freed my husband's hands, which were rubbing circles on my scalp. It was, by far, the best feeling of the day.

"Hey, what's up?" Finn answered casually.

"Chief," Hawk replied back and then immediately stated

a necessity, especially when it came to someone of celebrity. "I need to let you know, you're on speaker."

"Oh," With just that one syllable, I could tell Finn was already a bit more reserved. "Okay. Whom am I speaking with?"

"Just my better half." Never mind the sweet words, if Hawk kept up the small circular motion above my eyebrows and around my ears like he was, my headache was going to go completely away and I might even sleep.

"Ain't that the truth," the country crooner jabbed back. "Speaking of … mine has been trying to reach you, Maya. Did you get her messages?"

"Yeah. Sorry. Things have gone a little haywire here." I looked at the phone as if he could see us, but, of course, we weren't on video.

"Oh?"

"Yeah, hey man, that's why we're calling." Hawk took lead again of the conversation. "Is Lara there? We need to talk with both of you."

"She's … Yeah. She's working on something for your shower get-together this weekend." On Finn's reply, my shoulders responded with a droop, and I felt Hawk's lips press against one of them in encouragement. "I'll get her." He changed his voice to call out to his wife. "Lar, Hawk and Maya want to talk with us about something." Finn was still speaking and I thought I heard Lara in the background, but I was a little distracted by someone entering my hospital room.

"Hi, Mrs. Brannigan." The woman was wearing scrubs and looking mostly at a tablet in her hands. "I'm Barbie. I'm the nurse practitioner tonight. I'm gonna check your—"

"Did she just say nurse?" I for sure heard Lara's voice that time. "Finn, where are they?"

"I don't—" her husband started to reply.

"Sorry." The woman—with golden blonde hair piled high above her head—looked in the direction of my stomach as Hawk grabbed the cell. "I didn't realize you were on the phone."

"Go. Go talk with them," I encouraged Hawk as he gingerly made his way off the bed.

He began to deny my request, and I knew why. Hawk wanted to be in the room. He wanted to hear whatever needed to be heard.

"I'll tell you," I reassured. "Go let Finn and Lara know what's going on." I motioned toward the phone in his hand. "You won't miss much."

"Hey, you're off speaker," Hawk spoke back into the phone. "I'm going out to the hall. Give me a sec."

Before exiting the room, my husband gave me a kiss. Did he know he was doing a lot of that since initially arriving at the hospital? Not that I minded, but I had a feeling what its origins were. It was love for sure, but there was also definitely a dallop of apprehension mixed in.

***

It was a long night. After hearing the nurse practitioner's report, Hawk went to the restaurant next to the hospital to get us a late dinner since I had missed the time when the hospital served it. I wasn't particularly hungry, but I knew the importance of eating and staying hydrated. So, we did.

When every conversation between the two of us ended up somehow leading back to the baby and the situation I found myself in, we knew we needed a distraction. The television provided that for us for a little while. A senseless sitcom even brought a few laughs. I liked seeing Hawk smile. He had a gorgeous one when he was carefree, and I longed for him to have more opportunities to be that way. I could picture him having such a grin while lifting our little boy in the air after hitting a homerun or eating melting ice-cream cones together. We would get there. Everyone just had to be patient and chill, including Collin, who needed to stay put for a little longer.

My daydream must have turned into a real dream

because the next thing I knew I was waking up. The room was darker and everything seemed a lot quieter. The hush of night had fallen over the ward. It was a good feeling … a peaceful feeling. I had felt like I'd been on the go the entire day—from the video conference, to the phone call with Oaklee, to the car, to Dr. Edgewood laying out the options, to Hawk pleading with me, to even the laugh track on the television. I needed the pause. No noise. No one else's opinions or thoughts … no matter how good intended. Silence. That's all.

I looked over to where Hawk's cot was laid out near the window. He had managed to go to sleep and, for that, I was grateful. He had a tendency to run on very little rest, and it was always a concern of mine, considering how my dad had died. And Hawk's "cute" thing about making sure I was asleep before him, didn't necessarily help. He needed his time, too, even if he was too proud and protective to admit it.

As if he instinctually knew I was awake and thinking that very thing, his eyes fluttered open, and he looked directly at me. "Mai, go to sleep, sweetie. You need your sleep."

My soft smile was accompanied by a whispery chuckle. "So do you. I love you."

CHAPTER FIFTEEN

"Good news, Dr. Edgewood." I was trying hard to keep a positive outlook on everything. I had been in the hospital for twenty-four hours and nothing had changed besides the fact that I was already getting a little punchy. I wasn't sure how many days or weeks I could handle solving online crossword puzzles and making small talk with nurses, aides, and orderlies. But I would have to find a way. My baby was counting on me.

"Oh, yeah, what's that?" she asked while continuing my exam.

I nodded at the monitors I was already getting used to reading. I knew where the blood pressure was. It wasn't really any better, but also not any worse. Plus, I didn't feel the tingling sensation in my body like I sometimes had. Shouldn't that count for something?

"Those are at status quo."

"They are." She went along with my positivity, despite knowing that staying at the same numbers was not the goal. "Where's your bodyguard?"

"You sure have gotten to know him." I chuckled. "I convinced Hawk to go home and check on things. You know … pick up the mail, get my pillow, put the garbage out. I told him to nap and shower at our place instead of here, but I'm afraid these accommodations are better than the ones when we are on tour. So, that wasn't going to fly as an—"

"Excuse to get him out of your hair for a minute?" She removed her gloves and threw them in the garbage.

"For his own good," I answered honestly. I knew he needed a break from our hectic day—birthing class, residents coming in for observations, and working a little on Team Murphy stuff. "You think *I'm* stressed? That man … That tough exterior takes in too much."

"Hmmm." As she entered something on her tablet, I readjusted my position on the bed.

"How we doing?"

"You tell me … besides status quo. Anything different? Pain anywhere?"

"Head is dull. The baby is moving around a lot. Really seems to be pushing on my lower back. Could that be about being in a different bed? I've been good about getting up, stretching, and moving around." I certainly didn't need blood clots on top of everything else.

The doctor's response didn't directly answer my question, but she did give a reason for the back spasms. "You're one centimeter, maybe a little more."

"Oh."

Oh. Oh, shit. Definitely not status quo.

"That could mean days or weeks yet, though, right?" We both turned in the direction of the voice—my husband's—coming from the doorway. He must have heard the latest as he was entering. Similar to how he held in stress, he also took in knowledge like a sponge, and I knew we had gone over the centimeter stages in birthing class earlier in the day.

"Every woman is different," Dr. Edgewood explained as Hawk touched my shoulder and I allowed him to swap out the pillow with the one he had brought from home. "You're gonna have to realize you're not in charge of this."

"Tell *him* that." I bounced my chin toward the man who

was used to being in control.

"Maya." He shook his head. "I haven't been in charge of anything since the very second you came into my life."

I appreciated the humor, sentiment, and irony in his statement. "Hmmm …" I countered. "Me, either."

"You mean, me, *too*." Hawk changed the last word and it made a world of difference in the perception of giving up something versus loving someone. And the kiss he quickly feathered on my lips helped alleviate some of the sting of the latest news. He then looked at Dr. Edgewood, who had placed her hands behind her back, obviously aware she was bearing witness to a personal, sweet exchange. "So, what's next?"

"Nothing different." Her hands went back to her front. "Besides keeping an even closer eye out."

"Don't know how much more of that is possible," I grumbled. "I'm already surrounded by medical personnel and beeping machines." The high I had experienced being in my self-proclaimed status quo had deflated as quickly as a pin to a balloon.

And then it was time for an even more serious Dr. Edgewood. The woman could certainly balance a multitude of personas and knew when to use which one. Besides her vast knowledge and experience, I believed it was her greatest attribute as a physician … even if I didn't always appreciate it. "When it's time, Maya—no matter how soon it is …" She paused and raised her eyebrows in a parental way. "If we say push, you push. Right? There won't be any of this he-needs-more-time and resisting business." Dr. Edgewood was a mom herself, so she knew how to lay down the law.

And I replied like an obedient child. "No. I know. I understand."

"Good. Because getting back to my original statement … Who is in charge now?"

Funny how I knew she wasn't speaking of herself. "Collin."

"That's right," she confirmed as Hawk sat on the chair

next to me. "We should really secure your birth plan, especially since both of you are here."

"As if I'm leaving again." He shook his head in a disapproving way since I had practically forced him out twice. I did note, though, how he seemed a little more relaxed since returning, and I couldn't help but wonder if it was because it appeared our son was coming earlier than anticipated, which was his vote from the beginning.

Dr. Edgewood broke into my silent ponderings. "I know your thoughts on meds. What about the room? What did we decide? Are you okay with whatever professionals are needed?" On my affirmation nod, she continued with a wiggly finger point toward Hawk, "And this guy? He's allowed?" There she was, back to her teasing bedside manner.

And, once again, I followed suit, as I'm sure was her plan. "I suppose. He just said he isn't going anywhere, after all."

"Not feeling the love, Maya," was my husband's sassy return comment.

"It's always about you, isn't it?" I retorted with obvious sarcasm of my own, knowing it couldn't be further from the truth. And then to the doctor, "What's next on the list?"

"Do you want to watch the baby come out?"

"I didn't realize these birth plans were so detailed." Before I could say *I told you so*, he continued, "But to answer the question, uh, I'm not sure. Maya?"

"Your choice." I meant it, but I especially liked the tease I got in, too. "Are you afraid it might ruin other things for you down there?"

It got the reaction I expected—an embarrassed and exasperated Hawk. "Maya … geez." He turned to the doc. "Can I make a game-day decision? I mean, if I end up looking, it's okay or—?"

"The question is really more for Maya." The doctor seemed amused. "Do you want a mirror or not?"

I knew the question was on the birth plan. Yet, I still did

not know which way I was leaning. I had gone on chats to see what other women did and their reasons, and it, honestly, didn't help. Their answers were about a fifty-fifty mix.

"I … I don't think so." There, I made up my mind. "If I thought something looked wrong, it might panic me, and that's probably not best."

"No mirror." Dr. Edgewood made a notation, and as much as she was trying to remain objective with my birth plan, the simplest pursing of her lips told me she was relieved by my choice. "All right, let's run through some of the room settings. Should be a quick checklist." She started with light options, birthing balls, and seats before she got to, "Music?"

It only took my husband and me a split second to look at each other before we announced simultaneously, "No."

The doctor outwardly laughed that time. "Really? Have enough of that normally?"

"Mayyybe …" Hawk's answer for *absolutely*.

I appreciated the relaxed mode as we discussed the birth plan. It certainly helped me not think as much about the fact that we were most likely getting to that birth sooner than I would have liked. And what it came down to was, I didn't really care about positions, who was cutting the cord, or much of anything else as long as there was a healthy baby as an end result.

When Dr. Edgewood left, Hawk and I started eating the food he had brought for dinner. It was another of my requests, and I knew he was happy to oblige. Hospital food had a reputation for a reason. We'd ordered from a sandwich shop—mine a basic egg and avocado sandwich with a cup of chili, and his was a side protein bowl and Italian sub with bacon.

"Far removed from my traditional appetizer and dessert likings," I sighed but at least it brought back good memories of the week we met.

"True enough," he agreed with a smile. "Maybe I should

have brought some of those cookies you made."

"Are they really half decent?" I seriously doubted my baking capabilities and also understood my husband's consistent desire to make me happy. But before he could answer, I needed to put the chili on the side table momentarily and shift my body. "Can you please tell your son to quit punching me while I'm trying to eat? No elbows on the table or the cervix or whatever." I was actually hungry, but with each jab of pain, I was losing my appetite.

Hawk laughed. "You know, Mai, I think we are really going to have our hands full with this kid. Forget terrible twos and teenage years, he's starting his rebellion prebirth. Let me finish this, and I'll give you a massage."

"Well, I hate to tell you, but I think the little rebel has been picking up on all the music. He definitely has rhythm. It's like he's going in waves." Knowing I needed to keep hydrated, I drank some hearty sips of water as Hawk finished his sandwich, washed his hands, and then climbed on the bed to sit behind me. I sighed with pleasure as I felt his knuckles start on my shoulders and in between the blades. "Thanks."

"You got it."

"Anything new at home?" With the perfect pressure of his hands, I was able to pick my sandwich back up.

"Uh, no, I guess not. The mail was all junk. I tossed it right in the trash. The package you ordered was by the door like you said."

"Did you open the box?"

"Did you tell me to?" His tone was in dutiful-husband mockery, and I took it in the lighthearted way he intended.

"Hawk …" I had. I wanted to make sure everything came and wasn't damaged.

"I did. We got more baby shit than room at this point." When he saw I wasn't really thrilled with his comment, he countered, "But I like the mobile with the little forest animals and the matching blankets."

"What about the outfits?"

"Uh-huh. But first Halloween already, Maya? Really?"

I laughed. That one had been too hard to resist. It was the cutest little cinnamon bun costume that made me think of Hawk calling the baby Little Bun all the time.

"What about the bottles?"

"Uh, five billion of them? I didn't count. I'm sure they're all there." I rolled my eyes at his exaggeration. "Anyway, it's there for when we get back. And I got Thomas to bring the trash cans to the garage door after pickup tomorrow."

"Oh, that's nice of him." I spoke of our next-door neighbor, and then wiggled a little to stretch. "Lower. Can you go lower?" When his hands traveled to that part of my back, my sigh that time was more like a heavenly moan.

"God, Maya." He chuckled. "You're starting to sound like we're doing something else in bed."

"You have no idea how wonderful that feels." Not quite as good as what he was referring to, but, in that moment, definitely what I needed more.

He rested his lips on my shoulder before moving his hands to my stomach and swirling them around. "The only other thing was, there was a message on our landline from the water company regarding the new house. I'll get back to them. But I also saw there was a call from Oklahoma. No message. It said yesterday afternoon. Were you home then? Do you know anything about it?" His lips met my shoulder once more.

And there Oaklee was … again, disrupting my beautiful life. I could have lied or at the very least danced around the truth. But you know what? I'd had enough. I'd had enough of Oaklee and her interference. I wanted her cleared out so she wasn't even a thought anymore. I had more important things to think about.

"It was Oaklee," I said plainly.

His hand motion stopped immediately. "What?"

I shook my head slightly and sighed, knowing it was the end of my magical massage. "Get up. I'll tell you. I'd like to see you when I do, though."

I moved the last couple bites of my meal onto the table as Hawk carefully got out from behind me and stood. He didn't sit. It was as if he knew the conversation was going to be one where he wouldn't be able.

"I picked up the phone when she called. I didn't know who it was … just saw the area code and knew it could be someone for you. She … she …"

"What?" His lips were already pressed tightly together.

"She's such a bitch, Hawk."

And then they exploded with air. "What did she …? Did she harass you again?"

"She kept trying. Singing the same song about how she knows you and what you want." Replaying and retelling the story was starting to charge me up, but, in a weird way, it was also doing what I'd hoped it would—releasing me. With each following word, I was speaking more calmly and with confidence. "I told her not to call again. Then I hung up, and I … I left."

Hawk, however, was going the opposite direction with his temperament. "That's why you left? That's why you went out yesterday?" He did a slow three-sixty in between his two sentences.

"I … Yeah. I needed to get out. She was a part of it. I did get my hair—"

"Shit! Damn it! What exactly did she say? God, I can't believe …" He was pacing with fury.

I closed my eyes upon seeing a couple of the nursing staff conscientiously meandering near the room. It was obvious they were trying to determine what the ruckus was about. I'm sure they were used to shouting and some choice curse words during labor processes, but they also had to know this scene was a little different.

"Hawk …" I cautioned in a loud whisper.

He looked in the direction I was, as a male hospital worker actually approached the door and made verbal contact. "Is everything all right in here? Do we need to get—?"

"No. No," Hawk reiterated and rubbed his hands over his face. "We're fine. She's fine."

"Ma'am?" Even though the man was skinnier and shorter than Hawk, I gave him credit for not taking the obviously stronger man's word and insisting on hearing from me.

"It's okay." I gave a quick closed-mouth smile. "Just bad news. Sorry to disrupt."

The man looked from me to Hawk and back again before signaling with his hand for me to press the call button if I was in any type of distress. He then slowly started to turn and leave. And I sighed.

"Hawk, come here. You're gonna get yourself kicked out, and I need you. Okay?"

With only a slight shake of his head, he approached my bed and climbed back into the position he was in before my Oaklee-telephone-call revelation. The massage wouldn't resume, at least not straight away, but if it had, it should have been *me* giving *him* one. I felt like putting my BP monitor on Hawk to read his numbers, but alarms would have surely gone off, and we didn't need any more attention.

Wrapping his arms around me with loving security, the words he spoke were no longer of anger. "I'm sorry. I know you need to chill. I'm just pissed my shitty choices in the past are affecting you. I'm having her blocked. She won't call us ever again."

"Remember, the doctor said there wasn't one thing that led to this, okay?" I didn't want him blaming himself, just as I knew he didn't want me doing the same, and I still did. If I hadn't felt a need to get out and get my hair done … Nope. I shook my head. I needed to stop thinking about it. Instead, I squeezed Hawk's hands with mine in front of my belly. "Besides, this isn't so bad, huh?"

When he blew out a gust of air that time, it was more of a relaxing one. "No. It's kinda nice."

When Collin decided he wanted to squeeze or shake or something on it, too, I directed Hawk's comforting hands to my lower back once again. Maybe it would be like rubbing a genie in a bottle. I wouldn't even need three wishes. I just needed one—our baby boy to be safe and healthy.

***

I didn't want to wake him. He was sleeping so peacefully, which was a rarity. I also didn't want to press the darn little call button. Goodness knows, after our scene so many hours before, the SWAT team might have rolled in. Plus, there was a hush in the hospital with the late-night time, and … the reason I needed someone was embarrassing. I knew hospital workers saw it all, but I wanted to hold on to my dignity while I still had it. I could probably just take care of it myself. I wasn't an invalid, after all.

I'm sure I wouldn't have even known if Collin hadn't woken me up. The baby was usually pretty good at night and didn't kick or move around when I was sleeping. I was hoping it was a positive foreshadowing of how he would be as an infant—a sleeping-through-the-night kind of kid. Regardless, he wasn't that night, giving me another of his wallops or maybe more like the squeeze I had felt at dinner.

I only made it out of the bed and had put the pillows on the chair when Hawk opened his eyes. In order to prevent him from waking, I had purposefully positioned myself on the side of my bed that was farthest away from his cot. But, of course, he still seemed to know I was up.

"Sweetie, what's going on? What time is it?" He batted his eyes. "Why are you—?"

"I, uh, I could use your help."

With that, he was definitely up—awake and physically standing. "What's wrong?" He glanced toward the monitors, which he, too, had become fairly educated in.

They weren't the problem, though. Again … status quo. Not good, but not worse.

"I … I …" It was humiliating. "I peed the bed. It's all the damn water they insist I drink. I was hoping to change the sheets, and *I* am going to need to change, too."

"Oh. All right. Come on. I'll do it." Hawk started looking through the closet and drawers for some kind of bedding. "We can put this on until housekeeping can change things out in the morning." I turned from where I was getting out a new pair of ever-so-sexy big-ass panties to see him lifting something that looked like padding rather than a blanket or sheets.

"Okay. I'm gonna go in the bathroom and change." But as I took a step in that direction, I felt something trickling down my leg. "Geez, I … God, I think I'm peeing again. I didn't even feel like I needed to go."

At that moment, a nighttime nurse entered our room. "Heard some movement in here. Everything okay?"

I looked at the young woman with medium-length brunette hair. She wasn't one I had met before, and I had been introduced to many in just over twenty-four hours. I knew medical charts detailed everything, but I hated having to keep explaining my situation to every new face coming in the room.

Ahhh … take a breath. I was tired and bitchy. I looked at my husband, who also had a reason to be but was gladly going on with the menial task of fixing my wet bed. God, that had to be the true symbol of love.

With that in mind, I changed my mental outlook and relayed the details to the nurse. "The baby woke me with some kind of … crunch." I put my hand on my back, still feeling the effects of the jarring wake-up. "And when he did, I noticed my panties and the bed were a little wet. Actually, I think I just peed myself again."

"You're sure that's what it is?"

"Yeah." I couldn't help but wrinkle my nose at the nurse's question. Goodness, you would think I would know what a light trickle of liquid rolling down my leg was.

"Sir, don't put that on there," she directed Hawk seconds before he placed the padding on the bed. Then turning to me, "Maya … It's Maya, right?" She continued on my nod, "You know those Kegel exercises?" She seemed to be examining the bed. "Go ahead and do a few of those right now, standing right where you're at."

It was late, I was woken up in the middle of sleep to pain, and I had peed myself. I didn't want to be doing strengthening maneuvers for my pelvic floor right then. I felt myself getting grumpy again. I wanted to be home. Why did I need to be in the hospital for any of this? I could be in my own bathroom. But I wasn't … and the nurse was staring at me with anticipation. So, I did the dang exercise.

"Did it stop?" She looked down to my legs.

"No. There's still a trickling. I really should use the bathroom." That time I squeezed and started to walk away.

"Maya, I'm pretty sure your water broke. That's what it is. Not urine."

On the nurse's proclamation, I immediately halted my stance and swung my eyes across the room to Hawk. I felt them widen in shock and horror. I didn't want that to happen. Yes, I was at one centimeter, but that hadn't meant much. Water breaking, though? Oh God, no.

"I'll get the sheets. We'll give you a quick exam to know for sure, but with the consistency, color, no odor, and contractions—"

"The what?" Hawk bit right on her last word. "Maya, you're having contractions?"

"No," I immediately replied to my husband but looked to the nurse for her response.

"Pain in the lower back … like a squeeze into the stomach area? Not the same as a kick or swimming around in there."

"I … Yeah, I guess. Could they just be Braxton Hicks?" Shit, I was in some form of denial.

"Not if your water broke. When did you first feel the contraction?" She was a multi-tasker, stripping the bed while asking more questions and recording them on my chart.

I know I answered all of them, and I know I changed my

clothes and listened to instructions, but everything was in some kind of mental blur during that time. Like seemingly everything else with the pregnancy—really from the surprising conception on—things weren't going to plan. I needed to wrap my brain around what the latest development meant. Mentally I made a list—a) the baby was coming. The nurse said probably within the next twelve hours but could be longer, b) we were strangely still in a waiting pattern. It was all about the timing and length of the contractions. Dr. Edgewood wasn't even coming in yet, and c) my blood pressure most certainly wasn't good.

It was right around the stroke of midnight when Hawk and I were once again alone in the room. And in the first seconds that we were, my flood gates opened. Not more of the amniotic variety, but tears. I started downright bawling.

"Awww, sweetie, hey … hey …" He came closer and wiped at my face before peppering kisses on my lips, but I continued to cry through it all. "Mai … Maya … stop, sweetie, please."

And when I still didn't, I felt his strong arms go between the bed and my bottom and back. When he scooped me up, I wanted to resist, but I didn't. For one thing, I didn't have it in me to emotionally argue. For another, despite the weight and awkwardness of my body, I trusted his strength. And more than that, I had complete faith in where his heart was.

With my arms looped around his neck, he walked us to the oversized chair and carefully sat both of us on it. Snuggled onto his chest, I could feel his circular caresses on my back. The crying was subsiding, even if the thoughts in my mind were not.

"I was wondering how you were keeping calm throughout all of this."

I looked at him, knowing my eyes had to be as puffy as seemingly every other part of my pregnant body. Just like he knew he could be vulnerable with me, I knew I could break apart on him. But I had waited to do it without any witnesses. "Dr. Edgewood kept telling us he was coming, but I somehow …"

"You thought you could still control the situation." He was echoing the doctor's earlier words.

But it wasn't exactly the truth. "I thought it was going to work out. I was trying my darndest not to think otherwise."

"Who's saying it isn't?"

"It's too earl—"

"Maya, I can't. I can't." His hands constricted a little on his grip, and his words were very abrupt. "I can't go through this again with you. It is what it is. You need to accept it." As if to punctuate Hawk's words, a definite contraction raced through my body at that exact moment. Since I was sitting on his lap, even though he didn't feel the actual pain, he definitely noticed it, especially with how hard I clenched on to his hand. "Should we be timing?"

I looked at the clock. It was a minute past midnight. I didn't count, but the contraction was over before the clock flipped to 12:02.

"I don't think we really need to yet."

Funny how him seeing me in pain automatically curbed his temper, and his words were once again soft-spoken. "Do you suppose you can get some sleep?"

"I don't know. I'm sure it would be best. It feels like it's going to be a long day."

"Our little boy's birthday."

"Hmmm … yeah, I guess so." A month and a couple days early, but I didn't say that part out loud. I knew Hawk couldn't take any more of my doomsday mentality.

He helped me get back into bed and then pulled the cot closer. We laid there in silence, simply looking at each other. I knew he wanted me to rest and vice versa, but it wasn't going to be easy … both because of my emotional state and the contractions, which were sure to come. I eventually at least closed my eyes. The illusion of sleep would have to do.

CHAPTER SIXTEEN

Every child has a birth story. Most people have probably heard theirs at some point in their lives—whether they asked or if their mother brings it up every time the child misbehaves … *It took me twenty-four painful hours to bring you into this world, the least you could do is pick up your socks.* I knew mine. It involved my mom laboring on her own, while my dad raced nearly four hours from Pittsburgh directly after a game to get to the hospital. He had arrived just in time. My mom was ready to push, and in four tries, I was born. It was as if I was waiting for him to get there. It wasn't my mother who told me the tale, though. It had been my grandma, who ended up raising me when my mom died at way too young of an age.

I didn't want Collin's story to be drama-filled. The months leading up to it had been enough. At least I knew his dad would be there. Steady as a rock, Hawk would not leave my side throughout that night and into the morning.

I'm not sure exactly what time Dr. Edgewood arrived, but I remember looking at the clock at 5:05 a.m. and thinking things were getting serious. The contractions were definitely closer and longer. And as the centimeters crept upward, they moved me to the delivery room.

Once there, the "fun" continued. Sitting didn't feel good but standing didn't either. I was hungry but feeling sick. I even threw up because of it. One time I made it to the bathroom, but the second round I did not. When I asked them to lower the lights since my head was starting to hurt, there was talk about keeping me hydrated and controlling my high blood pressure. And, sure enough, I watched as Hawk looked to the monitors. I didn't look myself, though. I didn't want to know at that point. All the sensations inside my body were telling me enough of the story as it was.

Hawk remarkably remained calm and collected as he turned once again toward me. He managed to rub my back while looking me straight in the eyes. "You're doing a great job, Maya. I love you. It's all good."

"Remember when you said the birth plan was going to involve me yelling at you?" I countered.

"Yeah …" His hesitant reply told me he was leery of my retort.

"Quit lying to me, or I am going to. I'm *not* doing good."

"Mai, you are," he argued. "I have never seen someone in such pain. I could not do this. You got it. You do."

Hawk was the strongest man I had ever known. And I'd known quite a few. So him saying that gave me the motivation to keep going—that I could be strong, too.

I was switching from the birthing ball, to the chair, and onto my side on the bed when things started happening even quicker. In the matter of ten minutes, I went from eight to ten centimeters. Dr. Edgewood's comment that it was particularly quick didn't exactly reassure me.

Just like it didn't excite me shortly after when she said it was time to push. I didn't deny her or Collin, though. I had to be ready because I knew, no matter what, my son was. I was looking forward to meeting our little guy, but that didn't mean the thought of his early arrival wasn't still daunting and dominating my brain.

My husband grasped my hand as I strained my body and the doctor counted. Between exertions, I took note that the number of people in the room had seemed to multiply since the labor process started. Besides Hawk and Dr. Edgewood, there was a labor nurse, tech, nursery nurse, and specialists who I believed were there specifically because of the unique circumstances of my pregnancy. I didn't feel claustrophobic, though. My sole concentration was on Collin.

Because everything else with his journey had happened at a quicker-than-usual pace, I was assuming the actual birth would, too. But I was wrong. Our son was not going to be a simple couple of pushes … definitely more than four.

It was after I had been pushing for thirty minutes when Dr. Edgewood started voicing some concern about my numbers and what we should do. I couldn't help but feel instant discouragement. How could we have come so far and have to switch the plan? But Dr. Edgewood said we would give it one more try. So, I squeezed with determination and immediately felt a strong pressure alongside a searing burn. And that was when she said she saw the head.

"As we thought, the boy has hair. He's not a baldie."

I appreciated the upbeat positivity she continued to have during the entire process. It really did help. It made me think about those types of lighthearted things, too. Collin had hair. I wondered if he would inherit his dad's dark-auburn shade that I liked so much or my golden brown.

I pressed Hawk's hand. It was a weaker grasp than the ones I did during an actual push, but it still got his attention. "Do you want to see? Have you changed your mind?" I still didn't want a mirror, but Hawk could go to my waist to see his baby boy come into the world.

He looked back and forth. "Uh, yeah, yeah. You good with that?"

"Uh-huh." I managed a smile.

As Hawk repositioned himself, I felt an urge to push. Ironically, though, Dr. Edgewood told me to take a breather. She explained that I needed to slow down and allow all my body parts to adapt. I'd heard about the fear of tearing … and pooping. So, I tried my best to follow her directive. Instead of pushing, I pursed out a breath and even fake coughed a couple times. It gave me a legit reason to make a let-loose sound because I was still far from comfortable.

But we were almost there. We were almost home. I rested my hand on my belly and whispered, "Collin, I can't wait to meet you." And then Dr. Edgewood gave me the green light, and I pushed. "Ahhh!"

"His head is out." Dr. Edgewood's eyes and cheeks lifted with obvious joy. "Probably one more push and your son should basically slide out. You'll have your boy."

Oh, the wash of feelings tingling all over my body right then were indescribable. It was a phenomenal combination of pain, nerve endings, and nausea seemingly everywhere. It wasn't just where Collin was making his grand entrance but in my heart, too. It was like every fairytale posting that every new parent made. Gaining momentum and beating a mile a minute, my heart felt like it was going to explode with pride, joy, and love. I looked at the clock, which read 7:02 a.m., smiled at Hawk, and I gave one more push.

***

They said I saw Collin … that he was actually on my chest as they wiped him down, covered him, and took his temp. But I didn't remember. How could that be? How could a mother not recall the first time she laid eyes on the beautiful creature she had been protecting and holding close to her heart for so many months? That was the most wonderful and miraculous part of a child's birth story.

The reason was actually simple and medical. I was told it happened immediately following the quick delivery of the placenta after birth—something else I did not have a recollection of. What happened to me only lasted about three minutes … under five. But it felt much longer because of the memory loss directly before and a little after—the times I should have remembered seeing my son … and them taking him away.

When I had regained consciousness and was aware, I was still in the delivery room, feeling like I was waking up from the oddest dream. Never mind the confusion over what I was being told. My head hurt, and I was so damn tired. Plus, God, I had just given birth. It felt like I had done two hundred crunches in the fastest world-record time.

"I know you want to see him, Mai," Hawk had one hand on one of mine and the other stroking my hair. "We gotta make sure you're okay, though. It was a full-blown seizure, sweetie. God, it …" I think he was breathing heavier than I had when I was in the transition phase of labor, which was something I definitely remembered.

"We're giving you meds and monitoring to prevent another one or worse from happening." Dr. Edgewood was standing with one of the specialists at the other side of my bed.

"But you said Collin is where?" I looked around the room as if he would materialize.

"They took him to NICU."

I closed my eyes. I knew that. Hawk was repeating what he had told me the first time … only minutes before when I realized I was waking up from something that turned out to be a damn seizure. Everything was still foggy. I needed it all repeated. Or maybe I simply didn't want it to be the truth.

"They're taking care of him." Hawk rubbed my hand.

"What's wrong? Why didn't you go with Collin?"

"The doctors needed to evaluate and help him. I couldn't do that." He paused for a second as if recalling the nightmare. "And because then you … It all happened at once."

"What is it? Is he okay? He's okay, isn't he? You would tell me if he … if he …" Oh God. I swung my head back and forth to the three people at my bedside.

"Maya, please, please calm down. I'm scared you're gonna—" My husband practically slammed his hand to his face.

Dr. Edgewood took over. "Maya, first of all, I agree with your husband. We can't have your BP rising."

"Then—"

She cut me off. "Second, he's a preemie, and his lungs aren't able to breathe correctly without some extra help. We had great staff in the room who were able to start him with that immediately. Now he's in the NICU getting all the—"

"Oh God, he can't breathe." It was something I was all too familiar with. I couldn't bear that my newborn was experiencing that particular terror of all things.

"He is. He's breathing. He just needs some help," Dr. Edgewood reassured.

As I imagined him with one of those damn masks suctioned onto his mouth like I had in the ambulance, I took huge gulps of air myself. Thinking of my son struggling was worse than labor. I wanted a redo. I wanted to reverse those past few days. I could do better.

"We knew it was a strong possibility, and we had everything and everyone set. The neonatologist was here with us when he was born and other pediatricians are there now, too. You know that."

"We do," Hawk agreed with the doctor.

Okay. Fine. Or, as fine as I was going to get.

Next question … "What about his heart?" I knew that was a concern with premature babies, too.

"My priority right now is you. Let us take care of you, and we'll let you know as soon as we can about Collin. Understand, it may seem like you have been out for a long time, but it was only a few minutes or so. They're assessing him and coming up with an individualized plan. Your son looked good, though, all right? We heard some cries. That's something we always want to hear."

It was also something they were going to *see* because tears were coming from my own eyes. Mostly everything Dr. Edgewood was saying was positive, or at least what was expected. But it was another case where I had thought,

Okay, so I go into labor early, but everything will be all right. What the heck in my life had led me to think that?

"Can I …?" Hawk was looking at the doctors but motioning toward me.

When Dr. Edgewood nodded, he crawled onto the bed and curled me onto his torso. God, did that feel good … and strange. Although my midriff was certainly still expanded, it was the first time in a while that I didn't have the feeling of having a baby there between my husband and me. And I cried some more.

"Maya, if Collin has a heart even half as strong as his momma, we have nothing to worry about." He kissed me on my cheek.

***

The second my exam was complete and the doctors went over what to expect as far as my recovery from labor and the seizure—which they told me were both a six-week process—I asked about Collin. "Can we see him?"

"One of his doctors or nurses will either come here or to your postpartum room to talk with you," Dr. Edgewood replied, as the other doctor had left.

I let out an exasperated sigh. "You have to be able to tell me some other info, though, right?"

"Like?" Dr. Edgewood was busy entering something on her tablet.

I started my query with fun stuff. I needed that. "I remember you said he had hair."

"Yes, dark, but it could change." Her index finger swiped across the screen a couple times.

"Eyes?"

Upon my question, she looked up and replied in a deadpan tone, "Two."

"Dr. Edgewood …" Her name came out of my mouth with exasperation, and Hawk did a two-bounce chuckle. I think the doc and he were bonding.

"He didn't have his eyes open. I guess the color will be a surprise," she stated more factually.

"All right. How much does he weigh?" I was ticking off the typical birth announcement questions, but I knew that particular one was more serious, considering his premature status.

"Five pounds two ounces." There was a soft smile on her face before she added, "Not that I am commending your decision, but you holding on for even a day and a half, provided Collin with some hearty ounces. Actually, more than expected."

With those words, I smiled. I knew every ounce mattered, and I would risk a seizure again if it meant helping my son gain the important weight. "What about his height or length or whatever?"

She conferred with her data before making a definite proclamation. "Seventeen point eight inches. That's pretty standard for his development."

I was trying to estimate with my hands how long that was, but measurement was not my math strength. Well, in all honesty, not much in the math family was. In contrast, I think Hawk had a tape measurer as a brain. When we were measuring things for the new house, he would do motions with his hands and spit out a number. I would insist we get the actual tape tool for accuracy, but nine times out of ten, he was spot on. The tenth time? It wasn't off by much at all.

Before I could even ask, Hawk parenthesized his hands to show me the approximate length of our son. "He's gonna grow."

I nodded and continued, "What else? What should I be asking? You said his lungs are developing. They're checking his heart? What else?"

As if on cue, the neonatologist who had been with us during the birth entered the room. "Maya, it's good to see you're doing better."

"She is, but she's extremely concerned about her son," Dr. Edgewood said with caution and a glance at the damn monitors.

Hawk stood and shook our son's doctor's hand. He was usually good about proper manners, but I wondered if he thought being polite would prompt better care for our sweet little boy. Even though we knew Collin was getting the best support possible, it didn't hurt. Heck, I would shake *Oaklee's* hand—even give her a hug—if it meant helping my son.

"Well, let's fill you in, then." Dr. Alish scooted a chair over to one side of my bed as Hawk reclaimed his seat on the other.

"How is he?" My eyelids opened wider and roamed around the specialist's face, anticipating the worst and praying for the best.

Dr. Alish started directly with the facts. "Let's begin with his heart." With mine beating to an extreme with nerves, she continued, "A common problem for preterm babies is a persistent opening between the—"

"A hole in his heart." The thumping in my chest intensified on those words. "God, he has—"

"Maya," Dr. Edgewood interrupted, looking again from the monitors to me. "You have to listen to what Dr. Alish is telling you. You need to be as relaxed as possible or else you aren't going to hear it correctly and you're going to risk another episode."

"Okay." I looked at Hawk, who, clasping my hand, was nodding slowly and pursing his lips to get me to mimic his breaths.

"What I wanted to tell you is, Collin's heart seems steady," the neonatologist proclaimed, and I breathed a little easier. "The only slight concern on those lines is his blood pressure."

Geez, did I pass all my bad traits onto this kid? First it was his breathing and then, *wham,* the BP. I was hoping more along the lines of not caring for most fruits or my dislike of all things exercise.

"It's low," she continued.

"Low?" Well, that wasn't exactly *my* problem. "Maybe I

could share some of mine." I tried to make a joke.

Hawk wasn't impressed. "So, what does *that* mean?"

"We think it'll only involve some IV fluids." Because the neonatologist said it with confidence, I didn't dare ask what the other possibilities might be. "He's in an incubator." Topped with blonde curls, she nodded slowly but forged on, as if anticipating me interrupting again. "He needs heat and oxygen. Our biggest concern is keeping his breathing steady. When you see Collin, you'll notice he has sensors taped to him to monitor all those things—his blood pressure, breathing, heart rate, and temperature."

Damn, another thing Collin and I had in common were monitors. "He'll be okay, though, right?"

Hawk piggy-backed my question with a similar one. "How long until he's clear?"

"Collin determines the timeline."

With my one-breath chuckle and eye roll, Dr. Edgewood informed her coworker, "They've heard that before."

Dr. Alish's eyebrows arched, knowing she was missing some kind of insider trading. "Well, it's true. Each baby is different. He is definitely going to have an extended stay here in our oh-so-spa-like facilities." I appreciated that she was trying her best to soften the blow of the unbearable news, but the image of my baby being hooked up to so much was making me sick.

"Are we talking a couple days?" Hawk seemed to pause as he let go of my hand and twisted his together. "Or like a few months?"

I swung my gaze in his direction. I could see the weary in his face. I knew he was holding it together for me, but he was concerned, too. I'm sure neither of us wanted our little boy to be in so much distress that his recovery would involve months. God, I couldn't handle that. And as I thought of those months ahead, I realized what it meant—the tour.

Before I could question my husband if that was what was on his mind, the neonatologist gave a frustratingly vague response. "I can't really answer that. I know it's not what you want to hear, but if I say something specific, you are going to hold me to it or look to that day on the calendar as if it was a magic cure-all. You can't do that. He needs to get past some checkpoints first in order to graduate to leaving." When I sucked in my lips and briefly closed my eyes, she retracted a tiny bit. "Preliminarily, what I will say is probably somewhere between the two extreme timeframes you gave." She acknowledged Hawk with a nod. "We're looking at weeks."

While that was still heartbreaking to hear, it did help me mentally organize the scenario. I was that kind of person. And, most certainly, so was Hawk. Whenever Collin did make his way home to us, it was going to be quite a shock to both of our structured systems, that was for sure.

As if to punctuate my internal thoughts, I think Dr. Edgewood enjoyed restating, "Collin is in charge."

"Exactly," Dr. Alish agreed. "One of the goals for him is to gain some weight, and that's where mom has some definite say."

Mom. I almost teared up hearing that word. Mom … that was me. I was the mom. God, it was really me, after so long wanting but not believing I could be. Yet, it still didn't seem real, since I had only heard a description of the baby and hadn't actually seen him, or at least that I could remember.

"You have a really important role. I understand you planned on breastfeeding." On my nod, Dr. Alish did one back. "Great. We're going to need you to nurse as much as possible. He might not be able to take to you directly or feed from a bottle because his lungs aren't mature enough yet to coordinate sucking, breathing, and swallowing. But a lactation consultant will help figure out how to get him your milk. It will not only help him grow but also fight off infections. We don't want to add that into the mix."

"No. Yes. I mean, yes. I will help. Tell me when." With anticipation, I shifted and tried to prop myself up. I wanted to help. I had to do anything I could. "Can I start now?"

"Once you're settled in your next room." The specialist got up from her chair.

Hawk did also. "Is that it? That's what we're looking at?"

I wanted to scream. *Is that it?* Is that it? Geez, our baby boy was in a tube connected to IVs and monitors. What else did he want to be wrong?

But the neonatologist seemed to go with the flow. "That's all."

Maybe I should have taken that as reassuring. I did not. If I went with the handshaking theory/superstition, I would shake hers a thousand times because I wanted to make sure my baby was being taken care of.

"Dr. Edgewood will get you to your room and whatever else. I want to get back to Collin and the other little ones there. But as soon as your doc says so, we'll get you down to see him. I'm sure that'll help everyone." On that, Dr. Alish left the room.

I felt like I wanted to slip back into the post-seizure state of not knowing … that momentary delirium. Because, that would mean nothing bad had pierced the bubble. I would not know everything I was just told. On what should have been the most amazing day of my life, I was overcome with fear, worry, and helplessness.

CHAPTER SEVENTEEN

I thought I was prepared. I had heard all the details from the doctors. I had watched a short video online while eating a snack in my postpartum room. I *should* have been prepared. I knew for sure I was ready, and I was definitely anxious. I had to see him. He was my baby … my heart … my soul … my very being. No matter where he was or what was attached to him, I was prepared.

But I wasn't. Oh God. I wasn't.

When Hawk and I first entered the NICU, I was still okay. It felt good that Collin was nearby. I was pleased to be bringing the neonatal team the milk I had just pumped using the hospital electronic pump and the assistance of the lactation consultant. I was helping. He needed me.

But when I really took in the scene, I started to falter. First, besides the sounds of the different machines running, there was an odd stillness that seemed to signify such a solemn state. Second, while the talk and faces of the hospital personnel were friendly and cheerful, the presumed parents who were there didn't give off the same vibe. They looked weary and worn. I wondered if I had the same haunted look.

When the nurse manager led us to Collin—all the while reminding us of what to expect—my feet did a kind of shuffle at the sight of my son encapsulated in a clear bassinette. Reality round eighty-five that our little boy was sick. Squeezing my hand a little firmer, even Hawk reacted by letting out the tiniest of gasps.

With the exception of a diaper, Collin didn't have anything on. Well, unless you counted all the medical equipment. As we had been told, he had a number of sensors connected to different parts of his body. There was a significant strap under his chin and a white wrap around his head. His one hand had some gauze. The other had an identification band around his wrist … similar to the ones Hawk and I wore to match with our child. His arms and legs looked small and fragile compared to his head and stomach. That was where one of the sensors—shaped like a gold heart—rested. I noticed how his little torso seemed to be working in overtime and not so rhythmically as it accepted air from the damn large tube covering part of his face. God, that was the absolute worst.

I took in a significant breath as if to will my own air to him. And then I closed and opened my eyes before nodding. "Okay." I needed to start the process of accepting.

"Okay," my husband echoed in a much softer tone than I was used to from him.

We stood there in silence a couple more seconds simply staring at Collin. That time, though, I really saw him. *Him*—my little boy, not the sensors and certainly not the breathing apparatus.

"He's so tiny."

Hawk's voice was also. "He is." Even though Hawk had seen him in the delivery room, I knew it wasn't for very long, and it had been under dire circumstances. It was like we both had blacked out our first real meeting of our son.

"And beautiful." I smiled.

"That, too." Hawk's lips rested on the top of my head for an extended moment.

"You can't hold him yet, but you can touch him." There was a nurse at our side instead of the manager. I had seen her approach, but I'm sure she waited to speak out of respect to our initial visit.

"I … yeah." I turned more definitively in her direction.

Hawk did, too. "We won't hurt him?"

"Gentle, of course. But the baby feeling mom and dad's touch is one of the best medicines." She led us over to the sink to disinfect our hands, despite Hawk and I having washed them only moments before when signing into the area.

We decided to put our hands in the incubator simultaneously. There wasn't really a reason, but when we did, I realized how significant it was. Collin could feel our love—the three of us—at one time together. I placed my fingertips on his stomach, imagining that I was giving him a hug and encouraging him to breathe like his father sometimes did for me. Hawk chose to put only one hand in, of which he softly caressed the top of Collin's head. The baby's eyes had been closed since we arrived and that didn't change, but I swear it looked like they were moving beneath the lids, as if he was having a good dream.

My son's determination to fight and live gave me strength in that moment. I managed a serene, soft smile at both him and his dad. And, somehow, I made it through.

***

I hadn't wanted to leave, but I pretty much had to. It had been the compromise between my medical team and me … and my concerned husband. They would let me go directly to Collin after my first pumping experience if I promised to make the visit short and come back to get much needed rest and recuperation. The team was apprehensive about my own numbers and monitors after the double whammy of giving birth and having a seizure. I had countered, though, that seeing Collin would only help. And it had, even if I had a minor meltdown when Hawk and I first got back to my room.

Sadly, the thing that set me off was self-pity. It was feeling the emptiness of my hands and midriff as we left Collin behind. It was hearing other healthy babies in the private rooms we passed on our way back. It was seeing the new mom in the room next to mine holding her baby as her husband brought their two older girls into the room. It was similar, I suppose, to how I had felt during the beginning stages of grief. It wasn't that I begrudged their happiness and good fortune. I simply, and admittedly, was jealous.

Without a word, Hawk brought me into his snug embrace. He did it for me, but I think we both needed it—to feel the comfort of each other and to do so in a room that was absolutely silent. We stayed like that for a good couple of minutes or so, as my tears subsided and I tried to focus on the blessings we did have.

When I felt secure enough, I pulled a little away from the rock I called my husband and wiped at my tears. "Collin's a fighter," I started with. "And, God, we're lucky he's not as bad off as some of those other little ones down there. Some …" I shook my head to stop the images and words so I would not get choked up again.

Hawk and I certainly had not gawked, but the NICU cribs were, for the most part, in a line and without an immense amount of space in between. So, we couldn't have helped but take note of a few of the other sweet babies struggling as they began life. There were blue lights, eye covers, surgical schedules, a baby who looked to be almost half the size of Collin, and bypass machines. We learned that some of the babies were considered critical. Collin was one step better at intensive, but there were still two other levels he needed to reach before the possibility of him being released.

"Shit, Mai, I'm not gonna lie. That was a little tough in there." His honest words matched the direct look he gave me with his knowing hazel eyes.

I put my hands up to his scruffier-than-usual beard. "It's been quite a day."

"Come on, let's get you back in bed." On my grunt of disapproval, he said my name with warning. "Maya …"

"You know, Hawk, you got the dad tone down already. I think you were made to be a parent."

"In bed," he reiterated in the same direct tone, but I could see his eyes lit up a bit in reaction to my humor. "Put the BP monitor on." He nodded to the lovely device I had become literally attached to, as he helped me onto the bed. He then read it immediately. "That's not good."

"It's better." It was both.

"You have got to be exhausted."

"I am." I admitted to the drowsiness my body reclaimed after the high of seeing Collin. "But the pain meds might be wearing off already." My head was fine, but my insides were starting to sing.

"It's not time yet."

"I know."

"Get some rest. I'll sit here and read you a bedtime story." He reclined back in the chair next to me.

"A what?" I chuckled, which I instantly regretted due to the soreness of my mid-section.

"The NICU welcome packet." He held up the document, which included rules and regulations, team job descriptions, some medical terms, and much more. Before going to the unit, we had gone through some of it, with the part I liked best being the twenty-four-hour parental visitation.

"Does it have a happily ever after?"

I waited in anticipation of his response. It seemed to hang there for a moment. I had said the question in a lighthearted manner, but I think we both realized immediately that it meant so much more. Not all preemies had a happily ever after. Not all babies had a chance to even leave the hospital. I closed my eyes, regretting the question and those thoughts that accompanied it. The brush of Hawk's hand against my cheek and his lips pressed against mine made me want to believe … even if he didn't actually give an answer.

***

His voice was low as he spoke. I didn't bother to open my eyes. I just continued to lay there and listen. I had managed to fall asleep, and, admittedly, it did feel good to stay in that rested state for a moment or two longer.

"Yeah, that's what I said. She had the baby." There was the slightest of pauses before I heard Hawk again. "It is." I couldn't hear another person, only my husband. "About a month." His voice seemed to drop even more with both sound level and enthusiasm. "He's in NICU, but we're hoping not for long." I looked then to see Hawk standing at the doorway of my room on his phone. "She had a seizure." He clawed his free hand through his hair as he listened to the other person. He wasn't turned toward me, but I didn't have to see his face to visualize its frustrated features that were, no doubt, accompanying his next words. "Yeah, I know. The doctor warned her it could happen. You know, it's probably best the baby came early."

I slammed my eyes shut on his proclamation. How could he think that? Our baby was connected to machines. We weren't able to hold him. He wouldn't directly take my milk. He. Couldn't. Breathe.

"It would have been—"

"Hawk?" I said his name so he would stop the obnoxious words I didn't want to hear.

"Hey …" He swirled around in my direction but still talked into his cell. "Hold on, Maya's waking up from her nap."

"Who's on the phone?"

"Momma."

Well, that made sense. She was one of the few people I could imagine my husband feeling comfortable enough to discuss such personal details with. Della was a good listener but would also tell it to you straight.

"Yeah, I'll let her know." He spoke again to his mom as he walked back to my bedside. "No. Not now. Maybe after Mai gets home." When he gently kissed me on my forehead, I let go of some of the anger of his previous comment. For being such a strong man, he had the gentlest of souls if he let you in. He listened to his mom some more, while looking at my monitor and then sitting in the chair. "Yeah. … . Yeah, tell—" He stopped himself. "You know what? How about only immediate family, okay? And tell them not to say anything yet. We'll let everyone know when we find out anything new."

I wondered why his answer seemed to change about them not telling others. Was he thinking of Oaklee's meddling? Or was it something else?

With a "Yep," Hawk hung up the phone and gave his full attention to me. "How are you feeling?"

"Can't really tell, because right now I'm as groggy as hell." I looked at the clock. From when I'd last remembered seeing it, I had slept for close to an hour and a half. The events of those last twelve hours or so must have really caught up to me. "What about you? Did you sleep?"

"A little." I suspected that was a lie, and he knew it. "Seriously. I drifted off. But they came in with your food." He motioned to the tray on the nightstand. "And the texts were multiplying on my phone. Momma had left a few general messages the past couple of days. And since I didn't respond in any way, she was starting to get worried."

I completely understood that feeling. I thought I already had when Collin was snug in my body. But the fact that he was in the greater world and helpless, made my mom instincts multiply by a thousand. Hearing that Della still had those fears and thoughts for her son made me realize those feelings never dissipated, even when your little boy was thirty-eight years old.

"I decided to call her so she didn't drive here herself or somehow track down one of our neighbors or, you know, whatever. She sends you her love." He started to lift the food container. "Why don't you eat something?"

But I stopped him. "Did you hear anything more about Collin?"

"No."

"Hmmm."

"Eat."

But I still had another question. "Why did you tell your mom to kinda keep things hush?"

"I don't know, Mai." He rubbed his hand along the top of his head again.

"Hawk …"

The reason behind his hesitation on telling others was dawning on me. It wasn't about his witch of an ex-wife. It wasn't even due to his nature to keep things private and reserved. It was that he wasn't sure. He wasn't sure about Collin.

"He's going to be okay." I meant to say it in a lot stronger, more confident voice, but it came out sort of strangled or gargled. I would love to have blamed it on my not-quite-yet-awake status, but I knew it wasn't that. I was worried that it wasn't the truth, but I so desperately wanted to believe in the fairy tale.

"I need you to be all right, too. Please eat. You have to keep your nourishment up and stress down."

I was quick to realize that—just like our happily-ever-after conversation—Hawk didn't agree with me directly, but, instead, proved, once again, his ongoing desire to keep me safe. His words were about me needing to protect myself physically. But I wondered if by holding back a full-out positive reply, he thought he was guarding me from potential future emotional heartache, too.

CHAPTER EIGHTEEN

Reality and a new kind of routine quickly set in that day and the next. It seemed to be a chain link of highs versus lows. There were failures and there were achievements—mostly involving my breast pumping. There was exhaustion and there were boosts of energy. There were moments of grumpiness and there were moments of kisses.

Hawk and I became quite schooled in the neonatal ward. We took notes and met so many people who played an integral part in the lives of Collin and the other babies there. That included other neonatologists, a physical therapist, a nutritionist, and a variety of nurses.

Learning so much about taking care of a preemie gave us little time for communication outside of the hospital. Hawk, however, sent a group text to his brothers and mother to let them know we appreciated their well wishes and we were sorry we couldn't get back to them, but we were overwhelmed. I helped word that because if I'd left it to him, he would have thrown the phone out the window with their constant questions.

Another person he didn't ignore—or maybe couldn't—was Finn. Not only did our boss and his wife know we were in the hospital, but they also knew the seriousness of the initial reason for the stay. Because Collin had arrived early, Hawk and I had to back out of job responsibilities. So, a quick exchange of texts updating the Murphys on our status had done the trick. Or, at least we thought.

It was a complete shock when—over twenty-four hours after I gave birth—Finn and Lara appeared at the door of my hospital room. Donning pajamas and diaper panties, I had just finished pumping and was looking forward to washing up and visiting Collin again. Hawk had miraculously fallen asleep on the chair beside me. I think it was a combo of the rhythmic sound the pump machine made, the fact that he was already over looking at my breasts and not being the recipient of touching them, and that my blood pressure seemed to be better than it had been in a while that aided in his rest.

"Oh, hey … I didn't know you—" On my words, Hawk's eyes sprung open, and he fumbled a little to sit up properly.

"Sleeping on the job, I see." Finn continued into the room, followed by his wife.

"F-U," Hawk jagged right back while standing up. "What are you doing here, man? I told you we don't need anything."

Ignoring the men, Lara approached my bed. "How you doing?" On my partial smile and nod, she set a small picnic basket on the nightstand. "We're still going to shower you with gifts. But for now, here's a bunch of nonperishable snacks for both of you. Coffee and cocoa packs, granola bars … that type of thing."

"You raid the tour bus?" Hawk jested about what were, indeed, staples while on tour.

After *tsking* my husband, I said thank you to Lara, who handed me some papers. "Vanessa and Carter are watching the kids, but they have some pictures for Collin."

"Awww, that's so sweet." Feeling a tear leave my eye as I looked through the children's colorings of babies and hearts, I quickly passed the papers off to Hawk.

"Tell Carter he needs to brush up on drawing in the lines," my husband teased and set them down.

"Tell the *kids,*" I corrected, "we said *thanks.* You guys really didn't have to come." I felt a weird mix of not wanting to feel like I had to entertain versus being touched that they were there for us.

"She insisted that it's what she wanted to do on her special day."

My eyes grew big on Finn's proclamation. It was April fourth. That meant it was Lara's birthday.

"Oh, shoot, Lara, I completely forgot. I knew it—"

"Do you think you have other things on your mind?" she blew me off. "If he waited one more day, Collin could have been my birthday twin."

"I wanted him to be mine," I noted with a twinge of sadness that my babe's actual due date had been my May fifth birthday.

"How is he?" Lara continued.

"He's … yeah … little." I looked at Hawk, who tried a smile. "He's hanging in there. Do you want to see a pic?" After a little debate, I had taken Collin's first photo and video that morning. I hadn't wanted it to be one with tubes and cords, but we decided it would be a good memory in the future to show how far he came. "Or we're about ready to see him again. He's allowed a visitor if one of us is with them," I noted the rule from the infamous welcome pamphlet. "It's, uh, up to you. But it's pretty … it's pretty …" I didn't want to say *sad* or *depressing* because it shouldn't be—those babies in that loved room were the lucky ones who actually made it. I didn't know exactly what adjective to use, though.

I recognized the strength of a mom who had been through a lot, because she didn't hesitate. "I'd love to see him. I'll only stay for a few minutes, though. I know you both want to be there."

Finn turned to Hawk. "I promised the hospital staff I'd sing a lullaby in the common room down the hall if they'd let us come to your room. Care to join me?"

"Pfff! What's a country lullaby? And I was wondering how you got in. Should have known … star-power shit." Hawk rolled his eyes and then turned to me. "Mai? You good? Go with Lara?"

"Yeah." On that, I got out of the bed and pecked Hawk on his lips.

As Lara and I started leaving the room, Hawk razzed Finn, "You are f-ing getting me to work for you right now, aren't you? I'm supposed to have some kind of paternity leave."

"Oh, shut up. Here you go." Finn took a blue-wrapped cigar from his pocket and handed it to the new dad.

Both Lara and I shook our heads as we continued to walk. It was good to have that quick moment of normalcy. I needed it, and I knew Hawk did, too. We just had to keep taking those baby steps—no pun intended—to get to a new and better normal with Collin.

***

Ranking the hard days/moments was difficult to do. They all seemed to be so damn tough. Initially finding out Collin was in the NICU was devastating. Seeing him that first time hooked up to so many devices was heartbreaking. But dealing with the doctor's orders for April fifth was definitely right up there, too.

That was the day they said I was discharged to go home. Most of the time finding out you were healthy enough to not need direct medical assistance and that you could return to your personal, peaceful surroundings would be a cause for celebration. For me, it was pretty much the opposite. How could I leave Collin? I couldn't bear not being in the same building as him … being able to walk down some halls and see him whenever I wanted. He needed me. The hospital staff had continuously promoted the importance of babies bonding with parents. Why would they send me away?

I was channeling Hawk from a few days prior when he had been coming up with excuses to stay at the hospital with me. "Don't I need to be monitored for seizures? I'm in the time frame of potential risk." I started with the one I thought had the greatest probability of working.

"No, we don't keep patients for that. We've talked with both of you"—Dr. Edgewood nodded to Hawk—"about what to do if a seizure should occur. But your numbers are good."

"I'm not sure how that happened, but that's good news." Hawk expelled a calming breath as the three of us strolled down the hall toward the NICU.

"Just take your BP readings like you had been during your last trimester, and no driving."

That provided a perfect segue for argument number two. "But I have to get the breast milk to Collin."

"Maya, come on, you know I'll be coming here, too, and will drive."

Dr. Edgewood plowed right along with both her feet and the facts. "I understand everything is set for you to use the hospital's pump machines and the meditation room here."

I did like that amenity. Plus, an additional side benefit of that hospital service was the nursing mom received a free meal to help support good health. That way when I was there, I needn't worry about packing food or finding something nearby or in the cafeteria. I could concentrate on Collin. Still, wouldn't it be easier if I stayed in the hospital itself?

"There's no way for me to extend, Dr. Edgewood? I mean, it's not like there is a reason for me to be home. We don't have any other kids or pets to take care of."

"Look, I would love to find a way for you to stay, but the hospital is at capacity and you live close by." She cited our approximate twenty-minute commute. "Some families, actually, have to get a hotel. You're lucky."

"Yeah," I sighed, not exactly feeling fortunate.

"I know it's hard, Maya. Every separation is. When we dropped ours off at college for the first time this fall, her dad and I cried the entire way home. It doesn't get any easier." *Great*, I thought sarcastically, as Dr. Edgewood continued, "Hey, listen, we're here, and this is a big day for Collin and both of you. Glad you get to do this before you are discharged. I've got more patients to see, but I know I'll be seeing you soon, Maya. Collin's lucky to have such a fighter in his corner." She then teased Hawk, "I bet you don't win many arguments at home, do you?"

"Only the ones she tricks me into thinking I want to win." He threw a wink in my direction.

I laughed. That wasn't true … in any sense. I wasn't a manipulator like another woman he used to call *wife*. I also didn't win all arguments. But, most importantly, I didn't think we really disagreed on a lot. Unfortunately, though, when we did, it was over significant things like whether or not to visit killers and when to give birth.

The event that we were *not* arguing about was the one Dr. Edgewood had alluded to. We were going to have a chance to actually hold Collin. He would still have the necessary medical attachments, but since he could regulate his own body temperature, he had advanced to no cover on his crib. We would be able to hold our little boy in our arms, not through holes in the side of a plastic box.

I was both excited and jittery nervous. Even though I loved children, I really hadn't been around a lot of babies. Sophia's youngest was born the year Jeff and I married. So, I did hold him a few times but didn't do any of the diaper changing and babysitting tasks. If Sophia and her husband, Walt, went out, their parents were on that duty.

Hawk pretty much was the same way. Raiden was born overseas, and Liam's kids were born after Hawk moved to Nashville. So, not a lot of infant experience with his nephews or niece. He probably had more of an opportunity with Chance and Arinn.

I sat on one of the large chairs as a nurse placed Collin on my arm cradle for the first time … at least the first time I remembered. He was pretty much all wrapped up and still connected to the hose, but I found a way to have my top down a little and give him some of the direct skin-to-skin experience that was recommended. That first feeling of having my baby embraced in my arms could never be matched. All the nerves went away and were replaced by absolute bliss. He was so still and peaceful, and so was I. Almost instantly, I felt myself naturally rocking him. It had to be instinctual because I hadn't realized I was even doing it at first. Nor did I know that I'd closed my eyes while performing the motion.

Hawk's soft voice caused me to open them. "He looks so tiny next to your hand."

I did note the size of my hand expansion compared to his back. But what was even more amazing were our son's little eyes, which Hawk and I had only seen once since Collin slept so much. They had opened and were looking right at me. A dark blue, they were definitely closer to my hue than his dad's, but, regardless, were so wonderful to see.

"Oh, my goodness I just love you," I cooed to our baby boy. It was a love so unique because it was a connection like no other. I looked then to my other love. "Hawk," I whispered because of the magic of it all. "Take my picture with him, please. And then we'll switch."

As much as I treasured the feeling of our little one against me, I couldn't wait for Hawk to experience that, too. While he remembered seeing Collin in the delivery room, he'd never had a chance to hold him. He needed to feel that physical bond, which somehow even more so enhanced the emotional one.

After snapping my first-time-holding-Collin shot on his phone, Hawk sat on the matching chair next to mine. The nurse told him he should open or take off his shirt completely, as it was the same for men as women with providing that special skin-to-skin contact. He opted for removal since the shirt he was wearing only had a few buttons on the top and wouldn't provide much space. I could see he was nervous, not only about getting ready to hold a frail baby but also about partially stripping in front of strangers. Both physically and mentally strong, he needn't be about either, though.

As Hawk removed his shirt, I loudly whispered to the baby, "And that, right there, is how it all started … how you came to be."

"Maya … geez."

As the nurse chuckled, she carefully manipulated the wires and transferred Collin from my arms to my husband's broad span. I'm not sure who was more in awe at that point—Hawk or me. I do know we were all perfectly quiet, though, letting the moment sink in.

"How you doing there, dad?"

He took a second and then looked up at the nurse, who had asked the question. "No one's ever called me that."

The nurse adjusted a wire and lightly touched the baby's face. "Well, first words are a little bit of a stretch at this point, but we'll practice with Collin to see if we can get *him* to say it, too."

I smiled, and it made me wonder. What *did* he want Collin to call him? I had not yet considered what our new parental monikers would be.

Hawk managed a witty comeback, all the while being completely captivated with our little boy. "Catching the football is up to me, though."

"Darn it, we'll make sure to cross that one off our list then." She smiled. "You two good if I go over to the desk?"

"Uh, I think so." Even his simple head movement of looking over at me was done gingerly with our newborn preemie in his arms. "Mai …?"

"Huh?" I realized then how entranced I was in the scene of father and child. I had been hearing the conversation and even sounds around me, but my focus was so specific on that bond. It was something I was overjoyed that my son would have. I swiped at the silent tear rolling down my face and gave a smile as a response. When Hawk grinned back, I inched a little closer and snapped the first family photo of the three of us, just as Collin's little reflexes grasped Hawk's finger.

CHAPTER NINETEEN

On the day that was supposed to be my baby shower, I was lucky I had even *physically* showered. We had powered through two nonstop days and were going on three nights since I had been discharged. Having our own, more spacious bed and not hearing the constant beeping hospital sounds was definitely a plus, but I'm not sure Hawk or I actually slept any better at home. No matter, the two of us were up each morning ready to start again. We may as well have been wearing one of those popular repeat shirts. You know the ones. Ours would contain the words *Eat, Sleep, NICU, Repeat.*

"You should have gone with Finn like you originally planned." I spoke of the benefit show the guys were attending that night while us gals were supposed to be eating appetizers, guessing a due date, and opening gifts.

"What?" The expression on Hawk's face when he looked up from the bowl of cereal was either confusion or frustration. Or maybe both. "What are you talking about?"

"It's not like we have a baby here to take care of." Yes, I said it with the utmost sadness. "And all I am doing is freaking pumping every couple of hours or so. If not here, then at the hospital. I feel like I'm a cow and you are the farmer transporting me back and forth to the milking machines."

He shook his head but still made light of our situation. "Mai, our courtship was pretty much me driving us around. Why should this be any different?"

I normally would have teased, asking him what historical British show he had been watching with his use of the word *courtship*, but I didn't have it in me. I only had the sad truth. "Because it *should* be different. All of this should be different." I wanted to pout, stomp, and run into our bedroom, but I lacked any energy to do so.

I knew it was bad when Hawk didn't try to lift my spirits. He simply agreed. "I know."

We looked at each other for an extended beat before I managed to pull myself a little out of the funk. "Why are you eating cereal for dinner? We have premades in the fridge."

There weren't balloons and teddy bears in our house like you'd expect upon the celebration of a child's birth. Instead, Lara had quickly organized a schedule for the band to make sure we had food—either prepped meals or groceries—delivered every day for a few weeks. I'd like to say it wasn't necessary, but it was, admittedly, helpful, as I certainly didn't feel like preparing food … unless it was the pumping variety. Yet, there my husband sat at the dinette at a little after six p.m. with a bowl of marshmallow-dotted cereal and a carton of milk.

"It seemed good," was his simple response.

He ate a few more bites, and I slumped onto the chair across from him, reaching for the box. After he poured the milk into my bowl, we both ate in silence. I could have blamed it on pure physical exhaustion, but there was more to it than that. It was us being together twenty-four-seven and having only breast pumps, oxygen numbers, and Collin's weight—which was down a few ounces but, supposedly, to be expected—to talk about.

Feeling the heaviness of those couple of days, I

chomped extra hard on the pieces of cereal that had defied the odds and remained dry. And I continued that way until silent tears fell from my eyes. Hawk closed his.

After another minute or so, he gathered the milk and his empty bowl, walked into the nearby kitchen, put the dairy back in the fridge, and rinsed his bowl in the sink. He leaned against the doorframe, looking at me for a second before speaking. “We’re not going back to the hospital tonight.”

“What?” My shock and frustration were louder than his had been mere moments before when we had been discussing the benefit concert. “Yes, we have to. We—”

“Maya, no.” He didn’t budge from his stance, both physically and verbally. “No. It’s too much. This isn’t good. It’s not good for you. You need to rest. You’re gonna run yourself into a complete mental break. We can’t keep this up for … for however long.”

I took a breath. Okay. But I knew what I was about to say was not the *okay* my husband wanted to hear.

“It’s fine. I’ll get a ride share. I know it’s a lot for you—”

“Maya!” It wasn’t a yell. It was exasperation. “That’s not what I said. I’m fine. I’m not the one who just gave birth, had a seizure, and is crying all the time.” No, but he *was* the one with dark circles under his eyes and wearing the floors out with his restless walking. He took the couple steps over to me, crouched low, and grasped both of my hands. “Sweetie, I love you, but we are not going back tonight. We’ll go first thing in the morning. You can pump here, and then we’ll call and ask them to set up the web cam.” He spoke of the technology option that allowed us to see Collin in his crib. Before I could argue, Hawk squeezed my hands and reiterated, “We’re not going.” He then pulled me up and brought me tightly onto his torso, encircling his strong arms around my back.

After I was done sobbing over the realization that he was probably right and that it was one of those arguments I wasn’t going to win, I pulled away. “You know I both love and hate you right now."

"I'm sure you do." And with that, he rested his lips on my forehead.

Not having to get more properly dressed and making the hospital commute did provide a little more down time and, if not real, the illusion of relaxation. We watched and talked with Collin and the NICU staff for a little bit. And although I longed to be there, it was, admittedly, easier leaving a screen than an in-person infant. Along those lines, though, I did make Hawk be the one to click the disconnect button.

Afterward, we snuggled together on the sofa to watch the broadcast of the live benefit show that was raising money to help fight childhood cancer. It was a mix of genres but taking place in Nashville. Finn was a big advocate of the cause and always supported it when he could, including performing "Boys' Weekend" that night. Having our own little one so sick certainly brought it emotionally home for Hawk and me.

It was as Finn was getting on the stage that my husband mumbled at the screen, "Je-sus, the f-ing …" His hand flew up in disgust, causing me to separate from his embrace.

"What?" I felt my eyebrows gather together. What was wrong?

"The …" He was pointing at the screen and watching intently.

"What?"

"They gave him the wrong guitar, but it's swapped now."

If I hadn't noticed it, I'm sure most of America didn't. But not Hawk. He had every precise detail down since he was the one normally backstage looking after everything.

I curled back onto my husband's side as Finn started singing. Everything was fine again … at least in the country music world. When he got to the part of the song that said "due sometime in May," his voice seemed to catch ever so slightly, but maybe that was just me being fine-tuned on things that were important to me.

"Might need to change the lyrics." I squished the one

side of my face at the words about our little one, who had been born in April instead.

But with Finn's next line about Hawk loving the baby and its momma, my husband very sweetly responded with, "That part's still true."

I gave him a quick closed smile. "Hawk?"

"Yeah?"

"It's almost time for me to pump again. I'm gonna go do that and work a little on a blog." I started to shift.

"A blog? Now? About what? You're on leave."

Had I not been in such a depressed, exhausted mood, I might have chuckled at that. Yes, Hawk and I were supposed to both have legitimate family leave. Despite the teasing at the hospital, Finn was most considerate about reminding us to take it. But at the same account, all three of us knew Hawk and I would continue to do what we could for Team Murphy. Not only was it our personalities, but it was also respect for Finn, and honestly, it kept our minds busy. A mobile world definitely helped, too.

"I want to write. I'm a little inspired by the song, and I … I need to get some stuff down."

"Maya, can't you just sit?" He was one to talk with his constant mobility. "You need to relax."

"You don't understand. That *will be* relaxing for me." I stood. "Enjoy the rest of the show, or text Finn and complain about the guitar or whatever, or have a beer since you're not driving. You relax, too." And I gave him a kiss.

***

When my alarm went off at three a.m., it was more startling than the previous days. I think that was because I was in a deeper sleep than I had been used to. I fumbled around for my phone on the nightstand and shut it off.

Hawk's words mimicked my thoughts. "Damn. Already?"

I swung my legs off the side of the bed and put my hand

on my husband's arm. "You don't have to get up." I could see that was his intention, especially since he had gotten up with me for the middle-of-the-night pump the other nights. "It's ridiculous. You're not—"

"Doing anything," he finished my sentence, which was the truth, even if it was beyond his control. "I just want to support you."

"I'll be back in like fifteen minutes." I kissed the same hand I had touched, and miraculously, he let me go.

I pitter-pattered my way down the hall to the room next to our master. The pump was there in the nursery/office. The lamp on the desk was already on, since we had it connected to a timer device so I wouldn't have to turn on the harsh overhead light in the dead of the night. I manipulated the pump pieces and sat on the rocking chair. The task was already something I could practically do in my sleep … and I nearly was.

As I started the process, I noted my laptop on the table right next to me. The sight of it open reminded me that I had started writing the blog the night before when I had come in to pump. When I thought of it, I didn't remember actually going to sleep or walking into the bedroom or saying good night to Hawk. I had finished the pumping and still wanted to write, but then what?

Not remembering exactly what I'd written or if I had even finished it, I wiggled the mouse pad a little and the screen lit up, showing me the writing document. Bringing my knuckles up to my eyes, I rubbed to get the last of the sleepies out so I could focus. Reading my words from the night before, I saw that they were loose and needed a couple switching of tenses and maybe some better word choices. But the message was real and honest. It began with me talking about sitting on the sofa with my husband and watching Finn perform "Boys' Weekend." I wrote about how it came across as a lighthearted song, but it was really about true love. And then I pondered the question of what exactly that was.

If you're, indeed, lucky enough to have a man who won't stop talking about you, then you've found it. Even more so, if you're lucky enough to find a man who still sees you as beautiful despite ice packs in unmentionable places, leaky boobs, and mood swings galore, you have doubled down. That's GIRL-code for don't let them go. Because men like these—like my husband—are rare and to be treasured and …

Ah, yes, I had been struggling for the right adjective to complete the sentence. I was pretty sure it was the last thing I had typed the night before. But it appeared I was wrong. There was something else a couple line spaces down, typed in a larger font size and bolded.

EXHAUSTED but completely and forever in love with you.
Don't you dare post this.
PS – It's easier to carry you again.

I chuckled, smiled, and felt a tear drop all at the same time. Hawk must have come into the room shortly after I had fallen asleep the night before and read what I had written. And then after carrying me to bed, he had "finished" the blog.

I shut the top of the computer, put the milk in the mini fridge we had bought for the nursery, and made my way back to our bedroom. My husband/guest co-blogger/wife-carrier had his eyes shut, but he wasn't in a full sleep. Not only did his breathing signify that, but I also knew he wouldn't let himself completely slumber with me out of the room.

Sure enough. "All good?"

"Hawk Brannigan, if I was allowed to and wasn't exhausted"—I emphasized that last word on purpose—"you would absolutely be getting some good sex right now."

His eyes opened and eyebrows lifted. "Is that so?"

"I love you."

"Me, too, Mai. Although, I'd prefer ice *buckets* over ice *packs*." He referenced the blog and then reached out his arm to curl me onto him.

***

I'd love to say it got easier over those next few days or so. But besides Hawk and I becoming fairly masterful when it came to changing Collin's diaper, taking his temperature, and switching out electrodes, it didn't. Because of the continuous days of feeling hopeless and exhausted, it maybe even got harder. For sure it was depressing.

It was depressing watching the pained faces of other families as they struggled with their little ones in the NICU and witnessing how the staff had such empathy, taking in every emotion from the parents in the room. The absolute worst was seeing a tiny, beautiful newborn arrive one morning and then gone when we came back the next. I ached for her parents having to find a way to survive such grief. Even though I knew that baby girl's case was vastly different than our son's—she was born pounds smaller than Collin and had a heart defect—it didn't help my anxiety.

It was depressing to only be pumping and not being able to have my baby be actually breast fed. I *did* feel like a dumb, used cow. And I thought I looked like one, too. Although my body felt generally better, the baby pouch was not decreasing as much as I would have liked, not to mention my pale skin and unconditioned, dry hair.

It was depressing—even though the intention was for it to be the opposite—seeing Collin's crib covered with little decorative eggs. In addition, the sweet nursing staff had somehow also adorned the cap that covered his tiny head with soft bunny ears. It was our son's first Easter. He wasn't with us dying eggs on the kitchen counter or looking at his basket full of goodies. He was spending it in a sterile hospital.

And ... it was depressing getting texts and calls from our

family and friends. I knew they meant well and were concerned about us and Collin, but it made me feel bad. I felt neglectful for not returning or acknowledging most of them. But my sole concentration was on our baby, and we were still very much engulfed in *Eat, Sleep, NICU, Repeat* mode. There wasn't a chance for much more.

I was looking through photos of Collin and having one of those moments where I was really missing my grandma. Having weathered a lot in her life, she had always been someone I could count on when I felt fear or weakness. She hadn't been much for prayer and, therefore, neither had I, but I hoped she was somehow looking after my son.

Breaking my thought, a cardinal flew past the master bedroom's window and landed on a tree branch just as the phone rang in my hands. I thought it might be Hawk asking or confirming something with me while he met with the construction people at our new home site. But it wasn't. It was Sophia. My hair was still wet from the shower and I knew Hawk would be back soon so we could go to the hospital, but not only did I want to answer the phone, I also needed to hear the voice of one of my best friends.

"Hey."

"I've been thinking of you today," she replied. "I'm sure it's hard."

It was. Of course it was. Every day had been since I'd slid off that damn road. But I didn't understand how she knew that. Their entire family—her parents and in-laws included—had been away for eleven days on an out-of-country spring break cruise. They'd had limited cell reception, so we hadn't talked since I'd been in the hospital.

Guessing that maybe Juanita—who did know via a text from me—had gotten ahold of her once they arrived back, I replied with a tired but honest, "I'm glad I have Hawk."

There was a beat of silence before, "Oh." It wasn't like her. Sophia was a talker, and I had counted on her positive words. But instead, it was followed by, "Well, okay then. I guess I'm gonna go."

"What?" My face punched back a bit in shock. "You don't even want to hear about him?"

Why wouldn't she want to know about my son who was fighting for his life? Why then did she call and make that comment to start off? She had been completely invested and supportive of my pregnancy. What was going on?

"No. No, Maya." Geez, she sounded mad even. "I've not begrudged you your happiness, but I don't want to hear about him today. He's a nice enough guy, and I guess your anniversary with *him* is the only thing that matters now."

What? Collin was a "nice enough guy"? Calling a newborn a *guy* seemed strange. My anniversary?

Oh … oh, shit! She wasn't referring to my precious baby boy. She was talking about Hawk. But, more importantly, she was talking about her brother. She was calling because it would have been my wedding anniversary with Jeff. Sophia had no idea that Collin had been born, and, damn it—just like Lara's birthday—I'd forgotten about everything else besides him.

I closed my eyes. "I forgot," I admitted softly and with sincere regret. It wasn't something that I would ever under normal circumstances forget. I loved Hawk, but Jeff would always have a place in my heart, too.

"Really? That's even worse than—"

Hearing her understandable fury, I had to explain. "Collin's here. I gave birth. He's … he's in NICU." Every time I verbalized that, it choked me up a little. "It's been rough."

"Oh God. Maya …" Her temperament instantly changed to being sympathetic. "I didn't know."

Then, as I watched the cardinal fly away, I got a chance to really talk with one of my best friends. It was exactly what I needed at that moment. We apologized, listened, and wept for the present and the past. But we were most definitely holding out hope for the future, too.

***

That was the feeling Hawk and I had when we arrived at the NICU later that day. We learned that Collin had achieved a couple small victories worth celebrating. Despite not directly feeding through me, he was taking in what he needed. He had regained one and a half of the ounces he had lost, which was definitely moving in the right direction. There was an even greater triumph, though. Just over a week old, our sweet baby was graduating from the CPAP to a different breathing device, which meant he still needed assistance, but it was less evasive and he was taking in more on his own.

"He'll just have the little nose thingy to help him breathe now?" I looked at the thin tube.

"Nasal cannula." The doctor smiled as she corrected my non-clinical "little nose thingy" term.

I didn't care what they called it. Invent a word with twenty-thousand letters, and I would pronounce and spell it correctly if it meant my little boy was breathing better. Truly seeing his entire face for the first time was incredible and beautiful. Suddenly, the NICU didn't seem so claustrophobic to me.

"And then the goal is to get him off that soon enough, too."

"I'm so proud of you, Collin." I gently pressed one of my knuckles to the corner of his mouth, which automatically opened on the touch. I knew it was too early for him to smile, but I took it as one. Me, though? *I* definitely had one on my face.

And the doctor did, too. "This also means that pretty soon we can look into having you actually breast feed. Let's get him used to this setup first, though."

I squeezed Hawk's hand and then placed the little note of love and encouragement we had written for our son on the outside of his crib. It was the first time we had both signed *Mom* and *Dad.* That's what we decided on. We certainly weren't the *ma* and *pa* type. Hawk didn't like *pop,* and he called his own mother *momma*. So, I didn't want that. *Mother* and *father* seemed too formal. *Mom* and *dad*, though, were simple, sturdy names just like the two of us.

It felt good to be them. It felt good to be happy. We finally had a day to celebrate. At least there was one.

CHAPTER TWENTY

"Hey, Mai."

It was Hawk's voice I heard answering his phone, but there were several others in the background, too. While it sounded a bit like a "boys' weekend" kind of gathering, I knew it wasn't. They—my husband, Finn, and the band—were at the studio ironing out the tour's setlist and what equipment, videos, etcetera would accompany each song.

"Hawk …"

As his name came out of my mouth, I immediately flashbacked to the last time I had actually called—not texted—him. It had been when I was laying partially sideways on the side of the road. Dang it! The two calls were going to be similar. Why? Oh my God, why?

"Can you hold on a sec? I can go in the other room."

"No," I denied him and went straight into my reason why. "I need you to actually get in the truck and come over here."

Like last time. Like—dang it—last time. The association wasn't good.

"Shit. What? The hospital? Why?"

"Something's wrong with Collin." I was pacing the hall outside of the NICU, wanting to have a secluded enough space to talk. "I need you to come."

"Okay. Shut up for an f-ing minute!"

"What?" I bounced back, shocked by his demand.

"Not you," he replied, while the guys on his end got quiet as the true recipients. "I'm on my way. What's wrong?" Hearing his panic made mine even worse, and I couldn't answer right away. "Mai?"

"Just get here. I can't be on the phone and be with—"

"Okay. Yeah. Damn it."

Hanging up with little else said, I noted the time on my phone and started counting the minutes until Hawk would get there. The commute to the hospital from the studio was even less than from our home. It was one of the reasons Hawk had agreed to our plan for the day. He had dropped me off at the hospital for my appointment with Dr. Edgewood. There was no need for him to attend since he knew my self-monitored BP numbers were nowhere near what the warnings were, and I had promised to relate any necessary info to him. Afterward, I could pump and then go see Collin. Lara was to meet me at the NICU after her own appointment with Dr. Edgewood and then we could go get a bite to eat before returning once again to Collin. By then, Hawk would have been done with the guys and could meet me at the NICU to spend some dad-son time while I pumped again. That had been the plan. Like most things, it had not worked.

The first part had, though. I'd gotten a positive report from Dr. Edgewood. Physically, I was healing nicely, and she was already discussing weaning me off meds because I was not showing any signs of the issues I had with the preeclampsia. The one thing she *was* concerned about, which was not a surprise at all, was my lack of sleep and how it promoted anxiety. She understood the emotional strain of having a baby in the NICU and wanted to set me up with either a social worker or a support group with families who had graduated from the neonatal unit and could relate. I had told her I was good. Since Collin was getting better, so would I.

With that in mind, I had pumped in the meditation room and then walked to the NICU. Going through the normal procedures at their front desk, I was feeling almost blissful, thinking about holding my baby and then actually enjoying a lunch out with Lara. I was pre-ordering the future appetizers and desserts in my head. But when I had walked in the room and saw a few of the staff huddled around Collin's crib, I instantly knew something was wrong.

It was like all the air from the room was sucked away. The day before had been too good—taking him off the CPAP and him gaining weight. I had fooled myself into thinking if he got to a week, we were home free. Why had I thought that? It had never been that way in my life. One minute you are alongside a sports star in a parade and the next a part of a funeral procession. One minute you are making dinner on the stove and the next you answer a call from the chief of police. One minute you're walking in with milk for your baby and the next doctors are talking about heart rate, oxygen levels, and were putting the CPAP back on.

It was horrible seeing that machine once again monopolizing Collin's face, but I had tried to ignore it and listen as the staff talked about how his little heart was jumping or skipping as he struggled to breathe. They would run some tests to hopefully rule out a heart murmur, but the CPAP would definitely put him more at ease. It did the opposite for me. Because of that sight and my lack of sleep, I had immediately felt weak and a little dizzy. All I could think about was how only a couple days before, there had been that little girl who was somebody's daughter for only a day and how her little heart gave out.

That's when I had made that call. That's when I knew he had to be there. Hawk needed to know and be there for his son. And when I hung up with him, I think that's when I started to zone out. It was like my exhausted brain couldn't process anything else. I knew my husband was on his way and he could be the ears for both of us. Because I seriously couldn't take any more.

And he did. He barreled into the NICU like a NASCAR driver in an invisible car. Meeting me at Collin's crib, he first looked at our son's little torso pumping up and down before scanning his eyes on mine. "What's going on?"

The doctor came over and re-explained everything to Hawk, who very calmly took it all in and even had his hand on Collin's head at one point. The baby looked peaceful. He was everything the doctor said—content and taking in his feeding tube. The neonatologist reminded us that sometimes it is an adjustment for infants to be completely free of the CPAP. They had told us that the day before. I somehow had missed that little bit of information in my elation to see him off it.

"But he's struggling." I realized I was pursing my own lips as if trying to get my infant son to breathe with me.

"He was, and we did what was best. We anticipate taking the CPAP off again soon." The neonatologist's words sounded encouraging, but I had heard and been witness to that before.

"His heart … What about his heart? You were talking about his heart rate."

"We'll monitor," she replied to my question. "I know you've gotten to understand these machines. Everything looks to be back to where we want."

"Maya, he's fine. He's fine." Hawk reached his hand across the crib for mine. "They told us preemies do this sometimes. And if he wasn't … if he didn't … if we … it would be all right. We wou—"

My arm broke instantly from his, and my voice was nowhere near his relaxed one. "What?" What did he say? How could he think that? It would be all right???

"I'm glad that's easy for you to say." I felt instant fury bubble up my arms and thump into my heart. His comment was making my eyes and brain blur. While I had been in a semi-silent, stunned mode before his arrival, I wasn't anymore. I was letting loose. "You were the one who wanted this. You wanted to have him come early."

Hawk took a step back from the crib and seemed to talk through gritted teeth. "I did not want him to come early, but you were so sick. I was worried about you and—"

"Then your concern was about how it affected the tour." *My* steps away from the crib were because I couldn't stand still or, apparently, let any of my thoughts remain that way either.

"The f-ing tour? Are you kidding me? What?" It wasn't gritted teeth that time—his irritation was quite evident and all the adults in the room took note.

And I completely broke. "You never wanted this baby. Not any—" I had heard it from Oaklee repeatedly, and anyone who knew him seemed shocked with his fatherhood status. Why hadn't I listened? "You never wanted any of this." I started to pull at my wedding and engagement rings to get them off, but they were not physically cooperating with my mental unraveling.

"God. Stop it, Maya. Stop it! You're acting insane." We had somehow made our way to each other at the end of the crib, and because of that, Hawk was able to grab on to my hand and halt the ring action. But then he quickly left go and, with even more emotion, hurled a verbal, "Oh hell." His fists went up to his eyes and he rubbed abrasively while shaking his head.

I had never, ever seen him like that. The honesty in his eyes was both disbelief and disappointment. And then he looked at the others around us. The already quiet room had become almost tomb-like. Even the constant whirling and beeping of the multitude of machines seemed to bow to the scene. Hawk turned from Collin and me, and then back again with a look of defeat before starting to walk away.

Whatever stillness had momentarily captured me evaporated as I recalled another time he had done so … another time regarding his feelings about my pregnancy. "You're leaving? Of course you are, just like you did when

I first told you I was pregnant. Everyone leaves. Go ahead. Go. I'm staying."

"Maya …" My name sounded like a warning, as he faced me again for that second. "God …" And then he did. He turned around and walked out of the room.

For the second time that day—heck, the second time that hour—I stood in a complete daze in the NICU. It wasn't because of Collin that time, though. It was his father. It was me. It was the whole damn mess. I couldn't think. I knew I was angry or upset. I couldn't tell the difference. I wasn't even sure about what bothered me the most or if any of it made sense. I only saw how quickly my world was falling apart.

It was both a doctor and another mother in the room who, after a moment, talked with me. They reiterated some of the same things Dr. Edgewood had said earlier about needing to take a break and getting rest. As hard as it seemed, taking care of myself was taking care of Collin. Somewhere deep down, I knew it was true, but how could I be a good mother if I wasn't with him?

I knew right then I needed to at least step into the hall and collect myself. I didn't want to give off the wrong vibes to my son while he was already fighting so much else. Plus, I was embarrassed to have lost it with Hawk in front of semi-strangers … in front of anybody, really. I didn't do that. I was a police officer's widow. I knew how to be tough and not show emotion.

Part of me hoped to find Hawk in the hall or around the corner when I left the immediate area. The other part of me prayed for the opposite, knowing everything was still too raw. The latter won. The only person there was the man at the main desk, and by the look he gave me, he had heard the commotion moments before, too. I lowered my eyes in shame, took a couple breaths, and walked down the adjoining hall. I needed a little distance from knowing eyes.

"Hey, Maya … Maya?"

I had my head way down and my thoughts even further,

so I hadn't seen her approach. But there was Lara, touching my shoulder to stop me. She was coming to see my baby boy, who wasn't supposed to have that damn machine hooked up to him. And she was coming to see her friend, who wasn't supposed to be on the verge of a nervous breakdown.

"God, Maya, what's wrong? Are you okay? Is it Collin?" She seemed to look past me and in the direction of the NICU as if that would tell the whole tale. "Maya?"

"He left." It was the first thing out of my mouth, and I instantly, internally questioned why of all that had happened, I chose to say that.

"Who?"

"I can't do this. I can't do this without him."

I was talking about Collin. No … Hawk. No … Collin. Damn it. I couldn't do it at all. I was losing it in every which way.

"Maya, what's going on?" I could hear the increasing panic in her voice, and I'm sure if I saw myself, I would be reacting the same way. "Did something happen with Collin?" She asked that one a little more softly.

"Hawk left. He walked out." Speaking in the same monotone, it was starting to dawn on me why that seemed to be my immediate focus. I was worried about so much, but Hawk seemed to be my top threat because, even though I didn't like the backslide, I knew Collin wasn't in any immediate danger. My relationship with my husband appeared to be, though.

"Huh? Why don't we sit, okay?" She pointed to the cushioned bench against the wall. "Tell me what's going on."

So, I did. I sat in the hall, with occasional passerbys, telling one of my dearest friends the horrible details of my time at the hospital that day. Lara simply listened. She was good at that, and I very much appreciated being able to just get my thoughts out.

"One little piece of advice," she said at the end of my

tale. "Know to let this go. Let this be one of those things that you both just forgive and understand what the circumstances are."

Although I knew that was sound advice, I also understood it wasn't an easy task. Having a few moments to step back from the disastrous scene with my husband, I was recalling the hateful things I had hurled in his direction. I was realizing the full impact of how that would affect him and our relationship. I still wasn't happy with his words, which had brought on my tirade, but that shouldn't have prompted additional ones that I knew, in my heart, weren't the truth.

"When everything happened with Arinn, Finn and I had a nasty blow-up. I blamed him. I felt like he was blaming me. It … it wasn't pretty." Lara admitted to her own past marital drama. "You know what it was, though? It was being a mom and dad. It was being scared. Remember what I told you at the airport? Hawk doesn't like seeing you hurt, especially when there's nothing he can do to help. And both of you, I'm sure, feel that right now."

And that … that right there was what made me cry. I hadn't the entire time. But she nailed it. Lara pinned down exactly what Hawk and I were fighting about. Or, more accurately, fighting *for*. I wasn't insane like Hawk had thought I was acting, but emotional for sure. The mental roller coaster ride my postpartum body was going through was already to be expected, nonetheless having a sick baby on top of that.

Lara gave me a side-arm hug, patted my leg, and stood. "Come on, let's go see that beautiful little one of yours for a few minutes, and then I'll take you to our place, okay? We'll eat there … not in public. Stay however long, and I'll drive you back here after. I'll call Finn and have him check on Hawk."

"He might actually be with him. I mean, I interrupted their meeting. Hawk could have just gone back to it."

"Hmmm, do you think so?" Lara seemed doubtful.

Although *I* knew Hawk more intimately, she knew him longer and had a decent insight when it came to him.

Even though putting work before family was one of the accusations I had hurled at my husband, what Lara said was true—I didn't think he went back to the studio. He was too upset. It was one thing to let *me* see that—and, God, the hospital staff—but his buds in the band? No … most likely not.

Everyone in the NICU pretended as if the last time I had been in that room a scene similar to one from *Marriage Story* hadn't taken place. Maybe they saw more of that in there than I knew. Regardless, I was appreciative. It gave me time to truly focus on who I should have been—Collin.

Given the baby's setback, I felt like I was having one of my own. I really didn't want to leave him. But everyone from the mother who had counseled me, to the staff, to Lara, encouraged me to do so. With a promise that the hospital would call me if there were any changes—no matter good or bad—I agreed. I did need something to eat, and I knew I would be back to pump shortly after that.

The fresh air in the car helped relax my manic brain a little. While it continued to circle between Collin and Hawk, I started thinking—hoping—that both would turn around. As we were getting closer to Finn and Lara's home, I felt a tug at my heart. It led me to make a request of my friend/driver.

"Hey, do you mind if we go the other way? I'd like to, uh, stop by our"—I partially choked on the word because of the emotions the location conjured up—"our new place."

I hadn't been there since the baby was born, and I wanted to see what progress was made. But it was more than that. I needed to stand where our hopes and dreams were … those of family, new beginnings, and happiness.

"Sure." Her soft, closed smile seemed to emulate the feelings I was having.

As we approached the property, we both saw the truck. There was only one, and it wasn't a construction worker's.

It was Hawk's gunmetal-colored pickup.

My heart jumped. My BP blipped. I didn't need a monitor to tell me that. I also, apparently, didn't need a tracking device on a phone to know where my husband was. We had an undeniable bond between us that did that … a connection between our souls. It was, I'm sure, what had led me to at the last minute ask Lara for the slight detour.

Hawk was sitting on the front stoop. It was the spot where we planned on putting the porch bench … close to the new welcome mat. Head in his hands, he looked up as Lara slowed the car upon our approach.

"You need me to stay or …"

"No," I practically whispered my response.

She put the car in park. "Call if … if you need a ride or anything."

I heard her voice, but I didn't see her. I was completely zoned in on Hawk. "Yeah." I hoped I wouldn't. Just as I hoped I wouldn't need the next thing she said.

"Good luck."

As I stepped out of the car, I knew Hawk was watching. More so, I understood his demeanor was definitely not his norm. Otherwise, he would have done the gentlemanly thing and helped with the car door or at least walked over and acknowledged Lara. He did neither. He simply continued to sit and stare at me upon my approach. He was not himself, and I obviously knew why. I just didn't know which emotion I was going to get from him because his face had such a blank look on it.

I stopped a few feet from where he sat, somehow sadly cautious of the man I loved with all my heart. I waited until I heard the sound of Lara's car disappear before I said his name. "Hawk …"

"You better think really carefully about what your next words are." It wasn't just the look of almost contempt but the fact that he had never spoken to me in that tone that proved how much he was hurting … how much *I* had hurt him. "Because, I will love you until I am in the ground, but we have some serious issues if you think I don't—" He stopped himself and stood to meet me face-to-face. "When you gave birth and had the seizure, you were so rigid. You were shaking and grabbing. There were so many machines and people. God!" His eyes seemed to be flitting, as if watching an internal flashback. "And then they were basically racing to get the baby to breathe … for him to live. God, Maya. God! I have never, ever experienced such fear … such utter distress."

The two of us had never talked about the exacts of what happened that day over a week before. I didn't remember any of it, and I was told I never would. While I ached to have the memory of seeing my son for the first time, I was realizing that it might be for the best that I didn't upon listening to Hawk's traumatic retell.

"Between you and him, I felt so powerless. I wanted to fix it. I want to fix all of it, but I can't do a damn thing for him or for you." When he swiped at his eyes, it was in a different way than when he had at the hospital. There he had been trying to stop his emotions from starting, but in front of our house and with just me, he did something I had never seen him do. He was openly crying. It wasn't vocal or uncontrollable, but there were significant tears rolling down his face. He was losing control because of exactly that—he couldn't control anything that was going on … and he was used to being able to do so. It was what made him so good at his job and as an overall stand-up human being. He shook his head with a sniffle. "I want you and Collin more than anything in this world. Do you really not believe that, Maya? Really? Still? After all—"

I couldn't let him go on. I couldn't bear for him to be in that pain, especially his doubt of our love. "Oh God. I'm sorry. I'm sorry. I'm so sorry." I stepped toward him and, with tenderness, put my hands up to the excessive scruff covering his cheeks. "You are the best thing that has ever happened to me. Ever." And on that word, I felt my own tears emerge. "I know you love me. I know you love …"

The image of our little boy in Hawk's arms suddenly struck my heart and mind, and I let out a muffled cry that time. Wanting to be strong, I brought my hands up to wipe my tears and continued, "Oh God, I'm sorry. I'm tired. I'm scared. I'm postpartum hormonal. I know none of that is an excuse, but I think I just needed something or someone to lash out at in the hospital. I shouldn't have done that, especially to you." I knew I had his attention then. "I needed to come here—right here—because I had to be somewhere where I felt you and us and our love. I'm so glad you had the same thought. Forgive me. It's … I hurt so much. Not physically." I made sure to clarify because I knew how obsessive he was about my personal health. "I hurt for *him*, and I feel such guilt. Just like you want to fix him, I know it was my fault from the beginning. I should have been able to protect him. I should have been stronger to keep him inside me to grow, and then he wouldn't be how he is now."

"You were sick, Maya. You were so sick. I don't think you even understand how much. The doctors believe you going early would have happened no matter what. I didn't want that. I didn't want him to have to fight for his life. But I didn't want you to, either. What I said in the NICU about if something should happen?" Hawk was beginning to gain control of his tears. "I was just trying to be strong for you … to let you know I'm here. I get that you're hurting because you don't like seeing him like that." When he paused for a second, I could tell it was because the emotions were ramping back up. "But God, Maya, I hurt, too."

"I know. I know. I do. You are strong, Hawk … so strong. When I see you seemingly being okay with everything, I wonder why or how. I forget how much you keep inside because you are being strong for me." Recalling me holding back about the anniversary of the day Jeff had died, I knew we were both a little guilty of that.

"And Collin." He made sure to emphasize that fact. "You both come first—before the tour … before anything, *anything* else."

"I know. I'm not sure why I accused you of—"

"I'm pretty sure *I* do." His head dipped slightly to make sure his gaze was meeting mine. And through that look alone, we both knew what—or rather who—he was referring to. "Oaklee put all of this back in your mind again, didn't she?"

"I …" I closed my eyes and took a breath. "I guess I let her get to me." I didn't think I had, but when you're tired and emotionally beat, things get messed up in your brain. "I know better, though. I know you."

"Trust me, Maya. And trust in our little fighter."

"I do." I nodded as a double confirmation. "He's just needing to use those kickass skills a little earlier than I thought," I recalled our talk on our honeymoon with a mix of sadness and encouragement.

Hawk obviously remembered, too. "Learned from his momma."

I managed a slight smile. "Everything's good at the hospital. He—"

"Yeah, I know. I just got off the phone checking on him when you pulled up." I wiped at my eyes … of course he had. "Neither of us is leaving. I understand you've had so much of that in your life, but we're here. Collin and I are going to be here. I'm sorry I left. I know I shouldn't have. But it, unfortunately, wasn't like before. It wasn't a time when I needed to reflect and appreciate," he spoke of his leaving after my pregnancy reveal, which I hadn't known then was just out of pure shock and not out of anger. He had needed to "reflect and appreciate" my completely unexpected announcement back then.

"It *was* for me this time, though. You were right to leave the NICU. I needed the space. Whether you knew that when you left or not, it was absolutely the right decision because I was barreling us down an ugly road."

His smile started as the soft, closed, sad variety type but emerged a little fuller after he spoke. "That's why I'm the one who does the driving. Come here."

He opened his arms and I plowed immediately onto him. His exhale was immense and extensive behind my back. It had been a horrific start of our day, but in a weird way, I think we both needed it to happen. We both needed to release so much and not feel like we had to be in control or strong for each other all the time. Strength came by being open, vulnerable, and honest together through all of it. We had to not just say it but believe in what seemed to be becoming our mantra—*It's you and me.* Every day. Even—and perhaps especially—the hard ones.

CHAPTER TWENTY-ONE

That day acted like a restart button for both Collin and me. Well, maybe not a restart but more like a series of buttons—pause, rewind, and play. Our little NICU warrior wasn't the only one who had to take a minute and learn to breathe again. I needed to also. My breathing wasn't physical like his, though. It was mentally regrouping and doing what everyone told me to from the start. I had to take care of myself, which would in effect help not only Collin but Hawk, too. My husband worrying about me was not good for his own physical or mental health. It all began with me, and the starting line was to lose control in the right way—by accepting that Collin was getting the best care and he would be the one who'd set his own path.

I say all that as if it was an easy thing to do … as if it was really simply pressing a button or two. It wasn't. But the emotional upheaval of the NICU and front porch scenes with Hawk provided me with the right incentive to try my best. I never again wanted to hurt him like I had.

One of the first changes I made was getting in contact with the mother who had counseled me in the NICU. God bless her, she was a single mom. I didn't ask the details, but to be doing all of it on her own? Talk about strength. We agreed to look in on each other's baby when we were in the unit and give a text update. It was almost like having another web cam available but, most definitely, it was our own little support group. It also meant that Hawk and I wouldn't be there as often. Yes, we'd still absolutely go every day. But in addition to cutting out the after-dinner run, we were going to get a later start in the mornings and not make two trips. Instead, we would go on walks—boy, did I need the exercise—watch some movies, talk a little work stuff, and try to be ourselves.

And as that next week went on, Collin made plans of his own. He hit another button. He was suddenly going in fast-forward. If he had a NICU report card, he would have been getting *most improved* marks from his teachers. And two of the first subjects he mastered were the best ones. The report on his heart was fantastic with no concerns, and he aced CPAP 1-0-1. Or should I say 2-0-2 since it was the second attempt at getting rid of it? Regardless, within a couple days, he was off the obnoxious machine again.

When Hawk and I entered the NICU on the second day after the CPAP was removed, Collin was awake. With his deep blue eyes open wide, he was looking at me. And I felt more hopeful than I had in a very long time.

"Hi. Good morning," I greeted our little boy, while Hawk tickled his belly. "Good morning. I missed you." It was still hard being away from him—the blessing who had hugged my insides for months—but I knew I was getting better rest, and because of that, a more positive attitude was shining through. "He did good, huh?" I asked the doctor as she approached. "No setbacks?" My physical hands were playing with his tiny feet, but my mental ones had fingers crossed.

"Real good night," she confirmed.

I hadn't realized I was slightly tense until my shoulders dropped into a much more relaxed state upon her words. "We can hold him, yeah?"

"Of course," the neonatologist agreed. "Let's get you

situated, and then I'll tell you *today*'s good news."

My eyelids expanded, and I switched my gaze to Hawk, who curved up his lips. "Let my husband hold him first. It's his turn."

"Oh, we're taking turns now?" Hawk teased. "I thought I had to duke you out for the privilege."

"I can make a tally chart if you prefer."

The doctor did not understand the sweet, cheeky, personal meaning of my words, but Hawk did. He gave me a wink and unbuttoned his top—he had learned quickly what to wear to the NICU—before sitting down to accept the baby. I watched as Hawk took Collin in his arms and nuzzled with him. There was nothing sexier … absolutely nothing.

Instead of embarrassing him for a change, though, I went for something more appropriate and what I knew would get a chuckle. "I am a complete fan of the nose thingy." I sat next to my two guys.

The doctor did, indeed, laugh. "Here, let's get his hat off. He's getting enough direct heat." She gently removed Collin's cap. "So, here's the good news. It's a two-parter." She seemed to wait for both Hawk and me to look at her directly. "He got his weight back."

"Yay! Yay!" I smiled. "And what's the second part?"

"We'd like you to try actually nursing this afternoon if you were planning on staying around for your next pumping."

"Doc," Hawk answered her before I did. "You know better than to ask that."

"Of course," I played off my husband's response. "That is exciting."

The doctor shifted on her feet a little. "Here's the thing, though."

Of course. Sigh. "There's always a thing."

"Maya …" Hawk *tsked* my negativity like a practiced dad.

"What's the thing?" I tried to lift my voice to a little more of a cheerleading type, but I'm sure I failed miserably.

"He might not latch right away. He's showing signs, but it could take some time … some practice for both of you. I have the lactation consultant ready to be here in a couple hours." She looked at the large white hospital clock on the wall as if to confirm. "And, of course, it is a complement to the feeding tube for now. So, he'll be well nourished no matter."

All I could do was nod. I was excited and nervous at the same time. It was a big step, but one I was, for sure, looking forward to.

Even though I was silent, I think Hawk recognized my emotions and offered a light lift-me-up. "I guess you get to hold him for that."

My belly bounced with silent laughter. "True." I reached my hand out to stroke the baby's hair. "You know, I thought I noticed this before but he usually has the little hat on or had all the straps … Does he have curly hair?"

"It takes a little while to determine," she informed. "But the fuzzies when they get wet do seem to be wavy. Curly hair is a dominant trait whereas straight is recessive. So, if one parent has curly, it usually wins out."

"My hair is only wavy if I scrunch it and have layers." I fluffed it, as if she needed a demonstration. "Then how—?"

"From me, of course." Hawk rubbed the baby's back so beautifully, I was almost a little jealous.

But that was overpowered by my shock about the hair. "You?"

"Yeah." He seemed almost offended. "I just never let it grow out to see it. My dad's side."

I furled my brows in thought. Huh. Jake's hair was cropped even shorter than Hawk's, so I couldn't tell. But Liam's definitely had some waves. Raiden didn't seem to, but I think his mother's side won that gene pool with his stunning slick-black locks.

"He's my boy. No denying."

"Wouldn't want to." I smiled and decided what better

time than to take another photo.

***

If Collin had already pressed fast-forward, he then did it repeatedly. His progress started accelerating at an even quicker pace. A big part of that was because he took to my breast expertly. Once I had him on my lap and brought him to me, his face immediately showed the correct motions for getting the milk and knowing when to take a breather. My initial worry was not knowing if he was getting enough. With pumping, it was easy to see how much was coming out. So, the lactation coach showed me how to weigh him before feeding and then after. And sure enough, he did great. Burping was the harder and messier of the tasks, but I didn't care. It was all progress.

With him taking my milk directly, he continued to gain weight. And then the staff started experimenting with taking the "nose thingy" off. I was careful that time to note and understand that it most likely would be a back-and-forth transition before being completely removed.

But when talk started about Collin being released, for the first time my tears were legit happy ones. He was checking off each necessary medical item. He had no signs of infection, was maintaining a consistent body temperature, was able to breast or bottle feed, had steady weight gain, and was breathing on his own.

The fact that the infant CPR course Hawk and I had registered for before Collin's unexpected early arrival happened on the day before he was set to come home seemed fitting. We both, more than ever, recognized the vital importance of knowing how to save a child's life.

After the class, we went back to the NICU so I could feed Collin and meet with the neonatologist to go over some final checklists. Whereas things felt like they had gone so incredibly, painfully slow after Collin was born, all of a sudden it seemed like those two-and-a-half weeks went by in a flash. We were really going to have our baby … truly. He was coming home. He was going to be in his nursery and held by us whenever we wanted—without driving to another location … without seeing him on a screen when we couldn't … without constant beeping sounds. But, also, without the help. And I realized then how I had very much come to rely on the staff's advice and expertise. Dad and Mom—aka Hawk and me—were it. Yay and eeek!

I was thinking of that as the doctor concluded with the tests Collin would get the next morning before being released. "No monitors at home, right?" I confirmed, feeling that relief, but then added, "What about any kind of oxygen? Should we have it in case?" Even though I was prepared for that possibility as a safety measure, it was still hard for me to finish the sentence.

"No. He's not at his due date yet so he's still maturing, but his lungs look good, Maya." Hawk squeezed my hand on the doctor's words, knowing I needed both the verbal and physical confirmation when it came to my child's breathing. "Your car seat is new, right?"

"Yes." A flashback of arguing with Hawk about putting it in the car slammed into my brain. That had been such a horrible day, but we had made it.

"Then he's fine. He exceeds the minimum weight," she spoke of Collin's ever-growing weight of five pounds eight ounces. "When we discharge him tomorrow, I'll have someone help you put him in the first time, making sure all those straps go to the right place."

"Appreciate that." It was the first minor glimpse that Hawk might have some nerves being in charge of our little human all by ourselves.

"One more thing …"

"Yeah?" I actually had a pencil and notebook out and was writing stuff down.

"Leave. Leave early today. We have plenty of your milk on hand. Go home or wherever you want and enjoy the rest of the day as a couple. Because tomorrow?" Her eyebrows lifted. "Your family experience really begins."

***

"I did. I did so win."

"Okay, Maya, you keep thinking that if it's what you need."

"What I need? It's not what I need. It's the truth." I fastened my seatbelt as Hawk started the truck.

"You know, I'm a little concerned you are going to be setting a bad example for our son if you cheat like you do."

"Hawk Brannigan! I did not cheat. It may have been by one point or whatever, but I won fair and square." On his laugh, I prompted, "How exactly do you think I cheated?"

He looked over at me after he changed lanes and gave me a wink. "You distracted me by being legitimately happy. It was so nice to see."

I smiled. I was, indeed, over-the-top happy. We had taken the doctor's advice and spent time away from the hospital that late afternoon. It was on the way home from that visit when Hawk had made the suggestion, and with a little detour of our route, we ended up at a miniature-golf course—a perfect, nostalgic nod to our first date.

"Your hands on me could most definitely be considered a foul, too," I noted.

"I was helping you line up the stroke."

"Mmmm-hmmm."

"Believe me, Maya, doing that did not help my game."

I leaned over and pecked him on the cheek. "Golf was a great idea. Thanks."

"You got it." He placed his hand on my leg. "Now call the food order in. I'm starved."

The second part of our impromptu date included ordering from one of our favorite eateries. Neither of us felt like being in an overstimulated restaurant full of patrons, music, and workers. So, we decided to have it delivered, and we could eat it in the solitude of our peaceful home. By the time I got the order placed, we were back at the townhome. I figured I had enough time to pump while Hawk got the drinks and silverware ready before the food arrived.

It was when I was changing into comfy clothes that I noticed next to our framed tally chart was the dual photo frame—the one Hawk had set out for me as a housewarming gift when I had moved in with him. On one side was a photo of the two of us, and the other said *Future photo of baby Brannigan.* We had yet to replace it with Collin's photo.

I made a decision right then to do something about it. Our little boy was coming home. He was going to be okay. I went back to the office/nursery, printed out the latest photo I took of him, and replaced it in the frame. It was perfect … just like him.

When I entered the dining area, the food had arrived and Hawk had it laid out on the table where he was sitting. "What took you so long? I was ready to dive in."

"Sorry. Got caught up with something." I liked that he would see the frame later as a surprise. "Everything looks good." I noted our identical food order of chicken sandwiches and pasta salad on the table. And after a few bites, I verbalized what I had started thinking about while in the bedroom. "I want him baptized, Hawk."

"You want him what?" He spoke mid-chew and then put his bun down.

I knew my proposition was going to be pretty much a shock. It was something we had briefly discussed months before but decided against. It seemed almost hypocritical since neither of us actively practiced any form of religion. Hawk grew up with it, but when he moved from Oklahoma, he created a whole new life and it did not involve attending any kind of church organization. My family was split. My dad's side was Catholic, but I wasn't raised by them. My mom's mom gave up on all things religious early on, and, quite honestly, with all the tragedies, I couldn't blame her. Jeff and I had gone to church with his family only on holidays. He had liked any downtime as a cop to not be in community settings because he was always questioned about wrong things that were happening.

"Maya?"

"I feel a need to do something. Collin needs to be protected."

"We're taking him home, Maya. He's fine. He's going to be okay."

His sigh on that comment told me he didn't want to have to keep reminding me about the fact that our baby was all right. It was essentially what had started our argument of arguments at the NICU, and I had a feeling he was remembering it, too. We had done so well since then, even rediscovering ourselves as loving partners that past week and especially that day with the mini-golf outing.

"I know." I did. Truly. I believed our little boy had made it out of the perilous stage of his after birth. "I can't explain it," I continued. "It will make me feel better."

His sigh was different that time but still a sigh. "What are you thinking, then? What religion? Who would even accept us? Would we need classes or proof of something?" His litany of questions were all legitimately good ones.

"I don't know." It was *my* turn to sigh and take another bite of the pasta so I could collect my thoughts before speaking again. "We got married by a non-denominational minister. So, something like that?" My shoulders lifted with suggestion. "Nothing too formal. Like, instead of the shower"—which Lara was still insisting she wanted to have—"we gather our closest friends and family and, you know, shower Collin with love and good thoughts, letting him know he has all of us."

"Okay. I'm liking this better." He took a swig of his IPA.

"I know it's bad timing with the tour and the ACMs right before you all go, but I'd like to do it prior to that."

The thought of him—and basically everyone else I was close to in Nashville—leaving was stinging on a whole new level. It had only been merely a thought and far in the future when I was pregnant. But there we were with the time fast approaching, and I already had a sense of the loneliness that would come with it. I wondered if that was, in fact, part of my sudden need to have some kind of ceremony for Collin.

Hawk's face pinched a little and, with his adamant words, I understood why. "I told you, you and Collin come first." Although we certainly had healed after our blow-up, it would take some time for a few of those trigger words to not make an impact.

"I know," I reassured. "Sorry, I didn't mean—"

He eased my mind with a better remembrance. "Family before fame, right?"

"Yeah, and forts. Don't forget those." I smiled. "I just know the tour is only weeks away."

He reached his hand out for mine and, with a squeeze, said, "We'll make it work, Mai."

"Good. Yeah." I picked up my sandwich. "Nothing big … just your family and Finn and Lara. They're like—"

"They *are* family."

Another grin. I thought so, too. I knew Finn was like another brother to Hawk, and we used the term *road family* loosely, but there was heartfelt meaning to it, also. It was the anyone-would-do-anything-for-each-other kind of feeling.

"Should they be the godparents?" I wondered out loud. "I mean, Sophia would be kind of weird as Jeff's sister, and then picking Juanita over her … I couldn't. Although, what about your brothers?"

"Same thing about choosing one over the other. Naomi's belief system didn't do godparents. But Liam had Jake be Landon's, and I am Neve's … simple birth order. I think if we need someone to stand up for Collin—"

"And take care of him if something happens to us."

My husband's bottom lip separated a little more from his top one. It was like a mental lightbulb had gone off for him. He understood then what I knew deep down was one of my main reasons for having the service for our son. It wasn't so much Collin that I was worried about surviving. It was us.

It was needing to make sure he was taken care of if something should happen to Hawk and me. It was my past. It was living that life.

"Yeah … yeah, sweetie. Yeah." He spoke softly and with great consideration. "Finn and Lara are going to be with us all the time. They know us. They already love Collin. Yeah. We'll do that, okay? Here …" He stood. "Let me get my phone. I'll look at the schedule, and we can call Finn." He started to take the step or two to go toward the charger in the living room.

"Wait." I got up, too.

"Yesss?" He turned.

"I want to kiss you first."

"You're making a lot of demands today." He chuckled.

I laid my hand on his chest, covered by the soft fabric of an orange T. "It's my prerogative." I'm sure he thought I was going to claim woman power on him, but I didn't. "It's my prerogative as the golf champ."

His laugh was a little bigger that time, and then he suddenly, swiftly lifted me. Wrapping my legs around his back and my arms around his neck, I appreciated how close we were without the significant baby bump between us. When our mouths met, it was done with the sweetest elements of care, trust, and love.

CHAPTER TWENTY-TWO

Two weeks before his actual due date and three weeks since I had first been admitted to the hospital, Collin was between Hawk and me as we had our photo taken in the hospital entrance. We were handed a pamphlet and list of doctors to call for different reasons, and someone made sure Collin was safe and secure in the car seat. And then that was it. Ready, set … go. We were on our own—mom, dad, and baby boy.

Collin was the most chill of the three of us on the ride home. He slept the entire time. Not one peep or even wiggle.

I think *I* was in shock. We were actually in the car and on our way to finally begin the life I'd always dreamed of. A few joyful, silent tears fell as I watched the baby ninety percent of the time. The other ten percent, though, had me taking note of the vehicles passing us by.

Because … then there was Hawk. He was nervous. And it was sweet to see, even if I knew he would never admit to it. He was not only going the speed limit, he was going under. And that was most definitely not his usual driving mode. Gone were the days of fast cars and freedom, which is what Oaklee claimed he wanted when they were together.

And he probably had. But I knew with every ounce of my being that he was no longer that guy, and the fact that I had momentarily lost my sanity in the NICU and suggested otherwise, still killed me a little. I knew he was *my* guy—the guy I loved and who loved me, our son, and our life tenfold.

"Sorry," he called out from his driver's seat.

"Huh? For what?"

"That bump I just hit. I should have went the other way … less potholes."

I shook my head. I hadn't even known we had hit anything. "No pressure," I teased from the back seat and then reached my hand that wasn't on Collin out for Hawk's. "Just the most important drive of your life."

He squeezed my hand quickly and then returned to having both of his on the wheel. "Mmmm-hmmm." It wasn't even a full, real word because he was concentrating so hard.

"Oh, you're so cute. You're so cute." I knew I already had the sing-songy voice of a newborn's mom down, as I resisted playing with our son's little feet so not to wake him.

"Yeah, I know. That's what all the pretty girls say." Hawk seemed to get his mojo back with that one.

"Ha! Not you, but you're pretty damn good looking, too." I noted his glimpse at me in the rearview mirror before I added with a warning, "And all the girls better not be telling you that."

"Good God," he exclaimed after a second, and by his tone, I knew it was not in relation to our current conversation.

"What?" As the car came to a complete stop and Hawk turned off the engine, I realized we were in our home's driveway. And with that, I saw what had caused his exasperated words.

"I asked them to do one little thing for me … not all this."

I got out to get a better look than the partial view I had from the back of the car. Covering the entire front yard—

which wasn't much since it was a townhome—was a blue *Welcome Home Collin* sign. Some balloons were attached on either side.

"Who did this?"

"F-ing Finn but probably Lara," Hawk mumbled as he got Collin out of the back.

"Look, Collin"—I bent down to the baby carrier in my husband's strong hands—"it's a sign for you." And on those words, sure enough, that was when our son woke and opened his eyes.

"This is overboard." Hawk shook his head.

"What *did* you ask them to do?"

"You'll find out. Come on, let's get in the house. The neighbors are looking." Hawk started walking and tossed me the keys.

"No, wait! We need a picture." On his grumble, I waved to our neighbor across the street. "Wakely," I called out to the young woman who was ready to enter her home. "Can you—?"

"That's her name?" Hawk loudly whispered.

"Yeah, shhh." I looked back to the dark brunette. "Would you mind taking a picture of us?"

"Sure, yeah, no problem." Her chocolate lab pulled at his leash strapped to her hand. "He's home, huh?"

"He is." I smiled at Collin.

"Give me a sec. Let me put Titan inside. I don't want him all excited around the baby." She patted the dog and started toward her front door.

"What kind of name is that?" Hawk was back in my ear.

"Stop! Shhh. How do you not know her name? She said she's lived here for a few years now." *I* knew her name because I introduced myself on one of my walks.

Hawk shrugged. "I don't know."

"I guess she isn't one of the pretty girls, then?"

"Only one I see is the one standing in front of me." He pecked me on the lips. "The same one who is going to owe me for getting this damn picture taken, by the way."

After I made a huge deal of introducing Hawk and Wakely—much to my husband's chagrin—the neighbor/Pilates instructor took a couple photos, and we finally made it into our home. We went immediately up the stairs since that was where the main living area was. Watching Hawk slightly struggle with the awkwardness of the carrier up the narrow steps made me very appreciative that our almost finished new house was only one story, minus the bonus room/man cave.

Hawk set Collin down in the middle of the living room, and we both kind of looked around and at each other. After a minute, he said, "Now what?"

"Huh." I laughed with nerves and appreciation.

Now what, indeed. Now … the rest of our lives. How did that look from there on out?

"I don't know," I admitted and we stood there for a moment or two more. I looked down at the baby, who was peering at us as if wanting to know the answer, too. "Welcome to your new home, Collin. I mean, not new, but …?"

"Yeah, new home," Hawk encouraged. As it turned out, we were both bumbling idiots when it came to the new-parent thing.

"Welcome home," I reiterated and carefully started to get him out of the carrier. "Sooo … let's take you on a tour." It was the only idea I had. Our baby should know his new digs. "This is the living room." I chuckled before the three of us ventured into the dinette and kitchen.

"You didn't even see it!" Hawk exclaimed as I started toward the same-level bedrooms.

"What?" I turned around.

"I mean, it's not as big as a gosh-darned yard sign …" He swung his hand outwardly to the kitchen counter.

On it was a vase full of red roses. Instead of adding lilies like he had in the past, this bouquet had baby's breath. Awww … I handed Collin over to Hawk so I could bring my hands to the vase and smell them. It was then I noticed next to it were two of my foodie favs—a bag of my favorite coffee and fudge from The Fudgery.

"*That's* what I asked the Murphys to have waiting for you when we got home. I wanted to get you something when Collin was born, but …"

"Hawk, I wouldn't have appreciated it then. Everything has been so … But now, I feel …" There were no complete, exact, perfect words for what having our son home felt like. "Now is perfect. Now is when he is born for real. He's home, safe, and healthy." Tipping up on my feet, I kissed my husband. "I love you. Thank you." I touched Collin's little hand, which seemed to be waving at us. "Come on, let's see what's next on the tour."

Hawk continued to hold the baby like a pro as we walked into our master bedroom. "This, son, is where your mom and I sleep. We're gonna have to teach you how to knock before you can enter."

I laughed. "That's something *I* would have said."

"What can I say, you're growing on me."

His belly rolling in laughter bounced the baby, and I thought about how nice it was to truly be relaxed again. I knew our life was completely changing and there would be sleepless nights and smelly rooms, but that overwhelming dread that came with being in the NICU was no longer there. There was breathing space. It was like getting out of a slow, moving, crammed elevator and finally having fresh air.

I took one of those breaths in with a sense of relief. "Okay, let's keep this thing moving." I led us into the next room. "Here's the best one of all, Collin. It's the one you've been waiting for. You have your very own room."

"Well, you share it with your mom," Hawk spoke to Collin. "She needs a workspace. But in the new house, you'll have your own."

"Then we'll get your name up on the wall and do some decorating … maybe a neutral-colored animal décor." I thought of the items that had already arrived. "And what do you think about clouds?" I looked at our son as if he really understood what I was talking about.

"Just say yes to the clouds for now, buddy." Hawk seemed to warn Collin that momma knows best. "But soon enough, we'll get you the sports stuff."

I shook my head but smiled, loving how Hawk already seemed to be talking directly to our son more than ever. Where he had done a little during my pregnancy, it became at a bare minimum in the hospital. And I wondered if that was because there were strangers around or he was afraid of forming too close of an emotional bond with our little boy in case something happened.

"We could add my first puck," I offered softly. When Hawk tilted his head in question, I continued, "My dad scored a goal the first game after I was born. He wrapped it with stick tape and wrote *For Maya. I love you* on it. My mom put it in a case, and it was always in my room as a child. It's been packed away for a while now, though."

"Where?"

"In that box in the bedroom closet."

"Hmmm." He knew I had memories of days-gone-by in there, and he'd always been respectful by not opening it or asking more.

I noted a decoration that already *did* adorn the current nursery. *The Dance* painting was the one my mom had painted of my parents wearing ice skates in a woodsy area. "I love that this is the first thing, though. I feel like his grandparents are looking after him."

I watched as Hawk ran his hand along our sleepy son's head. "And, he was, actually, born on *my* dad's birthday."

My eyes shot immediately to Hawk's. "Whaaa …? What?" I was amazed at how casually he had said such an amazing coincidence. "Why didn't you say something?"

Hawk shrugged. "Well, there was a lot going on for one thing, and my dad wasn't big on birthdays. But, of course, I remember it."

"Well, sharing a birthday with your grandpa is super

cool. It's one good thing about his early arrival. But the Brannigan no-birthday-celebration schtick?" I clicked my tongue, recalling my husband pretty much ignoring his own. "Let me tell you something …" Mom *was* going to know best when it came to this topic. "That ends here. This little boy"—I touched Collin's sweet cheek—"is going to have balloons and candles and icing and games and clowns." I didn't desire that kind of attention myself, but I wanted my child to have it all.

Hawk shook his head. "You don't think I had that growing up with Della as my mom? That's why I hate it."

"Oh!" I swatted his arm lightly, considering the baby was cuddled in it.

"I'm telling you right now, there will not be any more large signs in the front yard."

I let out a light chuckle. "Okay. No. Agreed. We'll start with a much more low-key baptism."

"Let's, actually, start with making sure he's fed, changed, and bathed."

***

A few days later, I couldn't help but take a photo of Hawk when he wasn't looking. His eyes, in fact, weren't even open. Having just finished pumping, cleaning out bottles, and taking a soothing long shower, I ignored the overflowing laundry pile consisting mostly of onesies, and walked down to the lower level to find him on the sofa with Collin … both sound asleep. It was such a beautiful site. Sure, my husband's naked chest was firm and built and so damn fine. But it was the baby snuggled softly and contently between it and his dad's big hand that was the real turn on. Hawk had taken to fatherhood with such ease. It was remarkable. He was gentle but not afraid of Collin. He was patient through the cries, even when I worried what they meant. And he talked to our baby boy as if they had been the best of chums for many, many years already.

Hawk awoke as I put the phone down and began carefully lifting Collin from the coziness of his father's embrace. "I got him," he claimed, and I wondered if Hawk ever truly fell into a solid sleep. He sat up a little more properly and reached for the remote. "I'll turn it off."

When I looked at the television, sure enough, there was a hockey game on. No wonder he had taken the baby to the family room instead of staying upstairs. He didn't want me to have to see it. I started to ask who was playing when I saw it on the screen—the Washington Capitals.

"No, leave it on." I touched his hand that was going for the remote. "I think Collin should know about the origins of his name, yeah? And I'm better with it. I promise." Hawk knew I wasn't one to watch hockey because of my childhood memories, but since going to the All-Star event, seeing Gus again, and hearing from his parents a few days or so after, I was focusing more on the positives of what the game meant to my dad.

Regardless, Hawk turned the volume down and gave his attention to me as I sat on the sofa next to him. "How about an update?"

"Are we talking about the score or poopy diapers?"

Hawk laid the baby between us. "Well, I managed to change one by myself without gagging." Admittedly, diapers were not my husband's strength. Although, he was a master at bath time and an ideal team player with lot of other baby things, too. "Man, this kid goes through an immense number of diapers and wipes. We're gonna need to buy stock in them." He chuckled. "But what I was talking about was getting some more RSVPs for the baptism gig."

I loved how Hawk would never simply call it the baptism or christening. He always added words like *gig* or *thing* to the end. It truly symbolized how we were making our baby's special day unique and not simply a religious ritual.

"Yeah, who?" I rubbed Collin's belly as he kept sleeping.

We already knew Della and Eli were coming. Goodness knows, after she continued to berate us for not having her at our wedding, we didn't dare not make sure Hawk's mom could attend before anyone else. She had offered to come immediately after we brought Collin home, but we politely said no. As much as Della was adored, we wanted that time to be just for the three of us, especially knowing how soon Hawk would have to leave on tour. We were determined to be able to take care of Collin on our own. And, besides some sleep deprivation, that plan was working. Ironically, I think it was because of the time the baby spent at the NICU. The two of us already had in weeks of certain experiences with Collin, not just a birth and out-in-days situation.

"Jake said he and Raiden will be here but will have to leave pretty soon after because of the flight schedules and needing to be back on base Monday morning."

"That's a shame but glad they're not driving." I don't think I'd ever get over my childhood trauma. Speaking of tragedies … "How does he seem? And Raiden?"

"Yeah, uh, okay." Hawk had kept me updated with how his brother and nephew were coping, and it seemed they were in the keeping-busy stage of grief … a part of denial but, I suppose, better than mentally losing it. "He thinks it will be good for Rai to be around family that weekend."

"Oh, damn, Mother's Day … his first without his mom. I wasn't thinking about that." Selfishly, I had been loving that it was my first with my son, though.

"They'll be with family," Hawk reiterated positively, and then, after a slight pause, added, "I guess we're getting all the Brannigan siblings in one room again."

"Yeah, Liam said they were—"

"Yep, but the other RSVP today was Annie." Hawk looked down at the baby, and as adorable as Collin was, I think it had more to do with avoiding my eyes in that moment … machoism and all that.

"Your sister is coming?" My voice pitched in slight surprise.

We knew Annie was iffy between her work schedule, short notice, and just the fact that she and Hawk barely had any interaction with each other. But a slight shift seemed to have happened after Naomi's funeral. Annie had started following my blog and private messaged me to say it was nice to meet me and see Hawk again. And when the baby was born, she contacted Hawk, wondering if there was any way she could help. It was sad that a tragic event like Naomi's passing was what had prompted a better relationship between the siblings, but, regardless, I was glad.

"Yeah." He looked up. "How about that?"

"It'll be nice to have you all together for something positive. It will be another reason to celebrate."

CHAPTER TWENTY-THREE

On a sunny day just two-and-a-half weeks after Collin was released from the hospital, we, indeed, had a celebration of celebrations. Since we hadn't had the time to send out thank-you cards for everyone's support during Collin's hospitalization, the gathering was meant to show how much we appreciated our family and friends. And also, of course, for them to meet and embrace Collin into their circle of love. The location itself was a third reason to celebrate. We set up a large tent, tables, and chairs on the grounds of our new home. While it was months away from us being able to inhabit it, we were able to tour friends and family through … and the plumbing worked. So, that was a plus.

The actual baptism was simple and beautiful. Standing next to the minister who married us—boy, were we lucky to get him—Hawk and I were across from Finn and Lara, who was holding Collin. The minister talked about welcoming our son into the world and how special it was to have such strong bonds of love around him. He strayed away from most religious elements but blessed the baby and encouraged him to always be honorable, respectful, and kind. In conclusion, he asked the entire group to vow to look after Collin's life journey.

I turned to our friends and family. "Thanks again, everyone, for coming on such late notice—or early notice from this one," I teased, nodding toward Collin, and was glad I could actually joke about it. "Especially because I know this is crunch time with the tour."

"How about if I sing a song, and we can count it as preparation?" Finn suggested. When I started to chuckle, he continued, "I'm serious. I'd like to sing something."

"Not 'Dark and Dusty,'" I cautioned my boss, who knew it was the one song in his repertoire I did not care for.

"You don't like that one?" Finn asked in mockery.

And when he did, I couldn't help but have another one of those moments where I thought, *How did I get here?* How was it that a year before I was on my very first run of tour stops with Finn and his team of musicians? I never would have expected that in my life, never mind the miracle of the year to follow.

"Something a little more fitting for the day," Finn offered.

"I don't have my drums," Carter yelled out, always the character. "I can beat on the chair." He did a little rap.

"No need." Finn waved his pointer finger at Carter. "It's a ballad … rough cut … new … not even fully finished. Took me a while to want to think about laying it down. It's something Maya might recognize a little bit."

What? I had no idea what he was talking about. It almost seemed like another surprise release like "Boys' Weekend." Nothing could top that, though. Or could it?

Lara handed Hawk the baby, who had been awake but peaceful during the ceremony. She then encouraged us to sit before taking her own seat with Chance and Arinn. Hawk shrugged in a way that I knew he was not sure what the song was, either. He then guided me to our chairs next to Della and Eli.

Right before Finn started, he said, "Sorry, I know it's Mother's Day. But this one is for another important person."

Within the first few lines of Finn's song, I knew why he said I would recognize it. I knew what the meaning was and where he had gotten the inspiration. I knew the background of why he said it had taken him a while to want to sing it.

I laced my hand with Hawk's, and I listened to Finn with my heart beating.

"I was born with his name. He passed it to me
Like those before him in our family tree
I wonder what he thought holding me that first time …
Was he scared, was he excited, was he calm and sublime
What I know from the photo in the living room
Is the look on his face was like a flower's bloom
But one thing for sure was my father's love

Just like me, he had his own dreams
He won some and lost some so it may seem
But the time when you'd really see him glow
Was playing with me in our modest abode
When I was sick, he held me tight and didn't give up
Although at times I'm sure it was tough"

I squeezed Hawk's hand on those lines. They very much mirrored our circumstances. And when I looked at my husband, I could see his eyes getting misty. The baby in his embrace prevented him from wiping, though.

In turn, the country crooner seemed to be a little emotional himself.

"But I made it through because of my father's love

Time doesn't stand still. We grow up too fast
And never know which day'll be our last
But I was blessed with one of the best
And when the time came for his final rest
I held his hand and was by his side
It wasn't easy, I cannot lie

But I was strong because of my father's love

Now I look at my own
And there's one thing I know
That feeling he had on my very first day
It wasn't just one … it was all three that stayed
Because being a father is both pride and some fear
Which repeats every minute of each new year
But nothing is better than a father's love

To my hero, my pal, my example, my pop
I'm sure glad to be born with your name"

Hawk handed me the baby and walked away. I was too stunned by the song itself to react to his departure. And because I knew him so well, I understood what caused him to leave and knew to give him that moment to himself. He didn't want to deal with the emotions the song brought up in front of people, even if they were his closest friends and family … or maybe *because* of that. The day was already hard on him because of those guests. He'd never said it out loud, but I knew he didn't like his worlds mixing. Most of his family had never met his work buds. Liam and Keita had attended a concert once and that was it. Hawk liked being Hawk and keeping Alex as Alex when in Oklahoma. I was really the only one who knew him as both … and what a beautiful mix it was. But he had agreed to have the two merge that day for me. And he also did it for his son. He was a father like the song for sure.

I realized after a second or two that I wasn't the only one speechless. Silence enveloped the entire gathering. I was sure the reaction wasn't because the song was disliked. It was quite the opposite. But how do you show your appreciation of the music when you aren't in a stadium or pavilion full of thousands? Waving cell phone lights or standing and cheering didn't seem appropriate.

As I tried to formulate my response, someone else took

care of it. Collin let out a coo/squeal that almost sounded like an *oooh* or *ahhh*, and I tacked on, "I think that sums it up from the guest of honor. We loved it!"

As an array of chuckles and light applause sounded, Chance and Arinn ran to their dad. Finn swallowed them both up in his arms. Sure, the song was almost like a gift to Hawk and me that day, but I knew there was a bounty of personalization for Finn in memory of his own father and as a dad himself.

"Uh, okay, well …" I stood and turned to our guests. "Please help yourself to sandwiches, sides, and drinks."

"Cake, too!" Della was in charge of desserts, while Hawk and I had ordered everything else.

On the mention of the sweet dessert, Chance's eyes seemed to light up. "Mom, can we have some cake?"

Lara joined me in walking toward her husband and kids. "Yeah, give me a second."

As Finn set down their two little ones, I started to properly thank him for the song. "It … it was amazing. I didn't know your dad, but—"

"He would have been so proud." Lara kissed her husband and grabbed Arinn's hand, who started tugging at it. "I better get these two—"

"I'll get Collin a piece." Chance peered up at the babe in my arms. He really seemed to be taken with my son, which was so sweet to see—two of my favorite boys.

"Get one for me, too, bud." Finn watched them walk away and then turned back to me. "Your dad would be proud, too, Maya. I know I didn't react well to the blog you wrote last Father's Day, but I told you I'd save it to use later."

"When you were ready." Remembering, I smashed my lips together to prevent tears, thinking there's never a time to be ready to lose a parent. "It made an even better song."

Most likely recognizing a need to shift the tone, Finn touched Collin's cheek. "Talk about a namesake. Collin Brannigan … so solid. He has both *your* family's name *and* macho man's over there." Finn raised his chin toward the creek bank, where Hawk appeared to be standing solitaire looking at the water.

"You know he's going to kill you." I smiled with a tease. "But only because it meant a lot to him," I acknowledged my husband's vulnerability that I was sure Finn was jokingly referring to. "The part about being there when sick? He's been so strong for Collin and me this whole time." I pressed my lips together and looked to the front porch just steps away, recalling with emotion the conversation with my husband after my meltdown at the NICU. "I should go over and see him." The baby letting out a wail caught me by surprise. I altered my arms to change positions and started a small rocking motion, which I had already come to learn soothed our son.

"How about if *I* go check on him while you get the baby settled?" Finn offered. "Need to confirm something with him, anyway."

"K." I bounced the baby a little more.

As Finn started his way toward Hawk, I reclaimed my seat and continued to caress Collin. When his cry turned to a sweet murmur, I put him in his baby carrier and lightly rocked it the way we would when Hawk and I tried to maintain some kind of semblance and have dinnertime together. Keeping the baby pacified during our meal was still a mission in progress but challenge accepted.

I took note of the group gathering at the buffet we had set up. Carter and Vanessa were mingling with Juanita and her boyfriend. Della and Eli seemed to be the kid magnet with not only Liam and his children but Chance and Arinn, too. And Lara was in a conversation with Keita and the minister. It was a beautiful kaleidoscope of our life, and I knew in that snapshot I needn't worry about Collin if something should happen to Hawk or me. Just like my grandparents had been for me, our little boy had support everywhere.

That included his aunt Annie, who slid onto the seat next

to me. She had gotten in that morning compared to the rest of the Brannigan crew who we had seen the night before. "I'm so glad I came. He is absolutely adorable." Annie held out her hand so Collin could grasp her finger. "Even better than the pictures, which are as sweet as can be."

"Would you like to hold him?" I never realized how many people were really into that until I had a baby myself. I didn't make it a habit and we hadn't really been anywhere, but I wanted to extend the offer to Hawk's sister.

Her body seemed to scrunch inward the tiniest of bits. "I've never actually held a baby."

"No? Well, neither Hawk nor I have much experience and, somehow, we are responsible for Collin's entire wellbeing." I made a look-of-horror face in jest, but there would always be—similar to what Finn's song said—some trepidation when you are a parent. "You never held one? Is that because you're not a kid person?"

"Uh, no, no. I like kids. I'm just not around them much. I see Liam's sometimes since they live kind of close but never held them at this age."

I took Collin out of his carrier and started gently settling him into Annie's awaiting arms. "The good part is, he doesn't really do much at this stage—eating, sleeping, bodily functions." I smiled, watching my son so calm in his aunt's hands but eyes on me.

"He's so tiny."

"Ah, but he's gaining weight." For that I was incredibly happy. "Do you want kids?"

Oh, geez, was that too personal? She was my sister-in-law, but I hardly knew her. Wasn't the whole kid question something that was kinda taboo or inconsiderate? After all, I remembered detesting it when Jeff and I had been trying without any luck.

But she answered. "I … Yeah. Just need someone to have them with."

"So … not seeing anyone right now?"

Well, I had already asked the baby question. Why not go

for it? I knew Hawk didn't know the answer, and it wasn't because of his relationship with his sister. He was simply a guy who preferred to stay away from too personal of info. Hence his escape to the rear of the property.

"You know the social media status 'It's Complicated?' That's definitely where I'm at."

Before I could react to Annie's comment, Jake and Raiden walked over to us. "I remember when *you* were this small." Jake placed a hand on Raiden's shoulder as he looked at Collin. "Goes by fast, Maya. Goes by real fast." His words seemed like yet another reference to the song and, of course, to his wife's passing.

Thinking of that made me double down on my need to see Hawk. "Hey, I … uh … Can you guys look after him for a bit?" I touched Collin's head and stood. "I need to check on your brother."

Jake said a Hawkism … or was it, actually, an entire Brannigan saying? "You got it." He sat next to Annie. "We have this little one covered."

As I started to turn, I heard Raiden. "I'm glad you and the baby are all right, Miss Maya."

"We are," I made a point to reassure the teen, whose words I'm sure reflected some residual guilt regarding the fire. "We are. I'm so glad you came to meet your new cousin. You both have such a strong family around you."

With that, I started toward my destination by first slipping off my heels. They did not complement the grass and weathered path, and I was, honestly, glad to ditch them. I hadn't worn heels in so long. I don't know what made me think I needed to that day.

As I neared the creek, I flashbacked to one of my first kisses with Hawk. We had been skipping stones at a small lake at one of the tour stops. I liked that our home was near similar water. I found it soothing.

When I got close enough to hear the guys' chatter, I was surprised that, while not particularly emotional, Hawk was speaking with full honesty to our boss/friend. "I can't do this, man. I can't do it without her … without them. I know … I'm whipped."

"You're a husband. You're a dad. That's what you are. Do you remember me that summer without Lara and the kids? It nearly destroyed our marriage. I told you, I'm good with it."

I'm not sure what gave me away. Maybe a stick I stepped on? Or had I actually sighed hearing their words? The men weren't talking about the song, but I was sure that was what had catapulted the current conversation. The tour. I felt it, too. I had already started preplanning some blogs about being a tour widow. Although, I needed to find a better word than that. *Widow* cut too deep. How could it be that I only had another week and a couple days with Hawk before he was set to leave for the summer? I was at least grateful that the tour was starting later than the year prior. And it was another good thing about Collin's early birth—Hawk got more time to be with his son before the tour began.

"Well, speaking of." Finn smiled in my direction.

"Hey, Mai." Hawk was definitely subdued but not necessarily in a sad state.

I adhered myself to his side and rubbed his shirt-covered chest. "How you doing?"

Instead of answering the question, my husband concentrated on another. "Where's Little Bun?"

"Geez, I thought we ditched that name. We have an army of family over there." I smiled, thinking I hadn't purposefully meant the pun in relation to Jake's profession. "He's well taken care of. Although, my arms feel weirdly empty."

"Hmmm." Hawk pressed on his phone already in his hand and then swiveled it around for me to see the screen.

"Yeah? What's that about, Griswald?" I teased while looking at the photo of an RV, albeit a much nicer and more modern version than the one in the *National Lampoon* movie.

While Finn laughed, my husband spurted out a "Happy Mother's Day."

Hawk had already bought me a beautiful gold necklace with Collin's name on it as my birthday present the week before. I had said that and having Collin's celebration on Mother's Day was gift enough. That's why I especially took the RV for the joke I knew it was.

"For me?" I sugared on the sarcasm. "What I've always wanted. What is it really?"

"I'm getting it to drive on tour so you and Collin can come, too." I could hear it in his deadpanned voice and see it with his steadfast eyes that he was being serious.

I pulled away so I could get a more direct look at my husband. "Oh, Hawk, no. You have too much already on tour, and the baby will keep us up." We definitely were already experiencing that.

"What's the solution, Mai? You heard what Finn said about when Lara and the kids weren't with us, right?" On my nod, he continued, "I watched it. I was there. It wasn't good. He wasn't kidding. They were … He was … It was bad." I'm sure both of us noticed Finn's face flinch on the truth of my husband's words. As a buddy, Hawk then threw out a comedic verbal jab toward our boss. "I could sue you for not giving me a long enough family leave." Both Finn and I shook our heads, and Hawk turned serious again. "Mai, I don't think I can be away from you and Collin for a whole summer, especially after all we went through to have him."

Flashes from finding out I was pregnant, to the preeclampsia, to the NICU bombarded my mind in milliseconds. "I know." It came out in almost a whisper.

"Look, I drove us most of the time during the second half of last year's tour." Hawk didn't say it, but that was because of him being considerate of my claustrophobia in the multi-person, small-quartered bus. Well, and the fact that we got to be alone.

"You didn't have a baby crying at night," I reminded again.

"It'll be okay. I'll wear earbuds and you get him, or we

take turns driving. A lot of times we don't peel out super early, anyway. Maya …?"

I knew Hawk was prompting me to simply agree with what my heart would have jumped on instantly, but my mind was methodically thinking of all the logistical issues. Which I should have known he would have worked through five times over before even presenting it to me. Still, I thought of what we would need to bring with us for an infant. Hawk and I knew how to pack light, but a baby involved more. Yet, maybe not. I had seen the Murphy's personal bus—admittedly bigger than the motorhome Hawk showed me—and their kids had plenty of room and didn't lack for anything.

There was also something I felt a little awkward asking in front of Finn, since I didn't want our already generous friend to feel any kind of obligation. "Hawk, can we afford this? I mean, building the house and the expense of a new baby an—"

My husband gave an immediate answer, as if he was ready for the question. "Not buying it."

"Renting can be just as bad." I really did sound like a spoil sport.

"Get this …" With those words, Hawk's voice lifted with enthusiasm. "The RV company is giving it to us for the months you're on tour with us this summer."

"Giving?" Like a complimentary gift? "Why?"

"Sponsorship," my husband explained. "You just need to mention it—in a positive way, of course—in the blog a few times. Maybe post a pic or some video. And they are taking out the bottom bunk for the crib. They want to show that feature."

"Really?" Admittedly, that was the first time I truly saw the crazy, impromptu plan coming together.

When I looked at Finn, he shrugged with a smile. "Seems like a win-win, right? I get two of my best employees with me, not just one grumpy one." He punched Hawk in the arm. "And we might get some extra plug from the RV company. I mean, I can see our followers liking the RV life."

"Okay ..." But I pursed out some air, knowing there was still one obstacle, and it was a big one. "When are you thinking? Collin and I can't go with you right away. Even though he did good on his checkup"—*Flying colors* were the words I had actually heard from the doctor—"we should be here for his second-month appointment so we can confirm that everything's fine. He—"

What were the lyrics in Finn's song? *Worry* and *fear*? Yep, from the day Collin was born—well, actually before even that—those two words were permanently embedded.

"Maya, I understand. I agree." Somehow throughout the conversation, my husband had progressed from emotional, to vulnerable, to calmly-in-control. "We're playing here the week of the Fourth of July."

Yes, I knew the schedule. I liked it originally because it meant I would be able to see all of them then and because ... "Well, more precisely, on your birthday."

"Normally not a fan, but last year was pretty nice." He gave me a wink before getting back to his agenda. "If Collin keeps getting good reports, that's when you two can join us. By then, we'll have all those beginning show jitters and kinks worked through." He knowingly side-eyed me ... us both recalling how anxious Finn got as the tour first started, and then after, it became a magical, beautiful summer of bliss. "It's still a little bit of a stretch, but Sophia's coming to be with you for a week during that time."

"Yeah." I was excited about that, especially since she wasn't able to make the baptism. "And Gia and I have some play dates with the kids," I spoke of the NICU mom I had bonded with and her healthy released little one. Hawk insisted that I had taken to motherhood like a pro, and I did love it and felt beyond blessed, but knowing there were support people in place once the tour started helped tremendously, too. "Finn?" I tilted my head at our boss. "Honestly, do you think this will work?" I wanted it to, but I didn't want to get my hopes up if there was any doubt.

"If I didn't think he could do it, I would say so. But I do," Finn answered with confidence.

I felt it. I felt myself getting excited about all of it. "And my maternity leave will officially be ending then. I'll be ready to take on more. I can help with Chance and Arinn again, and—"

"Awww, I thought big guy here was looking forward to doing that," Finn teased Hawk, who rolled his eyes. "Seriously, though? Lara would love that, and it will be reciprocal with Collin. You know we're a big traveling family. Everyone will pitch in. And maybe if you join us, you can help me iron out some of those lyrics I just sang, and we could see about getting you a writing cred if I record it."

While I thought of how amazing that would be, I knew it wasn't the reason the song was important. Instead of getting emotional, though, I went with a little sarcasm. "Yeah, we can record it in the camper. Collin's whimpering in the background will be a nice touch."

"Hmmm … that might actually be a good idea." Finn's eyes were bouncing from place to place, but I knew he wasn't looking at anything specific. He was thinking. He was legitimately considering my proposal. "I like it. Let me ponder some more on that." We heard the vibration of his phone before he pulled it out of his pocket, looked at the screen, and answered. "Hey, Beauty. … . What?" Finn swiveled around to look in the direction of the guests to see Chance jabbering about something while making his way toward us. "Oh, yeah, I got him," he spoke back into the phone. "Wait, hold on, Lar, he's telling me something."

"Daddy …" Bounding in front of us, Chance carefully handed Finn a plate. "Here's your cake, but Mommy says Collin can't have any." His mouth curved down and eyebrows furled.

"What a mean mommy."

We could all hear Lara's reply to her husband via the phone. "Finn!"

The singer laughed. "Mom's right, bud. Collin's too little

to have any cake yet."

"But maybe you can help feed him his bottle this summer?" I made the offer to the five-year-old.

The reaction was with pure boy enthusiasm, but it wasn't from Chance. It was my husband. "Yeah? You're saying you're good with this?" Hawk's eyes expanded with delight at me. "Yeah?"

"I am." I smiled back. "Looks like more miles and memories for you and me … and Collin."

GET TO KNOW MAYA'S PARENTS IN *THE DANCE*

Stepping onto the ice was frightening. Doing so required trust … and not just that of her feet. It also involved Cate's head and heart. Trusting meant she had to forget what happened in the past.

At twenty-two years old, Cate Lentz is starting to understand Noah's comparison of skating to a dance. The same, she realizes, can be said about life itself. You have to release the walls surrounding you in order to feel light and free. You also need the right partner. With the NHL rookie at her side, Cate is beginning to see a new and exciting life-canvas in front of her—similar to the paintings she creates in her art studio.

But as smooth as ice is, everyone tumbles and falls sometimes. When her ex, Leo, makes a reappearance in Cate's life, his mental instability creates such turmoil and heartache that it's hard for her to stand back up. Can she find a way to dance again after tragedy strikes?

Pulling at heartstrings and dealing with realistic issues, The Dance is a gripping tale that travels the reader back to the year 1980. This emotional story will leave you with a true appreciation for being both independently strong but also grateful for those who are by your side … no matter what.

EXCERPT:

Glancing at the paper, I mentally acknowledged it was, indeed, a local number. And I resigned myself to the fact of his new residency. "Okay. Um, Noah and I need to go."

There weren't any "nice seeing you agains" between us or "nice meeting yous" between the men. The fact was, I hadn't even introduced them. Although, I was pretty sure both guys understood each other's role in my life. There was only silence as Noah opened the passenger door for me and then walked around the car to get into his side. Leo stood once again against the gallery wall, with his hands shoved into his front pockets.

As we drove farther away, the image of my ex in the rearview mirror got to the small point in a perspective drawing known as the vanishing point. Even though I could no longer see him, I knew he was not gone. I could definitely sense him … and I wanted that to go away, too.

Like a near savage, I tore out the elastic band holding back my hair and flung it out the window. It was cathartic but not what I needed most. "Noah … hand." It came out part demand, part plea, as I extended my left arm in his direction.

Silent until then, he looked over at me, paused for a beat, and then spoke softly but directly. "You didn't want it a few minutes or so ago."

Available now in both ebook and print

HAVE YOU READ LARA AND FINN'S STORY?

CHECK OUT *COUNTRY ROADS*

A young woman content with her solitary life.
A rising country music star.

They were friends once …until their lives took them down separate roads.

Now, years later, when a child volunteers his uncle to sing for a fundraiser, LARA FAULKNER realizes it is none other than her college pal, FINN MURPHY. As the two get a chance to reconnect, Lara reveals to a compassionate Finn details of her shocking past and the traumatic decision she had to make.

Through trust and love, the bond between Finn and Lara deepens as the country singer manages to get an emotionally scarred Lara to let down her self-proclaimed walls. But will secrets, lies, and tragedy cause a bumpy detour on their road to complete happiness?

Emotional, dramatic, heartwarming… fall in love with COUNTRY ROADS – the first in a continuing series by author Grea Warner.

CHAPTER ONE

Back where I grew up, the roads went from cement to gravel to dirt and back again with no rhyme or reason. They twisted and turned. They intersected weedy railroad tracks and climbed hills with no guardrail to guide. These roads were surrounded by pine covered woods filled with Mother Nature's creatures who, only part of the time, knew their forest-like boundaries. People gave directions not by street names but by landmarks like a country inn or a local market. It was on these roads that I found my freedom...that I learned to escape. I could go miles without seeing a soul and get lost in the simplicity of nothingness.

It's funny how similar the city is. The subway's darkness burrows underground and leads you directly into a hub encompassed by the pure chaos of millions. Everyone walks fast among the buzzing noise and brilliant lights, not daring to make eye contact. Again, I have nowhere particular to go. There are masses around me, but I am still alone. I feel that sense of solitary freedom, and that is all that is important.

The truth is, it doesn't matter what your surroundings—be it the big city, suburbia, or a quaint country town—your heart and your memory follow you wherever you go. There is no escaping what lies deep down in your innermost self. And while there are things that you might want to forget, there are also those precious few keystones that you wish you could not just conjure up but bring back to life with a click of your heels. That only happens in fairy tales, though. And, every once in a while, when the cities and the towns become that cliché small world rolled into one, it happens in schools too.

***

"My uncle can sing!" first grader Wyatt blurted out in the computer club I was in charge of toward the end of each school day.

"Oh, okay. Well, that's a good idea. But maybe instead of your uncle, we can have a talent show and some kids can sing." I didn't want to totally douse his idea. "Your uncle can come and watch us perform, Wyatt. In fact, I'm sure he would like that better than singing himself."

The brown-haired child's offer had been in response to a sad topic we had been asked to talk about with the club classes. One of the students had been diagnosed with cardiomyopathy. The principal and school counselor wanted to develop a plan for helping the family. Because of the numerous hospital visits, they were trying to find ways to raise money to assist with some of the costs. And they also wanted the students to be aware, empathize, and help if they could with fundraising ideas. There were reasonable suggestions like selling popcorn or cookies, having a car wash, and making artwork to sell. But having a family member sing was surely not one of them.

"But he's good, Miss Faulkner."

"I'm sure he is, Wyatt. I wrote it down." I added his idea to the paper but had no real intention of having it actually make the official list I would give to Principal Lennock. Uncle "Joe Shmoe" could thank me later for the save, I smirked internally.

Available now in both ebook and print

ABOUT THE AUTHOR

Known for her emotionally charged, character-driven stories, Grea Warner is an award-winning and bestselling author of women's and new adult fiction. With a background in daytime drama, she brings a deep understanding of layered storytelling and compelling character arcs to every novel she writes.

Whether crafting addictive serials or powerful standalone books, Grea's work is rooted in realism, tackling life's complexities with honesty and heart. Her stories are told in an intimate first-person point of view, immersing readers in narratives full of drama, angst, and authenticity. From heartbreak, to trauma, to the hope of second chances, her novels resonate with readers who crave emotional depth and genuine connection.

Follow Grea Warner:

Facebook: https://www.facebook.com/Grea-Warner

Instagram: greawarner

Twitter/X: @grea_warner

www.greawarner.com

www.ingramcontent.com/pod-product-compliance
Lightning Source LLC
LaVergne TN
LVHW091119080826
845145LV00008B/1973

* 9 7 8 1 9 6 4 6 3 6 6 7 2 *